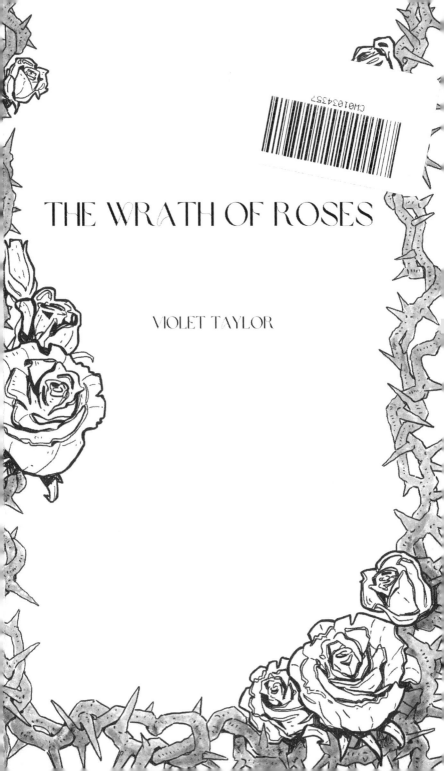

THE WRATH OF ROSES

VIOLET TAYLOR

To anyone who grew up fawning over noble princes, and now daydreams of devilish villains instead...

PROLOGUE

RENARD

*H*unting a human is far more exciting than hunting a beast. Especially one as deserving of death as *the witch*. The frost-covered forest blurs past as I ride my horse hard through the trees. My breath materializes in quick, clouded puffs and the world dissolves into a blurred frame of sugar-white snow. The frozen air tears into my lungs, rooting within them the cold presence of a reckoning that cannot be escaped. I let the chill of anticipation crawl through my blood and mingle with the lofty taste of bitter revenge as the icy flakes are swept into my mouth.

This day will end with blood.

The harsh wind rips across my face, biting all the areas not covered by my fur-lined riding attire. The hounds bark excitedly ahead and my hunting companions cheer as they catch the trail of her scent again. Evidence of her attempts to flee cover the forest floor. Bloody footprints paint a traitor's path along freshly fallen snow. *We're gaining on her.*

I work to adjust myself in the saddle. The thrill of the hunt sends blood rushing to my cock. These finely crafted trousers feel suffocating as they constrict painfully around

my engorged length. "Find the witch!" I command and the group gallops ahead. The moment of excitement is tempered with the realization that it never should have taken this long to find a lone woman fleeing on foot. Nonetheless, my erection twitches painfully and I urge my horse forward. Let us end this chase so I can bury myself in the closest nobleman's daughter. She won't object to me stealing her virtue. They never do.

The dogs howl in the distance, signaling they've cornered their quarry, and I grin. *Finally.* By the time I catch up to my hunting party, they've surrounded her. The snow seems to part as I approach, lifting a tenebrous veil from my sight and melting the ice from my lashes. There she is, the woman who has caused my family such pain. The witch. The dogs have her trapped up against a tree as their frothing jaws snap at her ankles.

"Tie her up." My voice can barely contain the well of fury and expectation swirling within me. By the time I dismount, the witch is strapped to the tree. Her pale face contorts as tears soak her flushed skin. I march toward her and soft-blue eyes lock onto mine. I thought her beautiful once. The thought drains the heat from my limbs as a sickening feeling claws at my insides.

"Please," she cries out. "I didn't do anything, I swear to you, my prince. I only tried to help. They were sick. I—" The sound of my palm striking her cheek echoes so loudly through the forest that snow falls from the branches above. Red wells up beneath the imprint my hand leaves behind and sobs wrack through her body.

"You have been charged with the murder of the King and Queen of Montrésor and have been sentenced to death." The sleek sound of steel unsheathing makes my heart beat with the thunderous pounding of a thousand wild horses. The sword feels weighty in my hand, different than usual. I flip it casually over but the strange feeling remains.

"I grow flowers, plants. I make herbal medicines, that's all. They were sick. I did everything I could, my prince, please..." Her crying becomes so violent that her words are lost.

I lean in close to the distraught woman, pinching her chin between my thumb and forefinger and forcing her to look at me. "You poisoned them. They died after drinking your floral concoctions. And now you will die." I raise the tip of my sword to her chest. The moment the blade touches her skin, something changes. The witch stops crying and her eyes harden. A golden glow surrounds her body, flaring to life and causing the men to shield their eyes. The witch's hair floats wildly around her face. Every vibrant, coppery strand writhes as if a mass of great serpents has suddenly awoken. I stumble back, unbelieving of the tricks my eyes play upon me.

"A monster has hidden beneath your angelic face for far too many years. Allow me to bring it to the surface," the witch sneers. The light around her intensifies, filling the forest with an unnatural daylight. "Mark my words, spoiled prince. My wrath you will taste and a beast you will become. Never again to know the willing touch of a woman, the love of another, or even one moment of true happiness. You will wallow in your beastly form but never die, and as the world withers around you, you will remember my face. Each time you look upon a mirror you will wish you had been more merciful toward me." Her grin sends a chill up my spine. "For you will find that none will be merciful toward a beast."

A dark fear buries itself in my gut. "That's enough!" I cry out as the blade of my sword thrusts cleanly into the wicked woman's chest. She gasps, her mouth gaping, drawing in one final breath before her body slumps forward in its bindings. I wrench the blade free. My shaky hands feel foreign and unwelcome. Blood drips from the wound and pools on the ground, tarnishing the snow as it darkens its pure white to a deep ruby red. A small flicker of light beams up from the steaming puddle. A new green bud pokes up through the frost, growing steadily from the ground below, twisting and writhing until a large crimson rose bursts forth from its peak. The rose shimmers as snowflakes land upon its blood-red petals. A darkness unfurls in my chest as I realize it's the most beautiful and terrifying thing I've ever seen.

A woman's laughter fills the forest. I whirl, spinning in circles as the witch's voice floats on the air all around me. *"Love, fair prince. Love will break your curse. But take care not to hope, for who could ever love a beast?"* Laughter fills the air once more, feminine and musical, moving away from us until it's nothing more than the hushed tinkling of bells in the distance. A soft red glow brings my gaze back to the witch's rose.

"It's the devil's magic," one of my men whispers as the flower continues to open.

"God protect us," another whines out.

"Let us leave this place, Prince Renard. I have an uneasy feeling in these woods."

I finally pull my gaze away from the unnatural flower as the words of my closest friend, Louis, begin to sink in. He's right. Something does feel wrong about the forest. The rose stares back at me accusingly and a shudder ripples through my flesh.

"To the castle," I command. My horse moves swiftly the moment I mount him and we begin the frigid trek back home. The snow thickens in the air as our group pushes onward. We make great haste at my request. I am eager to put some distance between myself and that cursed rose.

We're no more than a thousand paces away when the horses come to a halt, whinnying and trotting anxiously in place. "What has happened?" I call out. Louis circles back toward me, leading his horse to stand by mine.

"You need to come see this." His face is grim. I urge my horse forward, stopping at the front of the pack. Chilled air sucks deep within my lungs as my eyes fall upon the single red rose blooming at the forest's edge. *It can't be.*

"She's sending signs from beyond the grave," one of my companions murmurs while signing the holy trinity across his chest.

My fear turns to anger and I dismount my horse, stomping toward the flower. "Fear not, men. The witch is dead. She holds no sway over us now." I reach for the flower, wrenching it from the snow. A stabbing pain radiates through my fingers and forearm, forcing me to drop the unusual bloom. Confusion wells within me as I remove my glove and find an impossible sight beneath. Blood trickles from where the rose's thorns have punctured my flesh. *The flower should not have been able to breach my thick gloves.* My knees hit the cold ground as a new pain spreads through my body, spidering beneath my skin with a fiery heat that sends daggers of agony racing through my every cell.

"My prince!" One of my men dismounts, rushing to my side.

I can't tell who it is, my eyesight is turning watery and gray. My heart beats harder. The frantic rhythm threatens to splinter my ribs and send my pounding heart tumbling into the fresh snow. Sweat coats my brow as wave after wave of nausea ripple through me. The sensations become too much. I retch, staring down in horror as blood pours from my mouth, staining the frosted-white surroundings. Warmth spikes through my body. It raises my temperature until the scorching heat becomes unbearable. *Dear God, make this stop.*

Crack. A scream tears through my raw lungs as my spine snaps into two, forcing me to hunch forward. The nightmarish cracking comes again as more bones break and reform around me. *Why is this happening?* The world won't stop spinning. An explosive pressure radiates outward as my face begins to stretch and grow.

Through the tears streaming from my eyes I can just make out a pile of small white items dropping into the snow. I reach for one, grasping it with a shaky hand and opening my palm toward the sky.

They're teeth. *My teeth.*

It is only then that I realize I'm still screaming. The cries of terror and pain deepen, shifting to something altogether inhuman and feral. A wet, ripping sound torments my twisted ears. *Am I growing?* My body bursts through my clothes as massive limbs overtake the sturdy fabrics. The pain never ceases. My skin splits open. Pieces of pale, ragged flesh hang tattered and oozing from every inch of my body. The meaty exposed muscle and sinew below begin to sprout hair. It's not my familiar fair blond, it's brown and so dark it could almost be black.

No, not hair. *Fur.*

My twisted body grows and bends. More fur sprouts, stealing any remaining traces of my human form. Thick, sharp fangs descend from the raw, gaping spaces in my bloody gums. The oversized teeth crowd my mouth, forcing my jaw to accommodate to their punishing size.

A final burst of searing pain shoots through my entire body and I throw my head back, arching my neck and howling to the gray, snowy sky. And then it's all over.

* * *

Time ticks by. Each falling snowflake a grain of sand in the hourglass of horrors that cages in my new existence. I will my body to stand, flinching at the sight of the beastly, elon-

6

gated feet whose deep pads and talons remain imprinted in the snow. It's silent around me save for the easy sweep of downy flakes on flocked branches. My men are gone. They fled, left me in my time of need, abandoned me as I suffered a transformation so horrific it made their worst nightmares seem like lullabies and cloudscapes. Something dark stirs within my new form and bloodlust clouds my vision, turning it as red as the rose that has sealed my fate. Those traitorous cowards. They'll pay for their disloyalty. I throw my head back once more, bellowing with fury over the betrayal. My wide snout scents the air. *I can smell them.* Their fear is palpable, a trail that my new senses lock onto with ease. I race forward, propelling myself on all fours as I lumber through the snow. I'm surprisingly fast in this monstrous body, and I catch up to them quickly.

The men wail in terror as I take them down, one by one. My claws rake across their bodies, removing heads, limbs, and faces with little effort. Hot, metallic blood flings from their carcasses, painting the snow and causing steam to rise everywhere the viscous liquid lands. One final survivor gazes up at me, wide-eyed. Pain cleaves my heart as I recognize Louis. The sight of a loaded musket in his hand shatters the frail walls of my receding human heart. He fires once, but I'm faster than the fear that has addled his reflexes. Louis's head rips cleanly from his shoulders, ending his life.

I roar my victory and anguish to the forest.

Every last one of them is dead. My gaze scans the mangled human corpses. They're nearly unrecognizable in this state. Louis's eyes remain open, staring up at me, his features frozen in a look of horror so profound my stomach curdles at the sight. A sudden woozy weakness makes me stumble forward. My enormous body drops into the snow, fur and fear diving beneath crystals of ice, and a black veil drowns me in a dreamless sleep.

The courtyard's stone floor is cold beneath my cheek when I awaken once more. I roll, whimpering as my stiff body protests each movement. I rub at my throbbing head and recoil at the sight of my hand. Terror flickers through my muddled mind as I scamper across the floor. My gaze flits to the full basin of a fountain set in the corner of the entrance. My familiar blue eyes remain, but they're the only trace left of who I was before. The face of a monster looks back at me. I've traded handsome and warm for feral and fearsome. I slam a paw through the glassy reflection, distorting my face as the water ripples away. *It wasn't a dream.*

With great strain I rise to my feet and hobble toward the stone archway, stopping dead in my tracks at the sight before me. Vibrant, red roses now grow in the gardens surrounding the castle, filling every available trellis, archway, and patch of dirt with their devastating beauty. I stumble forward. The snarl that shakes the air as I rip a vine of roses down from the overhang must belong to someone else. My hands sting and bleed but I do not stop until the stone is clear of all greenery.

A sinking stone plummets to my depths as the space fills with thorny vines once more. Ruby roses sprout from the fresh foliage. The world darkens, and I sink to the ground in an unfamiliar state of despair. She truly has turned me into a *beast.*

CHAPTER 1

SIXTEEN YEARS LATER

The scent of roasting meat and fresh croissants hits me in my hiding place. My mouth waters on instinct but it's not food I hunger for today. I slink deeper into my favorite hidden spot among the trees. The villagers remain oblivious to my presence. Fools. I watch them, day in and day out meandering about with their ordinary lives. Baking breads, selling eggs, offering their services in poorly tailored clothes with self-righteous sneers upon their faces. They have always disgusted me, even before I became the Beast. And they taste terrible. Some far too plump, their bodies swollen and bloated from excess. Others spindly with wire-thin frames, nothing but a sack of bones to pick my teeth clean when the meal is complete. No, I long ago switched to animals. They taste better and they scream far less.

When I hunt humans now, it's for necessity. The neighboring kingdoms have been threatening to invade since my parents were murdered. News of the outside world reaches even the ghostly walls of my castle. War has ravaged the surrounding lands as the smaller kingdoms fight for power.

9

Without my rule, the world has fallen into chaos and ash. Messengers and scouts come riding through my woods every few months and I ensure they cannot take back any information that could put my land in danger. It's better for their men to never return. My hope is that fear of the unknown and rumors of the monster of Montrésor will keep the potential invaders at bay.

Of course the occasional ignorant traveler still wanders too close to the castle, and anyone who lays eyes on my enchanted rose gardens can never be allowed to leave.

Seconds turned into hours. Hours turned into days. Days turned into years. And years turned into lifetimes of suffering and heartache. The seasons came and went without a single joyous occasion. Life became nothing more than a waiting game for death. For years I spent all of my time locked away in the castle, but loneliness is a ghostly companion and eventually I wandered into the outskirts of the village. That's when I first laid eyes on her. The most beautiful creature I've ever seen. *Fleur.*

She walks out of the library, her nose buried in another fairy tale. Most days I can find her under a tree near the edge of town, reading her favorite books until the sun sets. What would she think if she saw my library? It more than trumps the tiny bookstore she frequents. The idea of her inside my castle makes my heart pound quicker. My blood warms as she nears me. Her hips sway as she walks, sending her pale-yellow and white dress swishing back and forth. My eyes follow the way her ass bounces as she strides past. Fleur remains completely unaware of me as I swallow the sight of her curves, my mouth watering as I dream of her soft body beneath me. Most of my nights are spent fantasizing about that tantalizing woman. I imagine her, bent over a chaise in front of the library fireplace, taking my thick cock beneath the many stories of books and artwork, crying out my name to the authors and poets long dead and forgotten as I am sheathed by her pussy.

The image makes my body thrum with desire. The strands of her light-brown hair are pulled up into a bun today. I'm overcome with the desire to dig my fingers into that hair, yanking her head back until her mouth falls open, and then force her to swallow every bit of my spend.

A low, slow growl releases from my chest. They're nothing more than fantasies. The witch has ensured I'll never enjoy a woman's touch or body again. I'll never be able to sink my cock inside her without ruining her. I'm far too large for humans. I learned the hard way that my pleasure would result in their demise. A shudder runs through me at the memory. I'll never forget the way the poor servant girl screamed. I'd only recently become the Beast when it happened. I had been new and desperate on that dark day.

I haven't touched a woman since, but as the years pass, that dark desperation begins to rise again to the surface. *There must be some other way.*

Fleur peeks her head up from the story just long enough to peer across the town square at the farrier tending to several stalls of horses. He meets her gaze, grinning. I know that look. I've watched the couple sneak around for months. But I'm not the only one watching the two lovers. Tall, broad, and everything I no longer am, Gabriel leans against the tavern wall, glaring in Fleur's direction. I've watched the dynamics long enough to know something is going on between Gabriel and Fleur. Gabriel pursues her in a way I would if I were still human. Fleur thwarts the dark-haired man's every advance, regardless of his actions. Gabriel is a ticking bomb. I can feel it.

My eyes settle on the nuances of him. The way his muscles pull tightly across his shirt, the way he towers over every other man around, the way his chiseled face draws the eye of every woman who passes. Envy sets a green flame alight in my gut. Gabriel is everything I used to be. But I won't waste my time focusing on a jealous man.

My hungry eyes turn back to where Fleur has slipped from sight. The farrier moves casually, not far behind. A grin splits my ghoulish features. It's the first of the month, which means I'm in for a treat.

It takes mere minutes for me to cut a path through the forest. The ferns and foliage are worn down from my many trips along this route, their delicate frames unable to recover from the trudging of my massive weight again and again. I'm close, and so is she.

I leer from just beyond the edge of the meadow. Fleur comes running through the field, giggling. She throws her arms in the air as the farrier gives chase. When he catches her, their bodies fall to the earth, disrupting the sea of dandelions and sending them floating up in a cloud of puffy, white seeds. The starry white mass floats past the couple, entering the forest on a gust of wind. Several of the feathery-soft dandelion remnants stick to my dark fur. The farrier's lips claim Fleur's and I swipe the seeds away as jealousy drips me in jade. I reach a finger up to touch my own lips. The massive maw has an array of sharpened fangs protruding from the menacing brown snout at all times. I'd devour Fleur's soft face if I even attempted a kiss.

The farrier slides Fleur's dress above her waist and slowly draws down the white undergarments beneath. I chose this spot because it gives me a perfect view of her glistening cunt. The farrier dips lower, extending his small, pink tongue. I lick my own lips instinctively. What does she taste like beneath those soft curls?

I will find out one day. I'll find a way to have Fleur, no matter what it takes.

* * *

Fleur

"Jean-Luc!" I cry out as his tongue dances along my seam. I can't believe it's been nearly six months since my favorite farrier and I started sneaking off for our monthly rendezvous. He comes to my little town once a month to tend to the animals and make house calls. We've made it a habit to meet in the field near my cottage the afternoon of his departure each month. We choose to keep our arrangement a secret. I prefer it that way. I've sworn off complicated relationships. Jean-Luc asks nothing of me in return, no commitment, no settling down. We simply use each other's bodies for pleasure and company.

Dandelion seeds cloud my vision as Jean-Luc continues his tantalizing assault between my thighs and I bury my hands in his wild, blond curls. Some of the seeds settle in his fair hair, giving him the appearance of a snow angel. He wrings a moan from my body as the pressure deep within my core rises to the surface, sending pleasure skittering through me.

Jean-Luc is gentle, sweet, and oh so giving. Experiencing sex with him is so different from… Well, I'm not going to waste my time thinking of *him* when another man's tongue is buried inside me.

Lingering memories of the past are burned away by the heat growing between my thighs. Jean-Luc latches onto my clit, sucking softly and pushing my needy body over the edge. His name spills from my lips on a note of ecstasy as my thighs squeeze tightly across his beautiful face. My chest is still heaving when he peers up from between my knees. His face is shiny as he grins.

"*Musique à mes oreilles.* I never tire of the sounds you make when you come for me."

"I never tire of the devilish tricks your tongue knows." I giggle out on a sigh. Jean-Luc crawls above me before flipping us both over. We land with his back in the silky meadow grass, my knees straddling his delicate waist.

"Now show me what devilish tricks you hide between those creamy thighs, *mon chéri*." His pupils are blown wide as he stares between our bodies. I bite my lip, taking him in my hand and lining him up with my wet entrance. Jean-Luc isn't overly large, certainly above average, and he knows how to please a woman. I slide down, my body welcoming the size of him as I drop down onto his hips. Jean-Luc's groans urge me on as I roll against him.

Sparks of sensitivity shoot through me. My body soaks up the residual sensations from the first climax. I rub against his pelvis, knowing it will be no time at all before another wave of pleasure erupts inside me. My movements pick up as I get closer to the edge. My moans cease as my body succumbs. I hold my breath, unintentionally falling into old habits as a fresh climax contracts through my core. It is only when my pleasure subsides that any sound releases from my lungs again.

The world turns upside down unexpectedly as Jean-Luc flips me over, driving himself inside my sensitive passage, chasing his own release. The sound of a musket cocking causes him to freeze mid-thrust.

"What do we have here?" Gabriel's deep voice thunders across my skin. My eyes snap up to him in shock. "Up," he orders Jean-Luc. "Take your trousers and leave my sight before I shoot you somewhere that will ensure you keep from ever violating what's mine again."

Jean-Luc scrambles to his feet, grabbing his clothes and running toward town. I slip my dress over my head, fore-going undergarments for the sake of speed.

"Jean-Luc!" I cry out. He gives me an apologetic glance over his shoulder before disappearing. And just like that, Gabriel manages to use fear to drive another of my lovers away. My cheeks burn hot. I glare at Gabriel. "What was that about?"

Gabriel's eyes darken. "Did you think your secret romance would go unnoticed? I have eyes and ears all throughout this village." A scoff is all I can manage in reply. *What a presumptuous ass.* "I better not see him in town again."

"If you don't want to see him, then close your eyes," I quip back. A vein throbs beneath his forehead. "What I do in my free time," I bite out, "and *who* I do it with are none of your concern. It's *your* fault I have to seek the company of foreigners to begin with. No one in the village will touch me thanks to you and your brutish threats."

"Good." Gabriel smiles cockily, putting his dimples on full display.

Those gleaming white teeth infuriate me more and I shove at his chest. "And storming up on us in such a state is indecent and rude."

"Rude?" Gripping my upper arm, he yanks me close. "*Rude*? On the contrary, I waited to intervene until you came. I think that was very polite indeed." He towers over me and I struggle in his grip.

"How would you know when I come?" I'm intentionally baiting him, but as I speak the words, something tightens low in my core.

Gabriel's big hand as he jerks me flush against him snares my skin with such force that I'm sure it will bruise. "I remember the way your breath hitches. How you grow silent and tense just before you scream out my name, and that sweet little pussy milks every bit of cum from me." His tongue slides out across his lower lip. "Like it or not, I know everything about you, Fleur." His eyes sear into me with an intensity that sends a shiver cascading down my spine.

"That was a long time ago." My voice comes out quiet and shaky.

"Maybe. But it doesn't have to be." Gabriel dips lower, bringing his face mere inches from mine. His icy-blue eyes are such a contrast to his raven-black hair. It feels as though I have spent lifetimes peering into that magnetic gaze. His lust blazes beneath those frosty blues. For a moment I'm falling into their arctic depths as I push aside every darkness that has separated us all these years. Then those unique eyes suddenly flick up and over my shoulder. The motion yanks me from my reminiscing. Gabriel tenses and my heartbeat quickens.

"What is it?" I ask, turning to peer behind me. My eyes slide along the tree line, noticing nothing out of the ordinary. Gabriel doesn't answer. Instead he releases my arm, raising his musket high and creeping toward the forest's edge. I take advantage of the distraction and dart away, sprinting past home and back toward the village.

Jean-Luc is nowhere to be found when I arrive. Gabriel must have scared him off, just like all the others. I may as well give up on ever finding a proper suitor. My chest heaves a cry of frustration and embarrassment as I think of the way Gabriel manhandled me. I should have slapped him right across that thickly carved jaw.

It seems strange now, but there was a time when I loved everything about Gabriel. We were young, barely teenagers when we became swept up in each other. My fondest memories are of the lanky dark-haired boy I spent so much time with. We spent hours running through the forests and lying beneath the stars. He took my virtue atop the wildflowers near my home and I gave it willingly. Something thin veils across my heart, stitching pain and loss into the depths of each memory-filled beat. I had loved him with all the endless depths and adoration a young lover's heart could give.

But as the years passed it became abundantly clear that our relationship was becoming nothing more than physical attraction. Gabriel learned of family dynamics by watching his own parents and expected his relationships to be much the same. He, the strapping husband, would hunt, drink, and boast of his conquests and trophies. I, the doting wife, would hide myself at home while I cooked his meals, bore his children, and pleased him whenever he asked.

That will not be my life.

As painful as it was, I ended things with him. We were just too different. Gabriel was devastated, of course. He left the village, embarking on a two-year hunting expedition. When he returned bearing forty more pounds of hard-earned muscle and an arrogant confidence that gained the attention of every girl around, he suddenly became the most influential and enviable man in Montrésor. When the neighboring wars broke out, he took up arms and trained the men of our village to fight and protect. Gone was the skinny boy who spent hours listening to me read beneath the crisp autumn leaves, and here to stay was the brawny tavern owner who could defeat every man in an arm-wrestling contest and have any woman he desired.

I don't know why he still pursues me so fervently. I deny his every advance and still he doesn't cease. One final sweep around the town square confirms Jean-Luc is nowhere in sight. More than likely that was the last adventure with my favorite visitor. Gabriel will use one of his many connections to arrange for a new farrier to take Jean-Luc's place.

What am I going to do about that overly muscled, arrogant, son of a bit—

"Good evening, Fleur," Pierre greets, dragging me out of my tempestuous inner rant as I approach his produce stand.

I offer him a warm smile. "Good evening, Pierre. I'm glad I was able to catch you before you left for the night."

"How is Henri holding up?"

My stomach sinks at the mention of my father. "You know Henri, as stubborn as ever."

"I'm sure he'll pull through," Pierre adds encouragingly. "What can I get you?"

I load my basket until it's overflowing with cabbages, carrots, and turnips. I'm going to cook a *garbure* for dinner. It's my father's favorite stew. I just need to get to the butcher to secure some ham before he closes for the night.

The sun is already beginning its evening dip behind the trees when I finish the rest of my shopping. I tuck a warm loaf of bread in my basket and head home. It will be dark soon and every woman in town knows better than to be out after nightfall. The night belongs to *the Beast*.

Something stops me for a moment, and I peer out into the shadowy trees. They say the Beast stalks the woods at night, slipping into the homes of beautiful girls and stealing them away to his cursed castle. It is best to be snug at home with doors and windows locked when the moon takes to the starry sky.

The vendors are tucked in for the evening and the village is quiet. With the exception of the tavern, of course. Light pours out from the stout wooden building. Booming laughter can be heard from within its wooden walls. I sweep past the gaudy entrance. The doorframe is decorated with a variety of antlers, skulls, and other trophy bones. My eyes roll at the garish sight. It's as ostentatious and absurd as Gabriel.

"Come to finish what we started earlier?" As if summoned by my thoughts, Gabriel emerges from the shadows of the alley between the tavern and the hat shop. "Don't you know pretty little girls should be tucked away in bed when the sun goes down? Lest the Beast get his hands on you." His unsteady gaze tracks down my body. He's drunk. It's only too obvious from the way his tall, broad frame sways as he slides closer.

I ignore his comment and sidestep him. Gabriel's arm snaps out with surprising speed considering his inebriated state. He blocks my path, using his body to crowd me against the tavern's outer wall.

"Why do you insist on fighting your feelings for me, Fleur?" His glassy-blue eyes stare down at me with a hungry light behind them. The scent of ale wafts from his breath. It mixes with his familiar, musky scent, creating a heady elixir of delightful past memories and present irritations.

"Feelings? Oh, Gabriel. Try not to use words you don't understand." My mocking tone is less than well received. Gabriel's fist slams against the wall next to my face and his nostrils flare as he growls out.

"You are mine, Fleur. The only woman for me. You should be home in my lodge, lying by my roaring fire, crying out in ecstasy as I fill you so fully your body has no choice but to bear my strapping sons." His dark hair falls loose from its binds, tickling my cheek as he nuzzles closer. "Not out in that farmhouse. Let me take care of you."

Empty words. I bark a mirthless laugh. "The only woman for you? How romantic. Is that why I hear there's a new girl in your bed each night? Because I'm the *only* woman for you?"

"Those women mean nothing to me," Gabriel grunts irritably. I spare him a tight smile.

"Let them bear your strapping sons and leave me be." I shove him backward and, still wobbly on his feet, he pitches over. The clumsy movement looks almost comedic on his muscular frame. Gabriel curses as he rights himself, but I've already left him behind.

"You're mine, Fleur," he calls out as I hurry off. I toss one more pitying look over my shoulder before turning down the forest path toward home.

CHAPTER 2

FLEUR

"I'm back," I call out, entering the farmhouse I've spent my entire life calling home. Aida hurries over from the fire, helping to take the basket from my arms. The kindly old widow does a wonderful job as my father's caretaker. After her husband passed, Aida had no place to stay and no one to look after her. In exchange for watching Papa during the day, I offered her the spare room in our home. She's been with us for months now. I enjoy the older woman's company. We've both lost more than we care to think about, and we bring comfort to each other in the little ways we can. "How is he?" I glance over to where my father sits still and statuesque in his seat by the fire.

"He is hanging in there." Aida's gentle eyes sadden. I'm hopeful, but I'm no fool. I know it's only a matter of time. His condition has been worsening with each passing day. The death of my mother and younger brother three years ago broke something inside him. He and I survived the fever that took their lives, but Henri has never been the same. He stopped speaking and barely eats. My vibrant and outgoing father has slowly faded away into a hollow shell of his former self.

Sadness tugs at me as I look around our home, my eyes landing on all the wondrous inventions he created over the years. He was quite famous at one time. I used his earnings to help keep us going in the beginning. When the money ran out, I started selling flowers from the fields behind our farm. It makes ends meet and ensures there is always food on the table and wood for the fire.

"I'm making his favorite for dinner." All of the cooking fell to me once my mother passed. I took care over the years to learn the recipes she loved to cook for us.

"Such a good daughter. I'm sure that will help cheer him up." Aida eyes the stew ingredients then smiles at me. I hope so. There isn't much that changes his state, but doing his favorite things at least makes me feel better. Aida unpacks the basket. "I'll prepare the vegetables if you will fetch the water. My poor back just can't handle the journey these days."

"Of course." I place a warm hand on her shoulder before wrapping a shawl around my shoulders and heading outdoors once more.

The short trek to the well is filled with the gentle sounds of night and a chilly breeze that cools me through my thin dress. This night is colder than the last. My palms chafe as I heave the water up, pulling the bucket back to the stone ledge. The forest quiets for a moment and a chill trickles down my spine. I turn toward the woods as the distinct feeling of being watched runs its shadowy hands across my skin. I often feel eyes upon me, especially when I am alone. *Make haste, Fleur.* The uneasy sensation urges me to grip the heavy pail more firmly and hurry back to the safety of home.

It's my imagination, surely. For who would spend their

evenings watching me from the dark depths of the forest? The idea is equally terrifying and thrilling.

Sleep eludes me tonight. It remains just out of reach, like a ripe ruby apple perched at the very top of the tree. I toss and turn, squandering my chance for dreams as the hours tick past. The soft, honeyed sun peeks over the tops of the trees, spilling into my room with its mocking glow. I take the hint and relent my efforts for a good night's rest.

Aida and Papa are still fast asleep as I sneak through the house. The gentle chill from last night has settled into a more malevolent cold this morning. Our full stock of firewood serves me well. We've barely needed to use it in the past few weeks. The seasons appear to have changed overnight. I build a fire in the small wood-burning stove near the kitchen, stoking the fire once before slipping quietly through the front door. The morning brings a bitter wind, forcing me to pull my cloak more tightly around me. My attire is less than adequate in these conditions. At least Aida and Papa will be warm when they rise.

What appears to be the last of the dandelions floating across the breeze is actually a light dusting of snowflakes, signaling winter's fast approach. The snow is early this year, cutting off fall before it's had time for a full season. I need to bundle and dry the last of the flowers before the first freeze seals them in its icy grip.

I quicken my steps down the path toward the bakery, where Emeline is already making her famous breads and pastries. The lack of sleep has my belly in an uproar before the sun has fully risen and I purchase more than my fill of the handcrafted goods. *"Merci!"* I call out as I carry the tasty treasures out of the quaint bake shop. I tuck the warm croissants and buttery madeleines away, leaving one particularly gooey chocolate croissant out for my journey home.

I've always had a taste for sweets. Truthfully, I spend far

too much time enjoying my favorite treats. It isn't ladylike, and certainly doesn't lend itself toward a trim figure. But I wear my curves with pride. I'd much rather enjoy a whole tray of *kouign-amanns* than fit into the same corset I wore as a teenager.

My figure is wider and fuller than most my age, but I've embraced it. I never allow myself to forget how lucky I am to be able to always eat my fill. News of war whispers across our village now and then. My life is a dream compared to those struggling in other parts of the country. I'll never understand the thirst for power and land that corrupts the minds of men. And to think, it all comes back to our kingless castle.

Another warm bite of croissant brings me back to the present. The chocolate dances along my tongue and buttery bits of croissant flake along my lips. This is the silver lining to not being able to sleep. You get the first pick of the freshest pastries in town.

A distraught wailing reaches my ears as I approach the farm. Aida is running toward me, her face red and puffy. I drop my satchel, spilling the freshly baked goods onto the cold, grassy earth. Aida's words are indeterminable through the sobs but I don't need to hear them to know what has happened.

A warm tear trails down my cheek, catching on the corner of my mouth where a crumb remains caught on my lip. I dip my tongue out, savoring the sweet chocolate and salty tear. The two clash, tasting of long-expected grief and an innocence lost. It isn't until I push inside the house and take in the wide, lifeless eyes of the man who raised me that it begins to truly sink in. My papa, my last remaining family member, is dead.

* * *

Black has never been my color. Funeral dresses and shrouds appear more like the shadows of death looming over the family members and their friends. Ghastly creatures who plant their talons in every mourning gown and dark suit, slurping up the sorrowful tears of each sad fool. No thank you. Papa wouldn't want to see me dressed like some shadowy, hopeless thing. He loved my strength, my perseverance, and my ability to always find the light in the dark. Instead, I wear one of my favorite dresses, knowing the moment I put it on that it will be forever stained with the grief of today. I've chosen a sky-blue dress with billowy sleeves and a thick white shawl.

The townspeople gawk at me, trying to hook into my self-esteem with their disapproving glares. I ignore them. This is just another scrap to add to the heaping pile of misunderstood moments that make me seem odd to everyone around. Papa never thought me strange or unusual. He was convinced it was all the townspeople who were odd. I remember giggling at his silly tales. I felt the true love of a father when he spouted, with great sincerity, the nonsense that the entire village was filled with unsavory characters, claiming I was the only normal one, all to spare his daughter the feelings of loneliness and rejection.

The priest speaks in solemn, emotionless tones that make it easy to tune him out. I'm cold, numb, and it has nothing to do with the steady flurry of snow accumulating on my shawl. My eyes stay fixed on the mound of freshly tilled dirt that butts up against the toes of my boots. A sudden unsteadiness rocks through me and I sway, watching the snow shift from vertical, to horizontal, and then back again. I feel the eyes of the villagers glued to every part of me, hear the murmurs, speculations, and pitying phrases tossed my way. It's all too much. The world presses in around me until it feels as if I'm the one entombed in that wooden coffin for all eternity. The air turns thin, as if the townsfolk are sucking it out from the space around me, leaving me to heave in deep, unfulfilling breaths like a rabbit with an arrow in its lungs.

I can't stand it anymore. My boots crunch through the light layer of crisp snow on the ground as I turn on my heel, racing off toward the forest, away from all thoughts of death, away from the scrutinizing stares of strangers, and away from my grief. Or lack thereof.

The fear settling deep in my gut stems from the icy detachment that has flooded my veins. I haven't cried since the day I found him. The murky feelings of my current sadness are muted compared to the overwhelming sorrow that nearly drowned me when I lost my mother and brother. Perhaps it's because Papa was gone long before his heart stopped beating.

Am I wicked for thinking such things?

My feet carry me deep into the woods and by the time I stop, my lungs are screaming from the exertion. The searing pain that accompanies each breath gives me pause, and I slow, resting my back against a massive oak tree. I allow my eyes to fall shut as my breathing works to even itself out, enjoying the silence and solace the forest provides.

"Fleur?"

My eyes open at the unexpected voice. Gabriel stands before me, his black funeral attire barely fitting his broad frame. How did he sneak up on me? He is a hunter. I suppose it's his job to sneak up on vulnerable prey in the woods. Arctic-blue eyes gaze down at me. I peer up into them, noting the lack of their usual haughty edge. "Are you all right?" His brows furrow in concern and it touches me to see him in a way I haven't for so long.

"I'll pull through," I sigh out. Even I recognize how small and pitiful my voice sounds. Gabriel reaches out to brush a loose strand of hair from my face. I lean into his touch, allowing my cheek to rest in his warm, large palm. A fresh tear rolls down my cheek and onto his skin. He draws me into his arms, and I don't fight him. His embrace is warm and comfort swells inside me as I bury my face in his strong, firm chest. I breathe deeply, inhaling his familiar masculine scent. His hand strokes down the back of my head as we stand in silence.

There are so many things I hate about Gabriel. The way he treats women like property, his arrogance, and his brutish mannerisms whenever I'm around. But I've been on my own for so long. Honestly I'm tired of fighting, tired of being strong and defensive all the time. Tired of being alone.

I pull back, peering up into his light eyes, and make a rash decision. Raising onto my tiptoes, I kiss him, drawing his warm lips to mine deeply. Gabriel's body reacts immediately. His hands fall to my hips and he drags me flush against him. Firm lips work over mine, diving into the kiss like a drowning man into a pool of life-sustaining water. I bury my numb fingers in his jet-black air, pulling him down, removing any remaining space between us.

"Fleur," the word ghosts against my mouth. I can feel how badly he wants me and right now I need to feel wanted. My nails tug slightly on the roots of his long hair and he growls into my parted lips. He backs me up, pressing my body against the tree and driving his erection into my stomach. I gasp when I feel the thick ridge of him through my clothing.

Shivers prickle along my skin as Gabriel's fingers dance atop my exposed collarbone before drifting lower. His hand dips beneath my dress. Warm fingers cup my breast in his strong grip. I mewl into him as his tongue snakes inside, claiming every part of my mouth. His other hand drifts lower. I grasp his hair more tightly as he reaches beneath my skirts and slides up. He knocks his knuckles between my thighs and I widen my stance in response to his touch, allowing him access to my heated core. The way he toys with my entrance makes me simper and writhe. When he finally dips his fingers inside me, I cry out in relief. My pussy sucks his thick digits in as he curls upward, stroking me with the skilled hand of a long-lost lover. His lips trace my neck, leaving an imprint of wet heat that is instantly chilled by the cold air. The fingers that were kneading my breast move to grip one of my thighs. My back arches as he raises one of my legs higher to allow himself deeper access to my already-dripping center.

His thumb brushes along my clit, forcing a moan from my lungs. I latch onto his neck, sucking on the skin above his pulse, needing something to steady myself. Gabriel releases a satisfying groan in response to my touch. His deft fingers work me harder. My whole body is shaking, whether from adrenaline, the damp chill of the snowy winter air, or the tantalizing assault of Gabriel's fingers, I can't be sure. "Come for me, Fleur," he breathes into my ear. He jerks his fingers at a demanding pace inside me, causing my body to grind against the tree's rough bark again and again. "Show me how good I make you feel."

I hate his dirty talk. It reminds me where I am and who I'm letting touch me. I move to protest, but his thumb presses down on my throbbing bud and I cry out as deep pleasure radiates from the places Gabriel's fingers touch, filling my body with heat. I resent the orgasm even as I welcome it. The wave of ecstasy crests over me and my limbs soften as I fall limp in his hold.

"That's my girl," Gabriel purrs in my ear. I am most certainly not his girl, but in this glowy daze I find myself unable to argue with him.

Gabriel pulls his fingers from me and raises them to his mouth. I bite my lip so hard it hurts as he takes the fingers inside, moaning when he tastes my cum on his skin. It sends a fresh wave of arousal blazing through me.

"Fucking addicting," he murmurs as he pulls the clean fingers from his mouth. "I missed the taste of you." His lips dip low and he captures my mouth in his, making me taste every bit of pleasure he's given me. Gabriel unbuttons his trousers and bunches up my skirts. "I knew you would come around." He grins as he works his thick cock free from its binds. "You're mine, Fleur." He pulls my hair back, exposing my throat to the sky, forcing me to cry out. "Submit to me, *ma petite fleur*. Be my wife, let me breed you, take your rightful place by my side, where you belong." He lines his engorged tip up with my entrance.

A sharp sort of clarity slices through my sex-drenched mind. All these years and he never changes. He still wants me submissive and dumb. Sitting at home, sucking his cock, raising his children. Shame cloys across my cheeks. I lost my wits in a moment of overwhelming emotion and animalistic desire, but they're back now.

I shove him away and he looks down at me in shock. "I'm no one's submissive bitch. I won't be bred like some animal and left at home to run a household. My life is worth more than time spent doing ordinary, menial tasks as my provincial life ebbs away." I drop my skirts and fight to put some distance between us. "I'll never be yours, Gabriel." And then I run. Gabriel just stands there, frozen where I left him, a dumbfounded expression on his irritatingly handsome features.

It's time to leave this town, to start fresh somewhere else. With my father gone I'm no longer tied to this place. I race home, cutting through the forest and taking the familiar pathways I've worn beneath my feet since I was a child. I slam the door wide, moving with speed and purpose. I fill my bag with a few important belongings, several dresses, a few loaves of bread and bits of cheese, and a spare cloak. I empty my satchel and fill it with some of Papa's smaller inventions to remember him by. My eyes catch on the baby-blue blanket tucked away in the corner of the living room. My mother made it for my brother before he was born. She would sit by the fire, her belly round and cheeks rosy, humming as she worked. My heart tightens as I think of them both. The fabric is soft and worn beneath my fingers. There's not much room in the small bag, but the blanket is thin and I'm able to fit it in my satchel when folded. The faces of my mother and brother float to the forefront of my consciousness. I pat the bag, feeling the weight of memories and loved ones lost in the gentle pressure that tugs across my body as I sling the bag across my shoulder.

"You're leaving?" Aida's sad voice floats in from the open doorway. I move to the other woman without hesitation, sweeping her up in a tight embrace.

"There is nothing left for me here. The house is yours, along with the farm. I left money on the table. Sell all the flowers we have left, and hire help for the next season if you need it. Thank you for everything you've done for us, Aida."

She rubs her hands along my back and sighs heavily. "Beautiful Fleur. Be careful." The old woman gives me one final squeeze before pulling back.

"I will." It takes less than ten minutes to saddle up my trusty palomino and tie the provisions and clothing to the side of his saddle. *Where will I go?* I peer around, assessing my options. *Anywhere is better than here.* I urge my horse onward, galloping into the woods and toward whatever adventures lie ahead of me. Some small piece of me knows there's no turning back now. Everything will be irrevocably and undeniably changed from this moment on. Why does it leave me feeling so uneasy?

CHAPTER 3

RENARD

J watch Gabriel and Fleur's unexpected tryst in the trees with primal fascination. Desire courses through my veins as Gabriel pleasures Fleur. She lets him touch her, taste her, despite the fact she spends nearly every day avoiding him and ignoring his advances. The sudden switch leaves me perplexed. Perhaps it has been too long since I've entertained a woman. Gabriel's body towers over Fleur's. He's built so very similar to the way I was before the Beast claimed my body. Watching them together, I can almost imagine it's me, driving my fingers into Fleur's wet snatch. Tasting her cum on my lips. I grasp myself, hidden among the trees, and stroke my monstrous cock until hot seed roars out of me in time with Fleur's cries of pleasure, covering the bark in thick, sticky ropes. It's an intense and incredible feeling, one I'm already desperate to recreate.

They're going to fuck, right here in the woods. The lasciviousness of the act starts my cock thickening again. But then Fleur shoves him away, snapping something venomous his way before fleeing. My previous confusion intensifies. Does she want him or not? She certainly seemed to enjoy herself

31

while Gabriel's fingers rocked her to climax. So why did she flee? The chemistry between the two is undeniable. Their passion awakens something seductively sinister in my great beastly chest.

A wicked idea takes root inside my depraved mind. Perhaps my manners and sense of propriety have been completely addled by too many years in this monstrous form, but I want them. Both of them. I want to command their bodies to act out my every twisted fantasy while I watch, pumping my cock close enough to spray cum on the two while my hand gives me the only release I'm allowed.

No. I don't just want them. *I need them.* And they will be unable to say no to the Beast.

Fleur is mounting her horse, armed with satchels of belongings by the time I reach her cottage. *She's leaving.* Every pounding hoofbeat leads her farther from the safety of home, and nearer to my castle. No villagers, no Gabriel, no one to snatch her away from me. It's just Fleur and I, alone in the woods. *My woods.*

I stalk Fleur as she progresses through the forest, riding farther along the forbidden path and unknowingly, ever deeper into my domain. She reaches a fork in the road and pauses. *What is she waiting for?* Fleur looks behind her, front teeth worrying her bottom lip. Her horse trots anxiously in place. The animal can no doubt sense what Fleur has chosen to ignore until this moment. The uncertainty of the path ahead, that eerie feeling of being watched. She turns forward again, allowing her horse to take several steps, before stopping him and glancing over her shoulder once more. *She's considering going back.* The realization brings a snarl to my lips. *Oh Fleur, there's no turning back now.*

Wicked winds disguise my approach as I drop to all fours, moving silently through the powdery snow. I'm a hunter and I've spent years perfecting the ability to catch my prey unaware. Anticipation storms in my belly and hot blood rushes to my groin as I close the space between us. She is so much closer than ever before. My claws twitch, protruding deeper into the ground with each step. My muscles coil with the realization that just moments from now, I'll get to touch her for the very first time.

I pause, breathing deeply. Fear dampens my excitement. Fear that this is all a dream. What if I'm home, asleep in that dark, drafty castle? Fleur's hood falls back and she shivers as the cold air reaches her neck. Her cheeks and nose are pink with the winter chill. *This is not a dream*. I take another step forward. *This is real, and Fleur is mine*.

Years spent pining over this gorgeous woman. Years allowing her to torment me in nighttime fantasies that can never come true. Now, at last, I have her. I'm mere inches behind her now, crawling low and slow. Poor little prey, completely unaware of the monster lurking in her midst. I raise up, bringing one of my massive paws high in the air, and quickly clamp it around the front of her face. She screams beneath my palm as I drag her off her mount, careful not to let her see my face. Her horse rears, whinnying mournfully before taking off back the way it came. In the presence of the Beast the animal's loyalty has been replaced with the desperate desire to survive. I would have done the same thing.

Fleur continues to struggle in my grasp, even biting the meat of my paw. I wince as her teeth sink deep into my flesh. But her attempts to harm me do not loosen my hold. I have her mouth and nose blocked. It will only be a few more moments now. The fingers clawing at my paw begin to slow before dropping weightlessly down. Her muffled cries of terror cease completely. I peer around, just as her light-green eyes slip closed.

She's passed out. I release my hold on her face. The last

thing I want is for her to suffocate. She weighs no more than a doe as I toss her over my shoulder, relishing the way her soft curves feel against my body. My paw slides up the back of her thigh, feeling the heat radiating from her core. I bite back a groan and my fangs pierce my bottom lip. I won't touch her now, won't soil her with my beastly claws and fangs. But I have other things in mind. Things I am very much looking forward to.

We reach the castle and I'm thankful I only have to put her to sleep once more along our journey. Her body is still as I lay her on the dungeon floor. I secure a thick shackle to her ankle. She doesn't fight me. Her body remains limp and unmoving. My eyes rove over her creamy skin and supple frame. Her lips are slightly parted as she breathes in and out. My erection aches as I gaze down at her, so still, sleeping, and so vulnerable. It triggers something predatory in me that I can't deny. I drag the tip of one claw along the soft pink flesh of her mouth. My fingers jerk back when a thin trail of blood wells up. *Patience*, I remind myself. I have the girl of my dreams in my castle. Now it's time to get Gabriel.

* * *

Gabriel

The headboard slams against the wall so hard it cracks. "Yes, Fleur." My need bleeds into my words as my cock slams to the hilt again and again.

"I asked you to stop calling me that." The woman I'm pile-driving from behind sighs in frustration. I bend forward, grabbing her face in my hand and squeezing until she winces. I turn her neck until she's forced to stare up at me.

"And I asked you to keep your mouth shut while I fucked you. Don't disappoint me again, or this will be the last time I take you. You are replaceable. Do I make myself clear?"

She nods in my grasp, tears pooling in her blue eyes. I release her and pick up my pace, thrusting savagely. She's pissed me off, and now I'm going to make sure it hurts. The woman whining beneath me is one of the triplets. Blonde hair, blue eyes, and big tits. I don't know which one, and I don't care. I fuck them all, indiscriminately. They're nothing but holes to be filled.

It should be Fleur beneath me, writhing as I wring every ounce of pleasure from her body. I want to bury my face between her thick thighs and then fuck her so hard she forgets how to speak. She's mine and I'll be damned before I let another man touch her again. I will have her, and when I do, I'll punish her thoroughly for keeping me waiting for so many years.

Tension coils at the base of my spine as my balls draw tight. I pull out, gripping my dick and biting back a guttural sound as I finish myself off. My cum covers the triplet's back in thick, white spurts. There's no way I'm getting one of those brainless blondes pregnant. No, that honor is for Fleur and Fleur alone.

I sink back on my feet. The triplet sits up, turning to face me. Watery blue eyes peer up at me through thick lashes. She didn't come. She didn't deserve to.

"Next time keep your mouth shut." She nods submissively. "Now get out." She leaves the bed hurriedly, grabbing her clothes and darting toward the door. It doesn't matter how poorly I treat the women in this village. They always come crawling back for more. Everyone except Fleur. The only one I truly want.

Sex with the triplet leaves me feeling less than satisfied. I need a drink. I stumble down the street and into the tavern. The men notice my arrival and a mug of ale is on the table in front of me before I even sit down. I chug the pint, then slam the mug into the wall, leaving a large hole behind. Shame burns through me as I remember the way she left me in the woods, slack-jawed and dumbfounded with my dick out and blue balls so bad I had barely been able to walk back home. The triplet had been loitering annoyingly close to my property and I'd pushed her into the cabin and shoved my cock inside her before I had a chance to rethink things. Fucking her did nothing to ease my fury. The men refill my pint and Laurent drops into the seat next to me.

"You okay, Gabriel?" My right-hand man gazes at me anxiously.

"Perfect." I drain my glass again, not caring that my sour mood has caught the attention of every man present.

"Is this about Fleur?" Laurent asks. My hand shoots out, gripping Laurent by the throat.

"Do not speak her name in my presence again." I release him and drown myself in another ale.

"Sorry, I just hate to see you like this, boss. She's really done a number on you."

My glare fixes on him. He shrinks back. "What is your point?"

Laurent downs his own drink before continuing. "I mean, what more could she want? You're the most handsome man in town." A group of girls giggle nearby, including the triplets. I toss an uninterested glance their way. One of them quickly looks down at her feet. It must be the one I just finished hate-fucking. Her clear discomfort makes me smile. "Not to mention the strongest, the best hunter, the bravest, the most popular—"

"Your point, Laurent?" I bite out.

"What more could she need?" He sets his mug down

thoughtfully. "Hell, I bet you're strong enough you could just make her do what you want."

The damp mug stills before my lips. I've never thought of that. All these years I've been begging and pleading for her to want me, waiting for the day she came to her senses. Why? When I could just take what I wanted. Who would dare to stop me? No man in the village is brave enough to challenge my authority to seize what I want.

"Laurent, you're a genius." I clap the other man on the shoulder and beer spews from his mouth. *All I have to do is take what I want.* I toss back one final round and push up to my feet. Laurent cheers me on as I walk past the giggling fan club of desperate women. I make sure to slap the ass of the triplet still staring at the floor. She jumps beneath my touch. The other women send jealous glares her way. If only they knew.

The snow is coming down harder now, cascading over every surface in a dense carpet of white. I barely notice. The ale courses through my blood, warming me from the inside out. My heavy boots thud loudly as I trudge through the crunchy mixture of snow and ice. I make it to Fleur's isolated farm in record time. Smoke rises from the chimney and I grin. She must be home. I kick in the door, not bothering to stand on pleasantries or pretense. A shrill scream comes from the elderly woman chopping vegetables in the kitchen. It's Aida, the old widow.

"Where's Fleur?" I demand, ignoring the ashen color of her pallid skin. Aida looks truly terrified. I march forward, leering down at the woman. Her spine is twisted and hunched from age and I tower over her with feet to spare. "Where. Is. Fleur?"

"She left," the old bat manages to whisper out.

"Where did she go?"

"She didn't say. But she left the village, for good."

My stomach churns. "When?"

"A few hours ago. But her horse came back soon after, alone. I've been worried sick, but the weather has me trapped here. I couldn't make the journey into town for help on my own." That information chills my blood. Fleur is out in the forest, at night, in freezing temperatures, alone.

I storm toward the stables, saddling the largest horse and jumping on before Aida can protest. My heels dig in, urging the animal forward. Time is of the essence. There are no other villages for miles. And everyone knows you are never alone in the forest. Wolves roam these lands. My mind revisits the dress Fleur was wearing when I last saw her. She'll surely freeze to death with no fire or shelter.

Snow whips through my eyes as the farm fades behind me. The thunder of hooves pound into the frosted ground, leaving deep prints in the powder. I pull the horse to a halt to search along the trail. Everything blurs into a messy world of white. I dismount, scouring the pathway for a sign, and there it is. They're shallow now, but if I squint I can just make out the tracks Fleur's horse left during their hasty departure.

I return to my mount, slapping the reins down hard and causing the animal to burst forward. My own body is already beginning to chill, and my concern for Fleur's safety deepens. I slow the horse again when we reach a fork in the road. I dismount, searching for the familiar tracks and clues. *Which way'd you go, Fleur?*

One road stretches completely undisturbed save for the small animal tracks that wind their way across the path. Likely belonging to a small fox. I peer at the other side and am stopped dead in my tracks. There are new footprints in the snow. They're massive, and inhuman. I place my own foot within one and swallow thickly. The unusual paw print dwarfs my boot, making my large feet appear no bigger than a child's. A foreign and unwelcome fear snakes through me. Beginning in my gut, it works its way through my stuttering chest and finally settles in the dark recesses of my mind.

The Beast.

So the legends are true. The size and depths of the tracks prove the creature is as monstrous in size as they say. And that monster has Fleur.

I leap onto my horse, turning it around and racing toward town. I'm going to need help if I want any chance at saving her. And mark my words, I will save her. Then she'll have no choice but to be mine. I smile despite the unforeseen turn of events. This may work out in my favor, after all.

CHAPTER 4

RENARD

The floor trembles beneath me as I pace back and forth in the great hall. I need to come up with a plan to get Gabriel to the castle. Try as I might, my mind remains as vacant of ideas as these old brittle halls. Fleur's solo travels through the forest were most fortuitous. I doubt Gabriel will fall into a similar trap so easily. I suppose I could go to the village and take the man by force. It would be tricky, though. Gabriel is never alone. He spends much of his time in the tavern, surrounded by others. When he does finally stumble home, it is usually in the company of a woman, or several.

I'm still mulling over my options when a familiar sensation creeps up my misshapen spine. *Someone is in my forest.* A heavy pounding reverberates through the castle as I rush to my private quarters, seeking answers from another of the witch's cursed objects. *The magic mirror.*

The mirror was originally a fixture of my dressing chamber, but upon arriving back in the castle in the form of the Beast, I found it moved. The enormous gilded mirror stands as tall as I am and covers nearly an entire wall of my bedroom. It cannot be moved and it cannot be broken.

Initially it tormented me, showing visions of what was happening in the world outside these miserable castle walls and forcing me to gaze upon my beastly form. The witch put it there to dishearten me, no doubt. To show me all the things I would no longer be able to do or have and places I could never again visit in this hideous form. But I learned to use the mirror to my advantage, finding it extremely effective in scouting my land for trespassers and then hunting them with thrilling precision. The mirror has become my main source of information and entertainment. I can see anything I want. But the price for a glimpse into the outside world is blood, and the mirror always collects.

My paw presses hesitantly against the cold glass. I grimace as the mirror shudders beneath me. It bites into my palm, its hidden teeth like a living being that dwells within the reflective depths. The familiar, painful sensation burrows into my skin as my paw remains flat against the cursed object. Crimson trickles down the smooth surface. The mirror swirls to life, satisfied with my offering. Its eerie voice rolls through my thoughts. *What do you wish to see?*

I need only to think it and the woods surrounding my home swim into view. A group of ten men march up the pathway that leads to the castle gate. They carry torches, muskets, swords, and pitchforks. I squint at the image. *What foolish band of imbeciles would walk so confidently into certain death?* A lone figure leads the group, riding atop a glossy, black horse. A smirk peels my lips back as I recognize the icy-blue eyes and raven hair of Gabriel. He's headed straight for the castle, willingly. And he brought snacks.

I peek over the edge of my balcony. The men have dismounted and successfully broken through the gate. It won't be long now. A dark chuckle echoes through my quarters. Those fools are going to march straight to the front doors. I know this castle and its grounds better than anyone, and I'll be on them before they have a chance to scream. A predatory hunger takes root as I move on all fours, crossing the castle's great distance with ease.

The gardens run all along the property, and one of their entrances leads me straight out the side of the castle. Heaps of cursed roses shiver and quake as I creep past, moving stealthily toward the front door where my visitors gather. I hear them now, just around the corner. The sound of so many low voices makes my mouth water. No, I do not enjoy eating humans, but I do take great pleasure in tearing them apart.

"The monster that hides in these castle walls is a threat to your families! He won't hesitate to eat your young and ravage your pretty wives! He's lived content in these stone walls for far too long! We've allowed him to fill our nights with dreams of fangs and claws! We've allowed him to keep us from hunting in some of the most prolific woods for miles!

"But no longer! Today is the day we kill the Beast!" Gabriel spouts his speech with such confidence and arrogance. The men hang on his every word, cheering as he finishes. It makes me smile. Once again, Gabriel reminds me of my former self.

"Kill the Beast!" one of the men echoes Gabriel's words.

"Let's burn the castle to the ground with the monster inside!" another cheers. Gabriel grips the man by his coat, jerking him forward before slapping him across the face.

"Fleur is inside that castle. Our priority is to save her. *Then* we kill the Beast, so I can mount his head in my tavern as punishment for taking what is *mine*."

My broad grin twists into a predatory snarl. What is *his*? Oh, Gabriel. I may be willing to lend Fleur's body to you so that I can watch the two of you enact my every fantasy, but at the end of the day, Fleur belongs to me. Gabriel will serve me until I tire of him. Then I'll snap his worthless neck.

I'm as quiet as the grave that refuses to take me, treading silently through the snow until I'm just behind the soon-to-be slaughtered army. I let the name Renard slip away as I prepare to taste flesh and fully embody the Beast. They think I'm a monster? I'll show them just how right they are.

It's almost too easy. I rise to my fullest height, casting a shadow across the oblivious trespassers. They freeze, turning as one to face me as I tower over their pathetic forms. They reek of fear, it's something the Beast craves, a tangible taste that floats through the air, ghosting along my monstrous tongue. Eyes widen and mouths gape as they take in my mountainous size and hideous appearance. I like this part. My victims taste different, better even, when terror flows through their veins. It's the same with animals. The fear sours their blood, like raspberries fermented too long, making it rotten and foul, but so unbelievably tart and irresistibly sweet as well. A death wine, begging to be drunk.

My first priority is to separate Gabriel. The last thing I need is one of these pompous imbeciles shooting my prize by accident. The man closest to me charges, pitchfork in hand. His courage is surprising, but ultimately pointless. My paw grips the weapon, yanking it loose from the feeble man's hold before turning it around and skewering the two closest victims on its sharpened points. Blood spurts from the mouths of both men as their bodies fuse into one when the pitchfork rams clean through their corpses and out the other side.

Two down.

I lunge for the rest, using my massive paws to split the group in two, knocking them aside and charging straight for Gabriel. A sharp crack blows through my ears as he fires his musket, grazing the thick skin of my shoulder. I grab Gabriel by the skull, slamming him into the castle's front door and knocking him unconscious. His large frame drops like a sack of potatoes, hitting the ground with a thump that's anything but graceful. Blood drips from the cocky man's forehead, tracing down the carved features of his face and pooling in the cleft of his chin. He will live, but it will cost him one hell of a headache when he wakes up. By the time that happens, he will be locked away in the dungeon with Fleur.

Frantic prayers bring my attention back to the survivors. They're getting to their feet again. A few decide to stay and fight. The others run for their lives. My right paw shoots forward and I bury my claws in the face of a plump, bald man. He shrieks in terror as the talons drive deep inside, pressing through his eyes and shredding his face before retracting. My other paw swipes hard across a tall, wiry man's throat, severing the head clean from its perch.

Four down.

Now to catch those who chose to flee on foot. I turn toward the forest, loping down the castle path, hunting each remaining man. I tackle two of the slower men together, then slam their skulls into each other, the concussive force scrambling their brains and killing both on the spot. I drop their corpses without another thought, and continue on.

Six down.

The seventh man is climbing a tree when I approach, clearly blinded by his fear in assuming the Beast cannot follow. Technically I don't have to climb it. Instead I wait until the man reaches the very top and then slam my body into the thick trunk. The shrieking victim shakes loose of the branch he's clinging to and falls to the ground. His neck breaks with a sharp and satisfying crack. The death is too simple, too quick. I put all my weight on the back of the man's limp head, increasing my pressure until the skull bursts like an overripe melon between my toes.

Seven down.

Number eight has given up by the time I stalk to his hiding spot. He cowers against the cold earth, crying and begging for mercy. Mercy is for men, not monsters. I open my jaws wide and sink my fangs deeply into the cowardly man's neck and chest. The sweet taste of frightened blood ladles over my tongue and runs hot and thick down my throat. The snow turns crimson as the blood drains from the now-lifeless corpse.

Eight down.

Gabriel makes number nine, which means only one man remains in the wilderness. It takes me longer to track this one. It's clear this man fled the battle the moment it began, not even bothering to stand and fight. Wide eyes peer over his shoulder as he runs. There's something familiar about this one. He's always hanging around Gabriel, one of his closest friends. He screams when I tackle him, splaying his shivering form in the snow.

"What's your name?" My voice is pure animal. Blood drips from my wet maw and splashes onto number ten's ruddy cheeks.

"Laurent," the man whispers. Yes, Laurent. That's right. Gabriel's friend. I grip the man's collar and drag him back to the castle. He may be of great use to me if Fleur and Gabriel put up a fight. I have a feeling they might. In fact, I hope they do.

* * *

Fleur

"It's no use," I grouse, frustrated. My ankle is bloodied and raw and my fingers stiff from frost by the time I stop trying to pull free from the metal shackle. *Where am I?* It's some sort of dungeon, that much is clear. Cold, gray stone covers the floor and walls of my tiny prison. A gust of wind blows a cloud of flurries in through the slanted window on the far wall, adding to the pile of snow accumulating in the corner, and further chilling my already-frozen body. Feeling vacated my nose, fingers, and toes long ago. Everything hurts as I get to my feet, limping over to peer outside. My muscles screech and protest as I push them to work. Every step burns as my blood tries and fails to heat my numb extremities. I need to find a way out of here before I freeze to death. Cold air bites at my face as I press it against the window's opening. I gasp, sucking in freezing air as I realize how incredibly high above the ground I am. *I'm in a tower?*

All I can see beyond the stone walls are woods for miles and miles. A faint glow in the distance gives me a flicker of hope. It must be the village. But if I'm this high up, so far from home, surrounded by trees and nothing else for miles around, then that means…

A sinking feeling tenses my stomach as I realize where I've been taken. "I'm in the castle," I whisper out loud.

"Yes, you are," a deep voice booms in response, making me flinch. I turn and am met with darkness. Whoever just spoke remains shrouded in the shadows.

"W-who are you? Why have you taken me?" My heart thumps against my ribs. I have a pretty good idea exactly who is lurking outside the cell. I utter a quick prayer, hoping I'm wrong. The man does not respond and my anxiety grows. It claws at my fluttering insides, flapping noiselessly amidst the eerie silence until I can bear the feeling no longer. "Show yourself," I stammer through chattering teeth.

A dark chuckle reverberates across the prison's stone

walls, making me immediately regret my demands. "As you wish."

The already-thin air is stolen from my overworked lungs as he steps into the dim lighting the moon provides. *The Beast.* He's at least eight feet tall and covered head to toe in deep black fur. Massive elongated feet end in sharply taloned toes. A pair of loose, tattered brown trousers cover his lower half. The threadbare fabric leaves his broad torso and hunched upper body bare. Large paws with claws that glint in the moonlight flex at his sides. A mouth packed full of hideous fangs smirks back at me. The largest of the teeth has to be at least four inches long, larger than any of the paring knives I use to prepare my meals back home. A wide, flat snout leads up to a thick, bristled mane where two vestigial horns curve upward, adding to the Beast's menacing stature.

The most unusual part of this monstrous creature is his eyes. They're blue. Not icy and pale like Gabriel's, but deep and saturated, like sapphires and the sea. They are also unmistakably human. There have been rumors of course that the Beast killed the prince and took over the castle. But there is another story, believed far less often, a tale that swears the Beast is the prince himself, cursed for some wicked deed carried out at his behest. I'm starting to believe the latter to be a more likely possibility. Those mesmerizing eyes pull me in, drowning me in their watery depths, and I find myself unable to look away.

"Speechless," he muses, cocking his head to one side. His voice is as surprising as his eyes. It resonates deep and smooth, but there is a dangerous, gravelly edge beneath every word.

"W-why?" I ask again, my body shivering so hard I can barely form the word.

"I need you to do something for me, Fleur. To give me

something I deeply desire. I've watched you for years and now I'm certain it was always meant to be you. Only you."

His words make no sense to my trembling mind as it slowly begins to shut down. *Watched me for years? Needs me?*

Frustration and fear bubble together like a poisonous tonic, filling me with a confounding mixture of bitter despair and foolish courage in the face of certain death. "I c-can't do anything for you if you let me f-freeze to death in this dungeon," I spit out with all the strength I can muster. He gazes down at me, his brows furrowing in thought.

"My apologies. It has been many years since I've had a human guest."

"Th-this is how you treat guests?" I glare back at him and he chuckles.

"Come. I will move you to a more suitable room for the task required." He crosses the distance between us with surprising speed, breaking open the shackle encasing my ankle in a matter of seconds. I gasp in shock as he stands mere inches before me. Heat radiates from his colossal body. Then he turns, exiting the cell. I stand, frozen in place. He turns back, snarling this time. "Make haste before I change my mind."

I take one step and crumple to the ground. My legs are numb and useless after too much time in the cold. A cry tears from my chest as I hit the floor. A barrage of pins and needles spider up my flesh. The Beast moves silently to my side, scooping me up in his massive arms and carrying me out of the dungeon. I want to fight him off, want to be repulsed by the monstrosity holding me so close. But I'm so weak and frozen half to death. I lean into his chest, soaking up the heat it provides. My fingers bury deep in his fur, seeking warmth to thaw them. The Beast growls low and slow and I shiver as the sound rumbles through me.

The air warms as we move farther away from the drafty

dungeon. I lift my head, attempting to familiarize myself with the new surroundings. I've got to find a way out of here. As soon as I can walk...

"Already planning your escape?" His voice makes my pulse jump. The Beast lumbers through the halls and his warmth continues to melt the chill and tension from my body. "Don't bother." His massive paw closes around my face in an instant. I struggle to breathe beneath the thick, soft fur.

My last conscious thought is that he smells of Christmas. Cinnamon and pine trees and juniper berries beneath the frost. It wraps around my senses as the world turns dark. Maybe I'm dreaming. Maybe this is all a dream. A few seconds later, my mind is forced into sleep and new dreams sweep in to take reality's place.

CHAPTER 5

FLEUR

"*F*leur." A frantic whisper wakes me from my beastly nightmare. What a horrible dream. A shiver skates across my skin as I replay the scenario. Sharp fangs, claw-tipped paws, a frozen dungeon, and cinnamon fur.

"Papa?" Sleep still dusts across my eyes as I take in some light from the room.

"Fleur!" The voice is more forceful this time. Its deep resonance triggers an uncanny familiarity within me.

"Gabriel?" Strong hands grip my shoulders hard enough to hurt. What is he doing in my room? Thick blankets surround my body, their weight keeping me wrapped in a cocoon of warmth and comfort. The velvety-soft fabric glides beneath my fingertips like petals. *This is not my bed.*

A whip of clarity cracks across my mind and I'm wide awake. Gabriel's crystal-blue eyes swim into focus. A loud slap echoes through the room as my hand connects with his chiseled face.

"Fuck." He snatches my wrist in the air and his seething glare makes me freeze. "What was that for?"

"Where have you taken me?" My eyes dart around the space. It's not my home, and it's certainly not Gabriel's. The lack of animal trophies and desperate women make that much abundantly clear.

"I didn't take you anywhere. The Beast took me when I was looking for you. I followed his tracks and attacked him with my men."

"The Beast? That's not possible. It was only a dream."

Gabriel's jaw clenches as he spits the next few words out. "It's very real, Fleur. Look around. We're in the castle."

I do as he says. The room is more spacious than my entire home back in the village. Rich, red, and smooth, gold dominates every wall, piece of furniture, and even the ceiling. The bed we're in is larger than my kitchen. The sumptuous ruby comforter that covers us is decorated with embroidered feather inlays. A snow-white canopy looms above, fastened to the ceiling on a wheel of ornate gold with white plumage around the top. Two gilded angels perch on either corner at the foot of the four-post bed. Their long arms hold the canopy fabric open wide. The center of the bedroom boasts a prodigious chandelier. Crystal teardrops hang from every inch of the fixture, and tall white candles glow brightly at each peak. The same design is mimicked in the sconces that line the walls.

Several chairs and an impressive wardrobe sit to one side of the bed. Blue and yellow fabrics peek out from beneath one of its closed doors. The last item to draw my attention truly should have been the first. A considerable throne sits across the room. Its high carved back and crimson-lined arms sit in direct alignment with the bed. I've never heard of a throne in a bedroom. Then again, I've never been in a castle.

"Why does he want us?" I wonder aloud.

"I don't know." Gabriel's eyes betray his fear, an emotion I haven't seen from him since we were teenagers.

Every candle in the room extinguishes as the door opens wide, plunging us into darkness. I reach for Gabriel instinctively, gripping his hand so hard his knuckles pop. A dark shadow moves inside. The towering silhouette can barely be seen from the illumination of the candles that line the hall outside our bedroom. Sapphire eyes glow in the inky shadows. *The Beast.*

"Welcome to my home. I will advise you first and foremost not to attempt an escape. If you refuse to cooperate, I'll have no choice but to chain you to the bed. Is that understood?" The voice is deep, and gruff, yet there is something posh and refined about the clipped manner of the words. It's not at all what I expected from a monster.

"Why have you taken us, Beast?" Gabriel is quick to speak. His loud voice makes me jump.

Those luminous blue eyes land on me in the darkness. My body shudders and Gabriel pulls me close. A soft growl comes from the shadows. "I need you. Both of you."

"What for?" I murmur, my curiosity bettering my fear.

"Though I am a monster now, I was once a man…and I have needs that my monstrous form prevents me from fulfilling. The two of you will help satiate my hunger. I will take great pleasure from your pleasure as you act out my every fantasy. Your flesh will be mine to command, your bodies tools to bend to my will. I have watched the village for many years and am certain now that it has to be you, the both of you."

Surely he isn't saying what I think. Our flesh? Our pleasure?

Gabriel's anger fills the room, making the air thick with tension. "Fuck for you? Be your living dolls? Your mind must be as grotesquely twisted as your beastly form. There's nothing you could say to convince me to act out your little fantasies. I'll kill you, and take Fleur back with me, where she belongs, with a man who can give her what she needs."

I tense, preparing for retaliation from the Beast. Instead he chuckles and the sound is far more terrifying than his rage would have been. "That is your final answer? You will not do it?"

Gabriel spits on the floor. "I'd rather die."

The Beast's silence sucks the air from the room. His ocean gaze pins me in its incandescent glow. "And you, Fleur?"

"She's coming with me," Gabriel saves me from answering. The Beast never breaks his gaze. A glimpse of something white breaks through the darkness. Fangs? The Beast is smiling.

"Very well." The candles light as the door swings shut. Was it by magic? Or some sleight-of-hand trick?

"We have to get out of here." Gabriel jumps into action but I remain in the bed, shock seeming to root me to the spot. He roars in frustration when the door won't budge. "There has to be another way out." He continues his search, ripping down curtains and opening every closet and bathroom door in sight. *Why was he smiling?* I sit here, mulling over the question as a bad feeling worms its way into my gut. "Fleur—"

The door to our room opens once more and this time the candles remain lit. The Beast enters, dragging something behind him. His true form is more mountainous and terrible than I remember from last night. Every part of him, from his enormous paws to the curved horns that adorn his head, screams danger. His eyes find mine again and there's a darkness there, a hunger, and I see him in that moment for the true predator he is.

"Let me go!"

"Laurent." Gabriel gasps and I free myself from the Beast's stare, finding a bloodied and battered Laurent at his feet. Gabriel's right-hand man struggles within the claws of the Beast.

"Where are the rest of my men?" Gabriel demands.

"Dead," the Beast answers dryly. "And he will die too, unless you give me what I want."

"You cannot barter with human life!" shouts Gabriel.

"I can and I will. Have you changed your answer?" The Beast flicks his gaze between us.

"No," Gabriel answers firmly.

The Beast appears disappointed, but unsurprised. "Very well."

Laurent flails violently as the Beast lifts him in the air. One great paw grips the back of his head while he screams.

"Wait!" I start, but it's too late. Laurent's neck snaps with one quick motion before he's dropped to the floor in a heap. A stunned silence fills the room. My mouth hangs open on a scream that never comes. The sound wishes to break free but my air supply is trapped behind a prison of fear.

"Murderer," Gabriel whispers, dropping to his knees. "You killed him."

"I have killed and I will kill again, and again, until you give me the answer I want. Perhaps I'll barter with the old woman next." My heart seizes in my chest. "She's all alone in that house. It wouldn't be hard for me to snatch her in her sleep. Though, the old bat might die of fright before I even get her to the castle."

"No!" My terror spills over, giving me voice. "Please, leave Aida out of this."

"You control what happens to Aida, and the rest of the townsfolk." He strides toward the door, leaving Laurent's body where it fell. "Next time I return, I expect a different answer."

The door slams shut, making the candles flicker. Gabriel rushes to Laurent's body, checking his old friend for signs of life. But I know well that Laurent is dead. His lifeless eyes gaze up at me with the same blank stare I found my father with the morning he passed.

Now all I can think about is Aida, and all the others who have ever been called a friend to Gabriel or me. I can't let them die for me, but can I truly give in to the Beast's demands?

Gabriel's eyes meet mine and I can see the same war raging within his own thoughts. *What are we going to do?*

* * *

Renard

That did not go as planned. The castle shakes as I bellow my fury, stomping through the halls hard enough to shift the very floor. That foolish Gabriel. I chose him for his similarities to me. How I am...or was. It appears his stubbornness is right on point with my own. And then there's Fleur. She was so quiet, so fearful. Not at all what I expected from the free-spirited woman I've fallen in love with from afar. Gabriel all but dominated her mind. He even spoke for her. And the way he pulled her close when she was afraid? It was irritatingly personal. Then again I selected the two for their history, including the intimacy and passion that comes with years of knowing each other in a way I never will.

I storm into my quarters and begin destroying everything I can reach. The west wing is all but ruined anyhow. My fist plows through paintings, fine china, glass vases, and any piece of furniture still standing and within my reach. Why does this have to be so difficult? Why can't those two just admit they're still attracted to each other and fuck? I need to be close to them. I need to feel the heat from their bodies, scent their arousal in the air, hear their moans of passion and desire—

"Excuse me, sir," a nervous-sounding Claude interrupts my tantrum. "Will the three guests be joining you for dinner?"

I whirl on him and he cowers in fear. Claude is a short, plump man with a ridiculous mustache, beady eyes, and an almost constant sheen of sweat across his forehead. Even now, he pulls his handkerchief forward, dabbing at his face anxiously.

"There are only two guests now, and no. They will not be joining me for dinner." Though they may well become dinner if they continue to test my patience.

"But sir." Lucien sweeps into the chamber. I feel a migraine coming on. He and Claude make for quite the vexing pair. "They have never been in a castle before, certainly not one as *magnifique* as ours." He bows with a flourish, his spindly arms and legs looking as if they may snap at any moment, and gestures around him. His over-the-top antics have amused me often over the years, but currently they only serve to aggravate me after today's unsuccessful events.

"I said no," I bark through gritted teeth. "They can starve for all I care."

"Oh pish, tosh, we'll not be having anyone starving while I'm still a part of this staff." Mrs. Perle rolls around the corner with her tea cart in tow. "Now take a seat, young Master, and have a spot of tea to soothe those nerves." Mrs. Perle is the oldest of the small group of employees that run the castle. Of course, she'll stay the oldest until this blasted spell is broken, which will never happen. The staff is frozen in time, as I am. None of us age, grow, change. We're all just living within the curse and its unspeakable repercussions.

Mrs. Perle is a short, stout woman with wild gray hair that always seems to be slipping out from beneath her uniform bonnet. Of all the staff here, she is the one who's least afraid of me.

"Sit," she commands, pouring a cup of tea and stacking a plate with freshly baked scones.

I find the only semi-decent chair left in this part of the castle and sit with a huff. "They did not say yes to my request." I squeeze the teacup hard enough to shatter it, sending the hot, brown liquid spraying across Claude and that absurd mustache. He lets out a long string of curses which I ignore. Mrs. Perle grabs another cup and repeats the same routine. She's used to my outbursts.

"No to what?" she asks. I ignore her question. Instead I toss the tea back in one swig and drop the cup back onto the cart. She frowns and fills it again. Mrs. Perle still wants me to exhibit the refinement of a prince, but that was a lifetime ago. Prince Renard is long gone.

"They said no, so what did you do?" Lucien pushes.

"I snapped the neck of the man from the dungeon to make my point."

"Renard!" Mrs. Perle scolds. "You will not make friends of enemies by killing their friends. What have you done with the poor sir?"

I grin behind my cup, knowing my words are about to send Mrs. Perle into a tizzy. "I locked him in their room."

She removes her bonnet and slaps it across my shoulder. "Young Master, that is not the way we do things. The guests need to be fed and not sitting in their room in absolute terror with a corpse at the door. Your mother and father would—"

"Fine," I concede. I'm eager to stop this conversation

before Mrs. Perle can dive into the past and drag my parents and their pristine hosting skills into the discussion. "But they eat in their room. You can drop the food off inside. And I suppose you can remove the body while you're in there."

Mrs. Perle gives me a satisfied smirk. It triggers something volatile and the little bit of man left in me quickly recedes. She thinks she has won this round, treating me like a child who needs to be put in his place. But it is she who needs to be reminded where she belongs.

"Right." She takes the half-eaten scones from Lucien and Claude before sending them on their way. "You heard the master, off you go, the both of you." The two men voice their complaints as they scurry out of the west wing.

The moment the men are out of earshot I grip Mrs. Perle by the upper arm, enjoying the startled look in her frail eyes as the teapot drops from her hand and shatters on the rug. "You test my kindness too often, Éléanor. Do not attempt to use my parents to manipulate me in front of the others again. You've been a faithful servant of this castle." I increase my pressure on her arm and she winces. "But if you forget your place again, you will join the rest of the disobedient staff…in the ground."

"Apologies, sir. I meant no disrespect." Her eyes go to the ground in submission.

I release her arm without another word. She cleans up the tea mess in silence then hurries out of the room. How much longer can I bear the company of such fools? Their everyday tasks are beneath me, and as much as I despise it, I need them. Still, I've removed a number of the household staff over the years and we seem to be getting along just fine. What's the harm in one or two more? Tension continues to build within me and my anger boils until I'm sweating from the heat. I need a release.

The castle walls rush past me in a blur of candlelight and

tapestries as I stalk through the halls. I pass not a single soul on my journey, and that simply serves to fan the flames of my fury. By the time I reach the foyer, a tangible rage is flowing freely from my pores, surrounding me in an aura that can only end in death. Snow blows inward as the front doors are opened wide. The ruddy, young stable boy comes shivering in. Everything about the pitiful way he shakes and sniffles grates on my nerves. What great need do we have of a stable boy when the horses are never ridden or harnessed to carriages anymore?

His watery brown eyes lock onto me and his body stiffens. He knows exactly what's coming. I don't prolong his death, my patience won't allow for it. I reach for him, savoring the squeak of fear he releases as I secure his head in my grasp. The whites of his eyes are littered with red as I increase the pressure, keeping my hands pressed to either side of his temples. His skull cracks and oozes as I crush it between my paws, enjoying the way it bursts between my fingers like a rotten bowl of fruit. His body twitches after I drop it to the floor. I stare down at it with morbid fascination.

A startled gasp alerts me to the presence of another. Lucien and Claude drop the body they are carrying when they spy the pulpy mess that is the remains of the stable boy's head.

"Get rid of this one when you're done with the first," I grumble, my temporary high fading fast. "And take care of the horses. They're your responsibility from now on."

My usual methods aren't cutting it. I need more. I need Fleur. My cock jerks with the promise of Fleur's wet, willing body, moaning and begging for more beneath the roof of my castle. Perhaps I'll drop in and see if they've changed their minds.

CHAPTER 6

FLEUR

"*H*ow can you possibly eat right now?" Disgust roils through me at the sight of Gabriel digging into roasted pheasant and guzzling down wine. Two panicky men dropped off dinner and dragged the body away nearly an hour ago. Gabriel may be more than willing to accept food and alcohol from the Beast. But I'm not.

"You took a bath, how is that any different?" he asks, food falling from his overstuffed jaw.

"I took a bath because I smelled like a dungeon and was completely filthy. You should consider it." I'm grateful the tub already had water in it, even if it was freezing cold.

"Please. I bathed just—" His words cease as his eyes settle on me. The icy blue of his gaze heats as it glides over the towel currently shielding me from sight. When his eyes lift to find mine again, there's a darkness in them.

"Don't look at me like that," I scold, but heat creeps up my neck nonetheless.

"What are you afraid of?" He moves nearer, towering over me close enough that I can smell the alcohol on his breath. "You wanted it in the woods."

"Stop. We have more important things to think about, like how to get out of here," I snap, but Gabriel only smiles.

"Come on, Fleur." His hands ghost along the top of the towel and the heat of his fingertips sears into my skin as he moves up to my collarbone. "We had something special. After all these years, I know you've wanted me." His lips hover just above mine and I inhale his masculine, woodsy scent. So many years of memories...

The door swings open and I hastily step away from Gabriel. The Beast enters with a wild energy about him. When his eyes meet mine, they house a touch of madness. He glances between the two of us. "Have I interrupted something?"

Guilt and shame bloom through my body. "Where is Aida?" I ask, my skin still warm from Gabriel's touch.

"She is alive, for now. Do you have a different answer for me?"

Gabriel stumbles forward but I throw my arm out to stop him. "We cannot let him kill anyone else," I whisper. Gabriel studies me for a long moment. Then he tucks a strand of hair behind my ear.

"This is what you want? He's a monster." He keeps his voice low, though I'm sure the Beast can still hear him.

My mind flicks to Aida. That kindly woman has only ever been helpful and giving. She was dealt a harsh hand by life and has thrived despite it. To waste her life in such a way is something I cannot live with. "We will be the monsters if we allow innocent people to die on our behalf." With that thought in mind, I make my choice. I reach up, coasting my fingers over Gabriel's strong jaw and his eyes flutter closed. "Are you with me?"

He sighs, melting into me. "I've always been with you, Fleur." When his eyes open again, I see some of the old

Gabriel flickering within them, the one I believed to be long gone, the one I loved with all my heart.

"We'll do it." My voice comes out surprisingly confident despite my fear. The Beast looks as surprised as I feel. He moves slowly to the throne, and sits down gracefully despite his size.

"You will do exactly as I say." His voice is low and controlled but I can hear the barely contained excitement behind each word. "Exactly what I say. Do you understand?" We both nod and he grins, revealing every sharp fang in his mouth. "Let us begin."

The Beast flicks his wrist and the room is plunged into near darkness once again. This time two candelabras remain lit, resting on either of the bedside tables. The part of the room that houses the Beast is a storm of black shadows. His body and throne vanish into the darkness, leaving only those glowing sapphire eyes to illuminate his position.

My stomach explodes in a swarm of butterflies as my eyes adjust to the dark. A concoction of anticipation and fear mingle in my gut and then slither up into my throat. I look to Gabriel, who stares down at me in silence. His expression is impossible to read and he hasn't spoken a word since the lights went out. The silence in the room takes on the tangible weight of a thousand hands in the dark, pressing in on me from every side. It's burning up in here, yet I shiver from the frigid cold. My body is unable to settle on one feeling or another as an endless loop of what may be about to happen spirals through my mind, transforming it into a whirlwind of broken thoughts and devious fantasies. The excitement simmering beneath my fear terrifies me.

Gabriel still hasn't moved. His lack of command puts me on edge. The quiet funnels down my throat, suffocating me in its grip of the unknown. I reach for the half-empty bottle of wine, swallowing all that I can in a matter of seconds. I expect the fire of the alcohol to simmer painfully through me but instead, a smooth richness fills my taste buds as the wine sinks into me. It's the best wine I've ever tasted and I regret guzzling it down instead of savoring the complex flavors. It hits my empty stomach fast and a warmth creeps through my veins. I pass the remaining portion to Gabriel, and he kills the rest. I can't help but watch the way his throat bobs and constricts as he drinks. He tosses the bottle aside and my liquid courage intensifies.

I take the lead, desperate to move out of this anxious silence. "What do you want us to do first?"

The Beast is quiet for a moment, as if he hasn't thought this part through. "Go to the bed."

Gabriel takes my hand, and the touch of his palm on mine sparks to life every memory I possess of the time I've spent in his presence, the good, the bad, the heartbreaking, the intimate... I allow him to lead me, my hand locked tightly in his hold. We crawl beneath the canopy, our bodies illuminated by the candelabras nearby.

"Undress her." The Beast's voice startles me out of my memories. Gabriel hesitates for a moment and it's so unlike him that I suck in a breath and hold it. His hands drift along the damp towel. He's gentle as he frees me of it, his cold eyes never leaving mine. I keep my gaze focused on his, drowning in those frozen pools. The moment my body is completely bare, his stare finally breaks. Roving over my nakedness, his eyes fill with a hunger that makes my core clench. A low rumbling spills across the room from where the Beast is watching. "Now him."

My hands shake as they begin to undress Gabriel. I drink in the sight of him, unable to help but fixate on the large muscles that stretch across his chest, filling up his massive arms and leading down to the trim waist and shapely V that disappears beneath his trousers. No other man looks like

Gabriel. No other man has a physique so flawless it appears to be carved from stone. He's already hard. His erection springs free as I remove the clothing keeping it restrained. Gabriel has always been well endowed. His thick, veiny cock juts out stiffly, and I swallow. A shiny bead of precum forms on the blunt head. My tongue sweeps across my bottom lip as I watch the clear liquid pool on the tip. Gabriel groans as his eyes track the movement. He reaches a hand down between us to grasp his shaft.

"Lay her down," the Beast grunts, his voice rough and tight.

Gabriel lays me back on the bed. I'd forgotten how large his hands are, how easily they swallow my waist in their hold. A louder growl sounds across the room and we both jolt.

"Now use your mouth to make her come. I desire to see how good she tastes between those creamy thighs."

Gabriel grins. "With pleasure, Beast." I watch the gentleness vanish from his eyes as the Beast commands him between my thighs. I think of all the times he pursued me, every single advance I ignored, all the times I humiliated him in front of his followers. I see those memories reflected off the pale blue of his eyes as fire dances behind them. I know Gabriel, maybe better than anyone, and in that look, I realize...he's going to make me pay. Maybe not now, maybe not tonight, but it's coming. It's been coming for years.

A shudder ripples through me as he pushes my knees up and spreads me wide. I chance a glance in the Beast's direction. All I can see in the darkness are those glowing eyes. What is he thinking? What is he feeling? Part of me wishes to see him. All of him. To know what he...

All thoughts of the Beast vanish the second Gabriel's tongue swipes up my seam. My eyes roll back as his thick, hot tongue strokes me possessively. My back arches as sparks fire up my spine and heat courses through my blood. Gabriel's tongue dips into my folds, drawing a throaty moan from me. When he pulls out, he trails light touches up my center, flicking at the top of my clit. I whimper and grind against his face. *More.*

"So needy, isn't she, Beast?" Gabriel's smirk makes me want to kick him right in his handsome face. What the hell is he thinking? A few minutes ago he was against this, threatening to kill the Beast and hang him on his wall. Now he's getting off on the Beast watching? On making me squirm beneath both of their gazes? Gabriel just likes a good trophy —bragging rights that he's the best. My arousal on his face should be evidence enough of his skill. I'm practically a puddle beneath him and he's barely touched me. "What do you think, Beast? Does she deserve to come?"

I look from one to the other. I can't tell if I despise this turn of events, or if it turns me on.

"More," the Beast decrees from his hiding spot, his voice noticeably strained. "Make her come."

Gabriel's perfect dimples come to the surface, giving him the irresistible mix of boyish charm and savage man. He slides his arms beneath my ass, jerking me forward. My pussy slams against his chin. He was savoring me before, testing the waters with carefully planned movements, but now, he devours my flesh, feasting on me with such ferocity I instinctively struggle against his hold. His grip on me tightens and he demands submission with his face against my center. Panic turns to pleasure and I lose myself in the overwhelming heaven that his mouth spreads through me, listening to the wet, slurping and lapping as his tongue toys with every inch of my womanhood.

I exhale moans, coloring the air with lascivious music as my orgasm builds and builds. Another sound catches my attention. Somewhere in the darkness I hear it, I hear *him*. A deep, steady groaning coming from the spot where the Beast's blue eyes are trained on me. I'm caught in his gaze, suddenly aware of the way his eyes are moving. No, his body must be moving. His eyes are just the only part I can see. He jerks forward again and again and the grunting grows louder.

He's pleasuring himself.

Revulsion flees from my thoughts before it has a chance to take root and is replaced by a wanton desire to see him, to know what he looks like as he works his monstrous length with his fist, what his cock must be like. Those images terrify and thrill me in equal measure, with the scale tipping more in the direction of thrill than I wish to admit at this moment.

Gabriel pulls my throbbing flesh into his lips and it's all over for me, the sights, the sounds, the feeling of his hot, wet mouth sucking on my most sensitive spot. I come, crying out as euphoria sends me tumbling off the edge before jerking me upward and depositing me in a haze of clouds. My thighs squeeze tight around Gabriel's face as his tongue flicks across my swollen clit, making my legs tremble as another, smaller orgasm ripples through my center.

A deep, desperate roar practically causes the castle to shake. The Beast's eyes must be closed, because I see nothing in the dark. I can only imagine he's found his own release in time with mine. With that thought, the scales tip ever further away from terror and toward a place I am desperately trying to run from.

Gabriel emerges from between my thighs, face shiny, eyes wild, and climbs over me, slamming his hands on either side of my heaving shoulders. "That's enough for today." The Beast's breathy voice stops Gabriel in his tracks.

"What the fuck do you mean, that's enough?" Gabriel doesn't even try to hide his annoyance.

The next time the Beast speaks, his tone is once again low

and controlled. "You agreed to do exactly as I said." His eyes raise up, indicating he's now standing and I'm once again reminded of his unbelievable height. "And I say, enough."

Gabriel moves to stand, gripping his hard cock. "What the hell do you expect me to do with this? What's the point of everything that just happened?"

"The point is control," he says matter-of-factly. "I have it right now, and you don't."

"You monstrous—"

"I'm sure the tub and your fist will be quite satisfactory. There should be water left over from Fleur's bath."

Gabriel glares at the monster, opening his mouth to speak but the Beast cuts him off once more.

"Do not touch Fleur again without my permission. If you do, you'll regret it more than you can fathom." There's something in the Beast's sure tone that demands compliance. He doesn't need to say what will happen if we disobey.

My mind fills with scenarios so unimaginably horrific, goosebumps prickle on my skin. Even Gabriel, who's as alpha male as they come, stills beneath the weight of the Beast's command. I imagine him envisioning the possible punishments as his dark brow furrows. Gabriel glares into the darkness incredulously for several moments before snatching up one of the candelabras and storming into the bathroom. I startle as he slams the door behind him, a string of curses following in his wake.

It's just me and the Beast now. Me and the Beast and the weight of a thousand words unspoken. His eyes bore into me a moment more, and then he turns, stalking out. The candles reignite as the door latches closed. And I'm left alone and more confused than I've ever felt before.

CHAPTER 7

RENARD

hy did I stop Gabriel from coming? I ponder the thought as I haunt along the ragged bones and endless corridors of the castle. I brought him here with the specific intention of watching him and Fleur come undone together and yet in the moment, I don't know, I panicked. I couldn't bear the thought of it being anyone but me inside of Fleur.

It's a foolish notion. I'm incapable of satisfying Fleur. The idea of me penetrating her, only for her soft body to split in two as she bleeds out and her organs tumble to the floor, makes me queasy. That visual will forever be seared inside my mind. The woman I destroyed was nothing more than a servant, but she was beautiful. Even as a Beast I can acknowledge it was a horrific way to die and one I do not wish to repeat with others.

But instead of watching Gabriel use his perfectly proportioned cock to rail Fleur into a new state of consciousness, I stopped him. Nerves got to me. That anxious, parasitic flapping in my stomach was a new and unexpected sensation. I have nothing to fear. I am the ruler of this castle, royal blood

flows through my veins. Still, everything feels new and uncertain. This plan always seemed like a dream, just out of reach and perpetually belonging to the clouds. Now that they're here...

"Everything all right, sir?" Claude's shaky voice alerts me to the fact I'm glaring at the stubby little man who's just crossed my path. I didn't even notice his approach. The fat, sweaty man must be working on his stealth. I can't fault him. I'd want to be able to stay hidden at my choosing as well if my master was an indiscriminate killer and literal beast. His nervous, dotted brow brings a smile to my face. I should never have doubted myself. All I need to do is come up with a plan to get Fleur alone, and avoid letting Gabriel get under my skin in the meantime. But I'll never have a private moment with her while she's locked in that room with him. What will happen if I let them out?

My gaze drifts along the darkened corridor. It would seem the spiders have made it their personal mission to decorate the castle. Silky, intricate webs cover nearly every surface. Sconces and candelabras stand bare, their candlesticks long ago burnt out. Dead leaves crunch beneath my feet, having been swept in through the front door and continuously piling up in the corners and atop the entry carpets as the years of neglect reach steep proportions.

This will not do for Fleur. No, she is worthy of a true castle. She is worthy of being a Queen.

"Prepare the castle," I command.

Claude flinches. "Prepare the castle?" he questions.

"Our guests will be leaving their rooms soon. I expect the castle to be better suited for company by tomorrow."

Surprise lights his eyes. "You're going to let them—" My sharp glare stops him mid-sentence. "Of course, sir. At once."

I smile and Claude's eyes go wide. He bows once before

hurrying off to do as I bid. It feels good to be at the top. Perhaps things are looking up at last.

"Master, come quickly!" Mrs. Perle calls from the end of the hallway. I do not enjoy being summoned so informally, but her unusually fearful tone sends me rushing toward her. What does she have to be afraid of? I am the scariest thing in this castle. I round the corner, spying her wild gray hair in the distance, and follow her outside. And just like that my carefully crafted bubble of tentative optimism bursts.

The roses are dying.

"What happened?" I demand.

"I don't know, young Master. I spotted it when I came out to pluck a few petals for an herbal tea."

Everywhere I look, red petals are raining down, coating the ground in a whimsically grotesque layer of decaying flowers. A dark worry seeds in my consciousness, and for a moment I swear I can hear the witch laughing inside my mind.

"What's happening?" Mrs. Perle asks.

"I'm not sure," I admit, despising how shaken this has made me.

"Could it be the curse? Has something changed?" There's a barely hidden layer of excitement buried beneath her nervous tone. She's hoping the curse will end, but I know better. There's only one way out of this nightmare: Love. And no one can love a beast.

Whatever is truly happening, it isn't good.

* * *

Sleep does not lend me its guise and the dark hours pass with little reprieve from the churning wheel of worry that dominates my mind. The sun rises more slowly, its colors muted by the thick clouds and blur of snow sweeping across the sky. Even so, soft pinks and oranges bleed through, and the delicate rosy colors remind me of Fleur.

My thoughts remain glued to her as I pace along the balcony of my private quarters. Is it possible things are changing because of her? Could she be the one who breaks this curse? Is that still an option? In the beginning, I convinced myself that love was no hard thing to come by. I was certain plenty of women loved me, and the Beast's curse would end up a short-lived cautionary tale spoken about over fine wines and pheasants. It hadn't taken long to realize just how alone I was, and how little I knew of love. Have I ever truly loved? Has anyone loved me?

Red rose petals flutter up on a gust of wind, floating effortlessly into my room. They scatter across the space, landing atop shattered glass and broken furniture. Each softly curled petal contrasts starkly against the destruction that abounds. They settle, mocking me with their vibrant darkness. My mind again wanders to the first of these cursed roses. The one that bloomed in the witch's blood after I ended her life.

If I knew then what I know now...

Self-pity drops me into the orchard seeded inside my mind, always flowering with overripe shame and planted on endless acres of regret. Something sad and simple and too human for the Beast brims behind my eyes.

I throw my fist into the great stone of the castle's outer wall, focusing on the pain. It works. I'm ripped free from the emotional turmoil threading its forlorn fate into the holes of my soul. Blood wells on my knuckles and I sigh in relief as the steady searing pain brings me into the present. Snowflakes decorate my dark fur like ash. A few tiny cold clusters drop onto my open wounds, sending steam rising into the winter air. I cannot allow myself to look back. Every visit to the past risks the ability to stay breathing in the present. But what if the future holds more than empty castles and dark despair?

Fleur's bright eyes illuminate the dark corners of my thoughts. If there's a chance to change things. To truly be with her…

I stalk to the wall that houses my magic mirror, feeling the enchanted chill before the familiar bite of pain passes through my palm as I press it to the glass. I hear the mirror inside my mind. *"What do you wish to see?"*

"Show me the one who torments my heart so. Show me Fleur."

The mass of the mirror swirls and darkens before revealing an image of the bedroom downstairs. Fleur is seated on the foot of the bed, her face buried in her hands. "What will we do?" Her ethereal voice is raspy and broken. Gabriel approaches, dropping down in front of her. It is an action I do not recognize from the haughty man. Lowering himself to another's level.

"We will get through this." His hand reaches out to take one of hers. A tick of jealousy winds the crass clock of emotions within me. My desire to be the one who comforts her grows stronger. "What can I do? Would you like books? Bread? I can ask for them the next time someone brings us food. I know those things always cheer you up."

A small smile tugs at Fleur's lips. "Books and bread. My weaknesses."

I snap my teeth in irritation. Why didn't I think of that? I know how she loves her visits to the bakery and bookstore. I know her routines and hobbies, her likes and dislikes. Hell, I've watched her every second of the day for months. Nothing about the way Gabriel acted during all that time led me to believe he would be, what, thoughtful? Caring? I assumed I would have the upper hand since Fleur treated Gabriel with daily disdain.

I underestimated how much their connection would rekindle under stressful circumstances and in close quarters. Now that things have changed, I'll have to step up my own attempts to sway Fleur to my favor. And Gabriel has given me the perfect way to begin.

CHAPTER 8

GABRIEL

"Well, I know better than anyone your love of books and bakery treats." I grin at Fleur who seems to be cheering up. "Do you remember when we stole a whole tray of macarons from that terrible old baker. Oh, what was his name?"

"Francois!" Fleur barks out, wrinkling her nose.

"That's the one. Horrid old man. We ran all the way past the Green and Acres before we even took a bite. And then the damn things turned out to be burnt. The reason they'd been out on the ledge in the first place is because he was going to feed them to the pigs."

Fleur laughs until tears fall, and her wide smile and the fact that I put it there makes the knot in my chest loosen a bit. Waking up with her in the same bed this morning was nothing short of heaven. It's been years since I had her so near while I slept. Maybe being put in this horrible situation together will turn out for the best.

I can see the future so clearly now. When we escape from here, I'm going to marry Fleur. My mind swirls with visions of her in my home, feeding me roasted meat from my latest

kill, chasing our young children around the field, and lounging in my bed, wet and willing anytime I want her. She's all I've ever wanted. She's the definition of womanly perfection, and the fire in her spirit keeps me on my toes.

Her lack of submissiveness makes her all the more attractive. Not like those desperate women back in the village. I bet they'd be willing to eat dog shit if I told them it would make me happy. That's not what I want in a wife. I want someone who's wild enough to warrant breaking in. I want Fleur.

"You're incredible." I stroke my fingers down her cheek and she frowns at me.

"Why do you do this?"

"Do what?" Her switch in mood is surprising.

"Act like this when we're alone. Why can't you just be this person, the Gabriel I know, all the time? Not the one who drives my lovers away and treats me like a prized cow to be won and bred."

"I hate to burst your bubble, Fleur, but your precious farrier has a wife back in his hometown. You were nothing more than a dalliance for him." There's a nearly imperceptible wince as she hears the news. I regret the words instantly, despite the fact they're true. Fleur swallows and the vulnerability vanishes from her eyes.

"Well you could do better. Instead of walking around being this manly man and God's gift to hunting and ladies alike." She pulls her hands away from mine, crossing her arms in annoyance.

"That's just who I am, Fleur. What do you want from me?" A moment ago we were laughing, and now she's pissed. The emotions of women infuriate me.

"I want the Gabriel I knew and loved before you became this macho, senseless man who treats women like livestock and is unapologetically unbearable most of the time. What happened to our days spent lounging beneath the trees, staring up into the clouds and speaking excitedly of our plans to leave this place? We were going to travel the world, tasting all the sweets and visiting the greatest libraries on Earth." The passion in her words burrows beneath my skin.

"I don't even read, Fleur." I stand, wanting to remove myself from this conversation.

"I could teach you. I've always wanted to. Plus there are other things in libraries, artwork, sculptures, inventions. You used to want to be a painter." The dreamy look in her eyes makes me turn away.

"That was a fool's dream that belonged to a boy without a broken heart. When you left me, things changed. I changed." There's a rawness to my voice I do not enjoy. "You left me, and I changed. So no matter how much you may fantasize about the old Gabriel, he's not coming back. None of us are who we were yesterday. The same can be said for you."

Fleur quiets. I close my eyes and rub my hands through the length of my hair as excess tension rages within me. I haven't hunted in days. I need to get out of this room. I need to breathe.

"I'm sorry." Fleur's voice draws me out of my own mind. "I know I hurt you. And you're right. We've all changed." Her gaze has softened. I love the way she's looking at me. I can see the past carouseling through her thoughts.

I reach for her face, brushing my thumb along her bottom lip. "I love you, Fleur. I've always loved you. Be mine. Even if I'm not perfect, I'm a man who will love you every day for always. I'll take care of you. I'll make sure you never go hungry or cold. I'll give you all the books you like and let you read them to me. I'll buy you pastries every morning."

She stares back at me, surprise evident in her gaze. "Gabriel…"

The door to our room opens suddenly, making Fleur

jump. The spindly man from earlier enters along with an older woman we haven't seen before. They push two covered carts a few feet into the room, keeping close to the open door. I consider making a run for it. The second I take a step forward, the door swings shut. Fucking enchanted castle.

"Good morning, honored guests. The master has sent us to deliver something special. Mrs. Perle, if you will." The older woman, Mrs. Perle, removes a silver dome from the first cart, revealing a large tea tray paired with a mountain of pastries and baguettes. The scent of fresh bread and sweet fillings wafts across the room. My mouth waters. "The master knows your passion for breads and sweets." *Does he?*

"And of course"—the over-the-top man pulls a sheet off the second cart with a flourish—"books." Next to me, Fleur gasps. "The master hopes he may cheer you up with some new reading." *Bread and books.* How the fuck did he pinpoint Fleur's favorite things so quickly? A scowl decorates my face. Something is fishy.

"Please help yourself to a spot of tea and cakes," Mrs. Perle adds cheerfully. "The master says he will be down to visit you in a bit."

With that, the two exit. Fleur wastes no time rushing to the cart of books, pulling each one out and gazing lovingly at the covers. How did he know that of everything he could give her, everything a castle has to offer, these are the two she would love most? *"I have watched the village for many years and am certain now that it has to be you, the both of you."* So he truly has been watching.

"Oh, how wonderful." Fleur scoops up a book and a scone and heads to an armchair in the corner, our earlier conversation seemingly forgotten. She looks so undeniably...happy. My distrust of the Beast grows, and with it, my desire to leave this place, and take Fleur with me.

* * *

Fleur has spent the last two hours silently reading. I spent the first hour staring at the canopy above our bed. When I grew tired of that, I switched to physical exertion. I need my muscles in peak condition if I am to defeat a monster like the Beast. Fleur's silence suffocates the space and I can bite my tongue no longer. I spit the words out, dripping them in sarcasm, "If I had known all it would take to make you happy is a surprise gift of books and pastries then—"

"You do know I like these things. Now stop your brooding. You had every chance outside these walls to give me something as small as a baguette or a book of poetry. I would have been equally happy receiving them from you."

"That's ridiculous," I scoff.

"What's ridiculous, Gabriel, is that you appear to be jealous of the Beast." There's a smug light in her eyes and I have the sudden urge to force her to her knees and make her choke on my cock until the light dims and she remembers who's in charge.

"There is nothing to be jealous of," I quip bitterly. An ugly green thing mocks me behind the untruth. "In fact, I've never been jealous of anyone, ever." I add that second part rather begrudgingly in an attempt to prove my point. Fleur just smirks. I stand so abruptly that the chair nearest to me tumbles over. Fleur looks down at the chair then back up at me, a startled expression upon her perfect features. "I swear, Fleur, if you keep…"

A knock draws both of our stares to the door. The Beast enters. He knocked? Why bother knocking? Everything about this feels suspicious.

"Good afternoon." Is it my imagination or does the Beast sound more refined? I scan my eyes over him. He's wearing a blue button-up and fresh trousers. The formal attire is garish on such a hideous creature. What is he dressing up for?

"Good afternoon," Fleur responds. What the fuck is this? Why is she exchanging pleasantries with the man who's keeping us hostage? "Thank you for the books." My mouth drops wide. *Unbelievable*.

"My pleasure. There's more where that came from."

Fleur practically blushes and my last glassy pocket of control shatters.

"Well done, Beast. Your stalking really paid off." The Beast glares back at me, but does not deny it. "In fact"—I stomp toward Fleur, ripping the book from her grasp and pulling her up to her feet—"she was just saying how grateful she is for these gifts, and how badly she wants to show you her gratitude."

"What are you doing?" Fleur hisses under her breath.

"Sweetheart," I coo, "don't be shy. Just tell the Beast. You want to suck my cock and let me fuck you while he watches, so he can pretend it's him." I turn to the Beast. "Isn't that what you want? Isn't that why you brought us here?"

The Beast remains calm, but his eyes glow ever so slightly as they flick to Fleur and a dangerous heat creeps across the room.

"Gabriel." Fleur pulls against my grip.

"Surely you wouldn't put poor Aida in danger just for the sake of a false pretense of feminine propriety."

She glares at me and I grin, realizing I'm back on top once more. I see the panic flicker through Fleur's thoughts. How easily I have them, both of them, all because I know their weaknesses. Fleur's decisions are influenced most heavily by her bleeding heart and the Beast is in love with Fleur. They're losing in a game they didn't even realize they started playing.

Fleur looks up at the Beast. "If that is what you want."

"Of course it is. Deny it, Beast. Deny your desire to watch Fleur pleasure a man and be dominated in return." Fleur cries out as she's shoved to her knees. I give the Beast one more look, knowing full well the challenge I hold in my gaze. He's a voyeur. This is exactly what he wants. "Stop me if I'm wrong."

The Beast shifts his sights between us and then quietly moves to his massive throne. The lights disappear in his half of the room, dropping him into complete darkness. "Proceed." The word is feral and rough and in that moment I know I've won. I can't hide my grin as I quickly unbutton my trousers and pull my stiff length free.

Fleur is seething beneath me. Her light-green eyes burn into me like the forest aflame. She forces a whisper. "One minute you're professing your love for me, the next you're trying to stuff your cock down my throat to humiliate me in front of a stranger. Which one is it?"

I grip a fistful of her hair, and drop my face so close that I can feel her breath on my lips. "You're mine, Fleur, and I'll have you. Whether by love or by force, that part is up to you."

She opens her mouth to argue back and I use the opportunity to stuff my cock in between her lips, using my hand in her hair to drive her down at the same moment I snap my hips forward. She gags, her free hands pressing against my thighs, pushing me away. I keep my voice low. "Come now, we have an audience. Suck it like your life depends on it. Aida's certainly does."

Fleur tenses. *That's right. You're mine.* She purses her lips, then drags them slowly along my shaft. The sound that leaves my throat encompasses all the years of need and neglect on behalf of Fleur's defiance. A matching sound spills from the darkness. I suppose we both need this.

"Faster," the Beast chokes out.

"You heard him," I murmur down to her. She flicks a

spiteful glare up at me and drags her teeth along my shaft. I nearly fall to my knees as pain and pleasure confound my fiery flesh. I thicken more and Fleur groans around me. Goddamn this woman. She's feisty, full of surprises, and endlessly fuckable. Her mouth picks up the pace, sucking and sliding me in and out. The sight of her head bobbing in my lap as I stare down makes my balls tighten. I take control, thrusting forward so that my hips keep pace with her lips. It pisses her off. I knew it would. My thighs bleed as she buries her nails in my flesh in retaliation. *That's it. Give me your rage. I want everything. All of it. All of you.*

Heat builds at the base of my spine as her drool dribbles down, coating my balls. The filth and excitement of this spur-of-the-moment situation have me climaxing before I have a chance to slow Fleur down and prolong things. I press hard on the back of her head, burying myself completely as my hot spend hurtles down her throat. She struggles against me and when I don't relent, she sinks her teeth into me, not enough to break the skin, but enough to hurt. I roar in anger as the pain cuts my euphoria off before it's finished flooding my veins. She gasps in relief as I jerk my hips back, removing my cock from her mouth.

"Oops, did my teeth get in the way again? Too bad I didn't taste any blood." She glares and grins and I practically have an aneurysm.

The Beast rumbles his approval from the darkness. "Now make her come. And then fuck her until her body relents and her smart mouth quiets."

She shoots an unbelieving look in the Beast's direction. I yank Fleur to her feet, tossing her over my shoulder and carrying her to the bed. Her body falls to the comforter with a thud. Those angry eyes shoot daggers at me. "Did you like that?" I smirk down at her triumphantly.

"No," she bites back.

"Find out if she's lying," the Beast growls out. "Check between her thighs."

The command is not what I was expecting. Fleur's cheeks become ruddy and she struggles against my hold. I shackle both wrists, my large hand swallowing the two with room to spare, and pin them above her head. My other hand slips beneath her nightgown. She squeezes her thick thighs shut. I bark out a laugh as my fist plows through the soft flesh until I find her hot center. Sticky, wet arousal greets my fingertips. I dip them inside her once and she turns her face away from me, biting back a moan.

When I pull my fingers free, I hold them in the air. They shine in the candlelight.

The Beast sucks in a breath. "She liked it." His words are nothing more than gravel.

"You have no idea all the things she likes, Beast." I drop my hand between her thighs again, driving my fingers in deep, and she whimpers. I bury two fingers knuckle deep inside her sweet pussy and then pump again and again. Fleur's mouth remains tightly shut, her face reddening. She doesn't want to admit she likes it. But I know she does. I know how to make her body sing like no one else ever will.

I add a third finger and spread my knuckles wide, stretching her. She's dripping down my hand, her juices sliding between her cheeks and pooling on the bed. I slide my pinky into her ass and her silence finally breaks. She cries out, unable to deny the pleasure any longer.

"I bet that flimsy farrier never knew you liked this." I work her in both places, delighting in the way her body squirms beneath me. "He has no idea how truly filthy you are, does he?"

More of her moans spill out, unguarded, and I've won again. One, two, three more curling thrusts into her cunt and ass and she tightens around me, her cries of pleasure filling the room and sending blood to my dick.

"Strip her. Take her." The Beast speaks between grunts.

I rip the nightdress from her body, wadding up the ruined fabric before tossing it aside. Fleur lays in a heaving puddle. I love her like this. Cheeks flushed, hair clinging to her forehead, eyes glazed. I push her knees wide, driving them up toward her shoulders. Her pink pussy spreads, allowing my gaze to devour every glistening bit of her. I drop low, unable to resist swiping my tongue through her sweet center.

She lurches beneath the touch. *That cunt is mine.* I mount the bed, aligning my knees with her body and guiding my tip to her dripping entrance. I slide the tip along her seam, rubbing my head across her clit until she seizes up with another orgasm.

The Beast releases a feral warning. "Take her. Now."

* * *

Fleur

Gabriel's first few inches press inside, stretching me wide. No other man I've slept with has ever been as thick as Gabriel. That's for certain. He works his tip in and out, groaning as my pussy sucks him in. His cock moves deeper, deeper, until he's fully seated inside me. Holy hell. I remember he was big but this…

A simper of pure pleasure slips from my lips as Gabriel rolls his hips.

"Tell me you missed me. Tell me you missed *this*." His next thrust carves a line of fire inside me. "Tell…" He slams his hips forward again. "Me."

"Gabriel." I mewl as his rhythmic thrusts push me toward climax. Deep grunts fill my ears and I turn my head to where the Beast is hidden. I'm again struck with the desire to see him, feel him, know more.

"Is that what you're after?" His voice is dominant in my ear. "A Beast? So be it." Gabriel ruts into me, his movements hard, quick, more frenzied. Our skin claps together as he fucks me roughly, all the while pressing my face toward the Beast. "Let's show him your favorite trick…" Gabriel's hand closes around my throat. Years of memories flash across my vision as his touch connects me back to another time, another place.

No one else touches me like this. No one else knows how much I like it. He squeezes, his fingertips lacing around my throat like a collar. I'm reduced to a pile of sensations. The strain in my lungs, the slapping in my ears, and the warm pressure detonating between my thighs. I open my mouth to cry out. When no sound comes, Gabriel grins. He releases his hold and the pump of fresh oxygen through my lungs is like an orgasm all its own. Dizzy daydreams and a sparkling effervescent shimmer bubble up through my bloodstream, hanging my body amongst the clouds while peppering it with sharp, stinging stimulation.

My body's had enough. It needs rest, recovery, a moment to bask in the glow. But Gabriel is relentless. He takes pleasure in dragging things out, he always has. My neck throbs where the imprint of Gabriel's fingertips paint my skin. I can't believe he remembers these things. Every dark dirty secret he and I have shared must be burned permanently inside his villainous mind. My pussy aches from the stretch of him, my core throbs with overstimulation. Gabriel's thrusts turn erratic and then his hot cum is flooding me, the warm sensation making me choke out a sob as my pussy pulses out a smaller, final climax.

The Beast bellows his own roar of completion from his solitude. I can't see him. His eyes are closed. Gabriel collapses onto me, his weight knocking the breath from my body. He quickly rolls, pulling me into him. His body is alight with heat. The swells of his muscles wrap snugly around me, holding me against him. His lips press to my temple, and he murmurs, "That is how it should always be."

Despite the reminiscent feeling of contentment that's washing across my skin, I turn, looking over my shoulder, seeking the Beast. He's standing near the door. How does such a massive creature move so silently?

"Bathe. Eat. And then you may explore the castle."

I sit up quickly, my voice unable to hide my delight. "You're going to let us leave this room?"

"Would you like that?" The Beast tilts his head in my direction.

"Yes. I would love—"

"You're not afraid we'll run the first chance we get?" Gabriel interrupts. He's on his feet now, standing gloriously naked and completely unabashed.

"I'm not afraid of anything." The Beast stalks away, but pauses in the doorway. He glances back at us. "Besides, this is an enchanted caste. I will know if you try. And know this"— the Beast issues a wry smirk—"no one leaves this castle without my permission."

CHAPTER 9

FLEUR

*O*ur next meal is delivered to our room promptly after the Beast's departure. The amount of food prepared for only two people is a bit overwhelming. We pile our plates high with smoked meats, pears, various cheeses, and even more bread. There's also a large terrine of fresh lentil stew with basil and rosemary. "Mmmm." The food practically melts on my tongue.

"Worked up an appetite, hmm?" Gabriel tosses me a smirk. What an arrogant ass. He's not wrong though. After our little performance for the Beast, I'm practically famished. I sip the same rich red wine from the night before, savoring the flavors. For a moment, none of this feels real. Dining in a castle, with Gabriel, after having sex, for the viewing pleasure of the Beast.

The pleasure was not entirely his own, of course. I enjoyed myself far more than I'm comfortable admitting. And as for Gabriel...

I glance up to find he's watching me. Something dark has settled beneath his frosty gaze. I have the distinct feeling

things have been altered to a place there's no coming back from.

His attentions cause a myriad of conflicted emotions to settle alongside the wine and fine cuisine in my belly. The momentary distractions are so…well, distracting. It's easy to forget what a less-than-favorable situation we're in. The Beast has us locked in his castle, threatening to kill those we love if we leave. It's stifling, restrictive, and yet…there is a strange sort of freedom here, as well. Perhaps I'm just a bird flying out of my cage and into an aviary.

And then I think of home. Grief threatens to drag me into darkness. I've barely had time to accept Papa's death. I've hardly had a chance to think of my former life at all. My fingers dip inside my satchel, pulling the powdery-blue blanket free. I hold it to my chest as I set my father's inventions out on the top of the armoire. The familiar stab of loss pries between my ribs and I breathe, accepting the pain and letting my guard down momentarily. *Nothing will ever be the same now.* How many times have I said that in my lifetime?

By the time the Beast returns, I've changed into one of the more casual dresses from the wardrobe. This one is a soft, petal pink with lace along the collar and wrists. It fits me snug in the waist and perfect in the chest and I wonder how the Beast was able to get such accurate measurements. The many mysteries surrounding our unusual host seem to grow by the minute. His gaze sweeps the length of me and he visibly swallows. I think he's about to say something, compliment my dress, perhaps. He opens his mouth, but closes it again. Gabriel eyes him curiously as he clears his throat.

"Let us explore the castle." I think I detect a hint of excitement in the Beast's tone. It may be my imagination but he seems to be standing straighter and speaking more eloquently. He's dressed in fine clothes and his hair even seems to be combed. Perhaps there is a refined man beneath the Beast after all.

Gabriel and I practically shove each other aside in an attempt to exit the doorway. Once we're out, my mouth hinges open. The hallway we're standing in is an impressive and towering space. Every inch is filled with light. Candelabras and chandeliers perfectly illuminate the great height and depth. Golden statues of beautiful women and fearsome warriors line the walls. Each piece is at least as tall as I am.

The cold stone floor is accented by an endless runner of ivory and pale-blue carpets. An intricate weaving of gold-leaf crown molding divides the ceiling into ornate squares. It's all so ostentatious and strange. We reach a chamber on the far end of the hall, which I assume is the castle foyer. I gasp as I spy the elegant colors reflected up above. Bright, gilded vaulting with scenes of the heavens cover the high, domed space. I spin, eyes toward the sky as I take in the absolute loveliness and detail of each triangular section. Every scene is more beautiful than the last. One segment begins with the sunrise, pale pinks and soft gold paired with fluffy clouds. The next tile shows the gentle blue of the sky coming into focus. The vibrancy of the blue intensifies as you make your way around the circle, until you reach the saturated twilight and deep purples of sunset. The very last painting is of the night sky, filled with stars and lit from within by a painted moon so bright and detailed it almost seems real.

"You are free to roam the castle. But you will not leave, and you may not venture past the hallways to the upper left of the stairs."

"What's up there?" I wonder, instinctively drawn to where I'm not supposed to be.

"My private quarters, which I shall request remain undisturbed." The bite in his tone leaves no room for misunderstanding. "I can give you a tour or you can explore on—"

"I'll do my own tour, thanks." Gabriel's snarky tone does not go unnoticed, and the Beast frowns. Gabriel heads fool-heartedly down a corridor at random.

"Remember what I said." The Beast's words stop Gabriel in his tracks. "No one leaves this castle without my permission." Gabriel huffs something under his breath and carries on.

"You're sure it's okay to leave him?" I ask, reticent.

The Beast nods. "I see everything that happens inside this castle. Even if he breaches the stone walls, he will not make it far." Well, that sounds rather ominous. We stand in awkward silence for a few minutes before the Beast speaks again. "What would you like to see?"

"Everything." I softly giggle. "I've never seen anything so wondrous."

His brows pull in as he ponders something. "I think I know where we should begin."

Our journey leads us up the grand split staircase and then a smaller side staircase to the right. My curiosity piques with every door we pass but do not open. When we do stop, it's in front of two enormous wooden doors.

"Where are we?"

The Beast grins. His terrifying display of sharpened teeth makes me take a step back. He quickly drops the smile and his eyes go to the ground. He clears his throat. "This"—he pushes the doors wide—"is the library."

I've died and gone to heaven! The library is larger than the entire town square. It's the most beautiful place I've ever set foot in. Dark, cherry wood dominates the room, warming the massive space and giving it a cozy feel, despite its size. A roaring fireplace glows brightly on one end, casting the library in a golden aura. Several lavish chairs and chaises in red and green velvets decorate the floor in front of the fire. The ceiling rises up like a part of the heavens itself, with paintings of great weeping cherry blossoms and lavender wisterias. The trees appear so real I feel as if the petals are raining down their beautiful blossoms all around me. Brilliantly gilded flowers bloom forth from every bare spec of wall, turning the library into a gilded garden from floor to ceiling.

But my favorite part are the soaring stories of books. There must be thousands of books, everything from pocket-sized poetry to great leatherbound tomes half my height. Eight immense bookshelves on both floors house the immaculate collection. The endless rows of books are separated by windows made from the most magical and colorful array of stained glass I've ever viewed. The windows depict scenes of the castle, its forest, and a sprawling rose garden. Sunlight peeks through the colored glass, casting rainbows across the library, drenching the inner world in jeweled blues, purples, reds, yellows, and more. I stretch my arm out, allowing the glass's reflection to bathe my milky skin in a deep crimson.

"Do you like it?" The Beast draws my attention down from the clouds to where his serious face is studying me.

"It's beautiful. I've never been anywhere so wondrously magical." The Beast smiles again, and this time I don't find the showing of teeth quite so frightening. "Thank you for bringing me here."

"You are welcome to any of the books, and you may come here as often as you like."

I wander to the bookshelf closest to where we stand, and gasp. "Nicolas Boughedir, Thibaut Guillon, Phillipe Vuil-laume..." This section is filled with some of my favorite poets. I select the shiny green cover of Ludivine Quillard and open it, flipping through the pages. I adore the whimsical beauty of Quillard's writing.

"Perhaps you will read to me some of your favorites?" The Beast's voice is soft.

I blink up at him. "You want me to read to you?"

"You do not have to—"

"I would love to." My grin broadens. The Beast gestures for me to be seated near the fire. I choose a velvety green chair with lily of the valley carved into the wooden arms. The Beast sits on a large couch that matches the green upholstery of my chair. The fire is warm beside me and I curl up, feeling right at home.

"I think we shall start with this one. 'Wildflower Skies'. It's short, sappy, and whimsically romantic. My favorite type of poetry." I clear my throat, acutely aware of his piercing stare locked onto me. Warmth simmers in my belly, and I turn my eyes down toward the page.

> *"In spring flower meadows*
> *My soul reminisces*
> *Of dandelion dreams*
> *And your fuzzy bee kisses*
> *With honey sweet smiles*
> *And pink petal sighs*
> *Let's stay hidden forever*
> *Under wildflower skies..."*

I blush, suddenly embarrassed. I've always been infatuated with love stories and poems of the heart. Reading them aloud makes me feel a bit like a fawning youth with a silly crush. The Beast does not strike me as a wistful romantic. Maybe I should have started with something more elegant and traditional—

"I've always liked that one," the Beast rumbles from his seat.

"You...read?" My hand flies to my mouth as I realize just how rude the question was.

"I do. I have read nearly every book in this library." His eyes sweep across the expanse of literature.

"Every book?" That would make him the most well-read person—or creature—I have ever encountered. What secrets his mind must possess. I don't know what I assumed he did all day and night, but it certainly wasn't reading. What use would a monster have of reading?

Unless, of course, he's not a monster at all...

I pick at my nails, uncertain if I should put my current thoughts into words. My curiosity betters my doubts and I find the question slipping from my lips before I can stop it. "Have you always been the Beast?"

The Beast peers down at me and the fire's flames dance like ghosts in the pools of his eyes. "No."

"What happened?" I'm swallowed up by the sadness in his sapphire gaze.

"I was once simply known as Renard. I was cursed many years ago. That is as much as I wish to say about it."

I ponder on that for a moment. So the Beast truly was human before? Why was he cursed? I have so many questions. The dark urge to pick at his scabs, reveal the truth despite his desire to keep it hidden, whispers on my shoulder like a demon. The stony set of his jaw and the way his eyes are cast down bring me back to some sense of propriety. I will be patient. But I will find out everything there is to know about my tragically monstrous captor.

"Well, Renard. Would you read me one of your favorites now?"

When he looks at me again, there is a whole world of thought flashing through his eyes. He rises, moving to fetch a small, dark leather book. The cover is ragged and torn, as if it's been handled many hundreds of times.

"Who is it by?" The bookshop in town held maybe a hundred books. Nothing like the grand collection of the castle library. The book in his hands is not one I recognize.

"Antoine Lespert." His voice is soft, different.

"I've never heard of him." Excitement builds within me at the thought of discovering a new poet.

"He writes...darker things." Renard traces his thumb down the spine of the book, fondly.

"Which poem will you be reading?" I encourage.

"This one is called, 'The Death of a Starling':

Starling skies
Metallic flocks dancing
Atop wind current whispers.
Tourmaline spectacle.
Of the hundreds above,
One descends.
Flying days behind him,
Drops like a feather-covered
Stone.
Grackles gasp, blackbirds bellow
As lone fowl follows southbound declivity
Burning like a starry beacon.
Violent violet reflects off the sun,
Fierce emerald sorrows cry out to the clouds,
And glossy black wings fall.
Radiant.
Dazzling iridescence gliding past,
Leaving sunset, sunrise worlds forever.
Obsidian plumage plummets.
Could death be so beautiful?"

My heart sits heavy. A second sorrow burdens my chest, as if my heart has taken on the weight of Renard's pain as well as my own. The poem is so beautiful, so poetically sad.

"You cannot die, can you?"

"No." Renard closes the book.

"Is that part of the curse?" Something compels me to move to him, to take his hand and offer a comfort I know he's long been denied. But there is still something about him, something dangerous. I've seen him kill. I'm sure he's done unspeakable things in his time in this form. Somewhere beneath the Beast, a man remains, but how much of him is left?

"I do not wish to speak of curses any more today." He heaves a great sigh and rises to leave.

"Wait." I jump to my feet, the thought of him leaving now hooks sharp barbs within my heart. "We don't have to talk about it anymore. Instead, let's order a tray of tea and cakes, and read each other our favorite poems? It's been ages since I've had anyone to read to." Not since death stole everything I loved from my life. I remember when Papa would bring us new books each time he went into town. My brother and I would spend hours listening to our mother read. Her voice was so beautifully melodic. The sadness I've been burying presses closer to the surface. What I wouldn't give to see them again.

He stands still for so long that I fear he's turned to stone. When his eyes again find mine, there's a fragile hope in them. "I would like that."

And so we do. We spend hours reading, discussing, eating scones, and drinking tea. I learn that Renard takes his tea plain, and his scones with jam only. I, on the other hand, prefer my tea with extra sugar and a dash of milk, and my scones are often buried by the mountain of jam and clotted cream I smear on. I reach for another and find the tray empty.

"I'll send for another batch." Renard rises and I stop him with my hands in the air.

"No, please. They are by far the best scones I've ever had but I'm quite certain if I keep this up, my figure will suffer to a place beyond repair." I giggle, envisioning myself as round as a blueberry.

"I think your figure is perfect. Soft, round, and filled with the things you love. I wouldn't have you any other way."

My mouth drops open at his words. A heated flush crawls up my neck and into my cheeks. "Renard…" My voice drops to a whisper. My eyes flit to the ground as I process the unexpected bout of butterflies fluttering around my stomach.

Renard clears his throat, sensing my discomfort. He stands abruptly, crossing the room and opening the doors before I can stop him. "There's something that needs my attention. I'll have another tray sent up. Please, stay as long as you like." A quick bow of the head, and he's gone.

My insides glitter with a tingly anticipation. Why did his comment affect me so? The answer to that question is unsettling in a way that makes my skin prickle and my lips part on a breath. I don't know much about curses, but I'm a resourceful, intelligent woman. I'll learn what I can.

Maybe there's a way to change things. My mind wanders back to those stormy-sea eyes. Such mysteries within you. *Renard.*

CHAPTER 10

GABRIEL

*A*nother dead end. In hindsight, exploring a castle of this magnitude on my own may not have been the best idea. I've wandered these halls for hours and not seen one living soul or a single exit to the outside world. Curse this place. Is it keeping the exits hidden through some magic? The thought brings anger boiling to the surface, heating my skin as I continue down another winding hall. Is it my imagination, or is it colder in this part of the castle? Darker, too. The extravagant decor has ceased and the candelabras and sconces are few and far between. Have I gone underground?

Voices reach me through the near darkness. Their words are angry and rushed. I slow my steps, adopting the silent stalk, the hunter's approach. The movements are familiar, my muscles falling easily into the stance I've perfected over so many years. I peer around the corner to find two figures in a small cupboard-like space. They appear to be males, in their late teens or early twenties. One is tall, with blond close-cropped hair and elongated features. The other is a shorter, muscular boy with shaggy dark hair.

The taller man grips the short-haired boy by the shoulders. "I know you are upset, but think, Elias. *Pense!*"

The smaller boy, Elias, pulls back from his grip. "You saw what he did to Èlliot. He crushed my brother's skull, killed him dead for no reason other than to ease the monster's temper tantrum. He should be punished!"

"Lower your voice," the tall man snaps. "Someone will hear you."

"What are you afraid of, Lyam? Afraid the Beast will kill you as he did my brother? You should be afraid. He is a murderer, a monster. We must strike him down!"

"We do not have the manpower to defeat him. Who will come to our aid when so many fear him? Who will help us to slay the Beast?" Lyam protests.

I seize the moment, stepping into the light.

"That, boys, would be me." The two turn white as sheets as I round the corner. My body blocks the doorway. Their wild eyes dart around the room, seeking a way to escape. "Never fear. I, too, wish to slay the monster."

Elias narrows his eyes suspiciously. "*Qui êtes-vous?*"

"Me? I'm a friend. You can call me Gabriel. And together, we can kill the Beast."

"It's *impossible*. No one can get close to him. He guards himself, guards his secrets, and he sees everything that happens in the castle. If you draw his attention, he will be watching you…us," Lyam insists, the color draining even more from his face.

"How? How does he know these things?" I demand. I am growing weary of these superstitions.

"I don't know. Only Lucien and Claude know." The portly and spindly men who bring us our meals. They're clearly privy to favors and treatments that the lower class of servants here are not.

97

"How many others are there?" I flick my eyes between Lyam and Elias.

"Others?" echoes Lyam, confusion evident on his young features.

"Others to your cause. Others who wish to see your master struck down?"

"There are many. Most of the staff have been wronged by him in one way or another. We're trapped here. The curse—"

"Curse?" I take a step nearer to the men and they back away. "What curse?"

"The curse that transformed Prince Renard to a Beast." Elias's voice quivers ever so slightly.

"The prince?" *So the rumors are true?*

"*Oui, le prince.* We have been trapped here ever since. Never aging, never growing, while the Beast picks us off one by one." Elias's eyes grow dark and distant but his sob story does not interest me.

So the Beast is the long-lost prince. His eloquent speech and unusual mannerisms all make sense. Excitement peaks in my gut. I've never hunted a prince before.

Elias continues, "We are all afraid of him, but no one will go after him—"

"I will go after him. I will distract him, gain his trust, and when the moment is right, we will kill the Beast, and take back this castle." My veins thrum with the thrill of it. "Spread the word, draw the others to our cause. We will meet again soon."

I wheel around, not sparing the two a backward glance as I stride away. My mind spins, turning end over end like a weed caught in the wind. I was already planning on taking down the monster myself. Knowing how deep the seeds of discontentment are sewn among the castle staff means the challenge will be all the easier. The servants aren't much in terms of strength, skill, or intelligence as far as I can tell, but if I can gather enough together for a proper distraction, it will buy me the time I need to sneak in and take *Renard* out.

A grin splits me from ear to ear. Perhaps Fleur and I will simply live here, in the castle once the Beast is gone. My mind saturates with visions of all the places I could ruin Fleur in a residence this large. I'll have her bent over tables, tied to the headboards of every royal bed, fucked against bookshelves, pinned in the dirt of the gardens, and screaming my name in every hallway of this enormous castle. I like that idea. I like that idea very much.

A cold wind bites into my flesh as I round the corner and there I find it: an exit from the castle. An open stone archway is revealed to me through a pair of ornate doors. The door on the right swings inward with the wind once more, having been left ajar or blown open by the snowstorm. I pull it wide, peering into the hazy gray and white wonderland outside. Something vivid and red catches my eye. As the wind dies down and the snow flurries clear, I spy the briars of a rose garden. Blood-red petals drip down from sagging faces. I'm shocked they've survived this long in the winter weather.

I bend low, picking at a pile of fallen petals and selecting one at random. The petal is soft and pliant beneath my touch, not frozen and withered. How unusual.

My eyes take in the wintery landscape ahead. I could leave now. Run as fast as my feet can carry me straight back to the village. I know what I'm up against now. This time I'll round up every man in town and bring them back to storm the castle by force. But what of Fleur? Can I leave her here, alone, with a monster? What wicked things will he do to her if I am not around for protection? What has he been doing with her in the hours since I left?

My throat feels sticky and hot as I swallow. In my frustration and desire for freedom I abandoned Fleur. What if the Beast has her now? The idea of her trapped beneath his deformed body as he defiles her with his monstrous cock makes me queasy. This is my chance to leave, to get help. But if I leave now, help may be too late.

No. I've seen the way that cursed prince looks at my woman. The Beast won't hurt Fleur. He's in love with her. Or as capable of love as an animal can be. Surely after going to such great lengths to procure her, he'll want to keep her safe, and alive. She'll understand if I leave now. She'll know I did it for her, to save her.

My boot crunches into freshly packed snow as I take my first step outside the castle walls.

"Gabriel." The deep voice sends electricity shooting into my skin as my heart rattles a startled rhythm against my ribs. I turn, already knowing who I'll find. The Beast stands mere feet away. He's close enough to kill me and I didn't even hear him coming. My jaw ticks. *I underestimated him.* "Going somewhere?" he asks, his voice irritatingly calm.

I have three options. *Flee*, run as fast as I can and hope I can outsmart the Beast, then lose him in the forest. *Fight*, take him on without the others, risk my life knowing I'm still the strongest man in the village. Or *stay*, do as I told the others, get to know the Beast, gain his trust. And when the time is right, kill him and take Fleur for my own.

The Beast steps nearer. He towers over me up close. I find it utterly unnerving.

"Just exploring. I got a little turned around earlier. You said we could look around the castle. I assumed the gardens were included."

The Beast does not move, does not speak, and the tension in my stomach coils like a serpent.

"I was about to head back inside, anyway. It's too damn cold out here." My voice bolsters a bravado I don't truly feel.

The Beast peers down at me, sniffing the air once before

speaking. "I'll escort you back to your room, so you don't lose your way again."

My body remains still, knowing that once I step foot over that threshold, my chance for escape is gone. I set my jaw, grinding my teeth as I paste a pleasant look on my face. My boots click as they exit the snow and clap down on stone floors again. Each step echoing the sounds of my posh prison. I bite my tongue and follow the Beast as he lumbers down the hall. *Stay it is.* I need to come up with a plan to get closer to him, some way to help him drop his guard. I have a few ideas, but none of them are ideal.

Just you wait, Beast. You're mine.

CHAPTER 11

FLEUR

I linger in the library until the sun sets and the stained-glass windows darken. My joints have grown stiff by the time I lay my current fixation down and stand to stretch. One side of my body is pink and toasted after so many hours near the fireplace. The flames gleam brightly, but are never tended to. The longer I'm here, the more I realize what an unusual place this is. Renard did not return after his abrupt exit. I admit I glanced up at the double oak doors more than once, hoping he would appear. Our hours reading and reciting poetry sit dewy and fresh in my memory. I've never met anyone with a passion for reading that can hold even the smallest spark of a flame to my burning passion for page after page of elegantly woven words and dreamy fairy tales. Until Renard, that is. My list of freshly consumed works has grown exponentially and there are at least a dozen new pieces I wish to share with him. I give up on that notion for tonight and head back to my room.

The castle is quiet at this hour, which is why I'm more than a little startled to find a man breezing out of a hidden

panel in the wall and past the bottom of the stairwell. "Good evening," I offer up courteously. Up close, the man does not seem much older than a boy, perhaps eighteen or twenty. He has silky-looking brown eyes and dark shaggy hair.

The boy stops dead in his tracks at the sight of me. I wait for a response, but he simply stares. Something prickles on the back of my neck and I'm struck with the sudden desire to make it back to the safety of my room. There's a tenseness in his stance like an animal caught in the wrong den, and a darkness in his eyes that makes me take a step back.

"Why do you stay?" he asks, his voice surprisingly deep.

"You mean here, in the castle?" I ask and he nods. "I have to. For now." I'm not sure how much I should say. What do the workers know about our arrangement with Renard?

"The Beast has something over your head? Something that makes you feel like you can't leave?" His voice is persistent, urgent. An uncomfortable sensation itches at my skin. I do not wish to speak ill of Renard.

"What's your name?" I ask, buying myself some time to think.

"Elias." His brow furrows. "What did he tell you? He lies."

"Nice to meet you, Elias. I'm Fle—"

"What did he promise you? Why don't you just leave? Right now. The entrance to the castle is just before you." His persistence is discomfiting. "Tell me." He takes a step closer. "Tell me."

"I'm staying here to keep others who are important to me safe," I blurt out, Elias's heightened emotions feeding my own nerves.

The darkness in Elias's eyes illuminates with a twinkle that sets my instincts to flight. I'm not sure what I expected from him next, but it certainly wasn't laughter. His stocky, muscular frame shakes as deep laughter bellows out of him. My face twists in disgust. I've had enough of this conversation. I spin on my heel to leave and his next words stop me cold.

"Those people are already dead."

My stomach bottoms out. "What did you say?" I whirl on him. My voice is as shaky as my hands.

"Those people are already dead. That's the reason you're still here, right? To keep them safe in your absence? The Beast promised if you played nice as his pretty new toy that he would spare the lives of those you love?" He chuckles to himself. "You're naive."

Horror awakens in my gut, sending the mass of scones and jam surging up into my throat. "He wouldn't."

Elias's eyes harden to glass. "You have no idea what he would do, what he's already done." His words strum frozen fingers across the musical strings of my well-hidden fears.

I don't move. A barrage of what-ifs and toxic doubts seep into my veins, polluting my blood until my heartbeats become thick and painful. A part of me refuses to believe it. Why would he lie? I just assumed he was a man of his word and if I did what he said, he would leave Aida and the others alone. Another part of me realizes he's not a man at all. Not in the way Gabriel is. The sound of Laurent's neck as it popped, twisted, and finally splintered under the unyielding grip of the Beast replays in my mind. What if this boy is telling the truth? I asked for no proof. I simply trusted a man, a monster, who kidnapped me and locked me in a dungeon. *You have no idea what he would do, what he's already done.*

Doubt pours down my throat, choking me. I need to know. I need to see for myself that Aida is all right. And if she isn't…

"You don't believe me? Go see for yourself." Elias strides to the front doors, flinging them wide. Snow billows through the opening and I shiver as the temperatures plummet. "The stables are on the left."

Can I possibly find my way back, alone? The snow is already piling into drifts at the base of the stairs. Every second that ticks by draws more panic from my thoughts.

"I would hurry if I were you. If the Beast catches you here, he won't allow you another chance to escape."

His words spur me on, feeding fresh panicky fuel to the adrenaline plowing through my veins. I dart forward, crossing into the deep snow beyond and treading left toward the stables. The collected snowdrift in the courtyard covers my knees, forcing me to use every muscle in my legs to cross the short distance. At this moment I'm more envious than ever of the physical training granted to men. If I survive tonight, I'm going to force Gabriel to teach me.

Snow hikes up my dress, freezing my inner thighs and making me gasp as it chills through my thin undergarments. Having snow up my lady bits is a rather unenjoyable sensation and one I need not repeat anytime soon.

The stable door is frozen shut when I reach it. I struggle, shaking the lock to loosen it, fighting to ignore the way my teeth are already chattering. It doesn't budge. I slam my shoulder into the rough wood, popping the door loose. It gives way with a creak of protest, sending me spilling roughly onto a dusty floor.

The ground is less than forgiving as it bites into my knees and palms, but at least the stables are warm and dry. The scents of hay and horses fill my senses and I find it strangely comforting. I thrust the door closed behind me, hurrying to the closest hanging lantern. I spare a few precious moments to hover my hands on either side, allowing warmth to draw pins and needles to my fingertips before removing the lantern from the wall.

The cubby in front of me houses a three-legged stool, a small tattered blanket wrapped around a pile of hay, and a wall of hanging leads. The jacket, mittens, and old mugs inform me this is where the stable boy resides while he's on duty. A pile of wooden figurines and a small carving knife sit on the ground beside a poorly put-together sleeping corner.

I don't have time to worry about where he is at the moment. I snatch the jacket, wrapping it around myself and buttoning it tight. The fabric is threadbare and has been patched more than once, but it's better than nothing. I scoop up a pair of dirty boots from the far wall. They're only a few sizes too large. I stuff the toes with extra hay before sliding them on. I surely look a bit clownish taking my first few stumbling steps, but I don't want my feet to succumb to frostbite on my journey, and so these will have to do. After a moment's hesitation I turn back, snatching the carving knife from the ground and stuffing it in my pocket.

Eleven curious faces peer out at me over the half-doors of their stalls. I use my instincts to choose a horse, having ridden nearly my entire life. The mare I end up saddling is a sorrel beauty with dark, wise eyes and a reddish-copper mane. The nameplate carved in the front of her stall reads *Marigold*. She stands at least seventeen hands tall and is well built, reminding me of my own large horse back home.

Muscle memory runs me through the motions as I tack Marigold and mount her. My hips welcome the familiar stretch of the animal beneath me as I hook my oversized boots into the stirrups. Velvety skin warms my stiff finger-tips as I stroke the mare's silky neck, patting once before urging her outside. Bitter wind sucks the breath from my lungs as we plunge into the elements. Hooves pound hurriedly away from the castle. The usual avalanche of familiar thundering *clip-clops* are swallowed by the powdery accumulation of soft snow beneath us, making our escape unexpectedly muted. My horse's breath blows out in steamy puffs as I push her faster, galloping into the forest and in the direction of the village.

Nightmares consume my waking thoughts as visions of the villagers swarm through my mind. Mutilated bodies, homes razed to the ground, blood lining the streets. Would Renard really massacre an entire town of innocent people? And what of poor Aida? I can't bear the thought of being her cause of death. She's too good, too kind.

Marigold moves swiftly, almost gratefully, and I wonder when she was last let out to run freely across the land. Bits of icy crystals pelt my skin, stinging my eyes and blurring my vision. Dense trees crowd the path, forcing me to duck to avoid several low-hanging branches. My face is wind-burnt and chapped already and there's still a good ways to go. I dig deep, searching my reserves, drawing forth memories of all the unimaginable trials I've survived thus far, letting them lend me their strength and determination. My thoughts are reinvigorated, my will stronger than before. No matter what it takes, I will find a way to check on the village. There's no turning back now.

Marigold stops so suddenly I nearly topple over her head. My fingers bury deep into her coarse mane as I hang on for dear life. It takes me a second to right myself, and as soon as I do, the mare rears, throwing me back. My oversized boots lose their purchase and I slip backwards, hitting the snowy ground with a muffled thud. I pitch to the left, narrowly avoiding the panicked pounding hooves as my horse turns tail and races back toward the castle.

"Marigold!" I screech, my tone desperate. Her ear twitches to the side but she does not stop. All I can do is watch as she gallops into the distance, disappearing and leaving me alone in the woods. Pain radiates up my tailbone. The snow is more firmly packed in this part of the forest. I rise, cursing myself for falling and biting out a string of very unladylike expletives that accurately express my feelings toward the current situation.

Trekking the rest of the way on foot is not ideal, but what other choice do I have? I take two stiff steps and freeze.

Yellow eyes illuminate the darkness around me. My head whips side to side, seeking a route past the terror confronting me. I've heard them in the night, but they never venture close to the village. I reach into my pocket for the carving knife and find it missing. My fingers thrust deeper into the pocket, revealing a large hole in the bottom. My heart sinks at the realization that my only weapon and chance to defend myself was lost somewhere along our path. There's no time to retrace our steps.

When the creatures begin to close in, I make a choice. I snatch a broken branch from my left and raise it high before me. If I'm going down, I'll go down fighting.

The first one leaps toward me and my breath stutters to a halt, fleeing my body as quickly as my mount fled this clearing. *What am I going to do?* I think back to the many books I've read over the years. Tales of action, danger, and adventure. I've always identified with the brave, independent main characters. Always willing to take risks, explore new things, and speak their minds on any occasion. Something stings in my chest. Perhaps I've lost sight of that girl over the last few days, allowing myself to be told what to do, when to do it, and hardly putting up a fight. Not anymore. Today, I reclaim my power, and if I die... Well then, death will be my last great adventure.

CHAPTER 12

RENARD

A new warmth flickers beneath the thick layer of darkness that guards my heart. My time with Fleur earlier today was so different, so unexpectedly wonderful. But is it too good to be true? As the hours pass, my worry grows. I begin to fear that the entire interaction was all a cruel dream, a fireside hallucination, something perfect and false created out of an impossible loneliness as I napped beside the licking flames of the library fireplace. Fleur's presence always feels too good to be true, as if at any moment her beautiful form will disintegrate, leaving behind a remorseless pile of undying rose petals. Another callous trick at the hands of the witch.

Fleur *is* too good to be true. Too good for me, at least. We shared stories, read poetry, and soaked up each other's presence for hours today. I can't remember how long it's been since I spent that much time with anyone. My staff keep their interactions to a minimum, choosing to spend their free time down in the servants' quarters instead. I've heard them before, laughing, cheering, enjoying themselves in a way that made me so deeply envious I was certain my eyes had shifted from blue to green.

But with Fleur, everything feels so natural, so right. My steps quicken as I approach her room. *Their room.* As much as I desire Fleur's company, I still need Gabriel. For now. I knock twice, hardly waiting for the second to finish echoing off the wood before I push the door wide. Gabriel sits in an armchair, his feet propped up on the cart that served them their dinner. His eyes narrow suspiciously.

"Fleur's not here." He flicks his gaze to the throne and then back to me. "And I'm certainly not interested in entertaining you myself this evening. I much prefer a partner when a homicidal monster is watching me fuck." Gabriel closes his mouth and furrows his dark brow, as if something has just occurred to him. Then suddenly, his sulky demeanor disappears completely. "Not that I mind your company, of course. I was hoping we could get to know each other better." He looks down at my cock and grimaces. "But not like that."

He's rambling. I learned long ago the power of silence. You needn't say anything to maintain the upper hand. Look menacing, stay quiet, and watch the world paint you as the epitomized portrait of violence and danger. Of course, snapping a few necks here and there helps to add to that fearsome reputation.

Gabriel is a charmer. He uses words to rile up enemies and inspire masses. The fact that he can back it up with muscle only makes him a more perfect specimen of a man. That's why he's continuing to ramble while I stare into his icy eyes. I assume he's trying to win my good graces after his pitiful attempt to escape earlier today. If he thinks I'm foolish enough to believe he had interest in exploring the rose gardens, he's sorely mistaken. I've watched his every move for months, from the way he guzzled beers with his dimwitted entourage, to the moments he had triplets choking down his cock like it was cuisine of the King. I see right through Gabriel. My gaze cuts to the dining cart where a large portion of food remains untouched.

"Fleur did not return for dinner?"

"No." Gabriel frowns. "I assumed she was with you."

Something is not right. I turn, leaving the room and ignoring Gabriel as he hollers out a question at me. It's late and the castle is growing colder by the minute. Nothing good comes from the shadows that materialize in the corners and darkened doorways of the castle at night. I know that better than anyone.

My first stop is the library. She isn't there. Perhaps she went to find dinner on her own. I'm well aware of her fondness for eating. The dining room and kitchen prove fruitless as well. Nerves worm awake in my gut. Has she gotten lost somewhere in the castle?

Blood pounds in my ears. I reach my personal quarters in record time, pressing my paw to the mirror and summoning Fleur's face over the glassy reflection. Everything inside me grows still and dead. The woman in the mirror is not simply cozied up in some other part of the castle with a book and a handful of pastries. She's not in the castle at all, nor on the grounds nearby.

Fear wraps my heart in thorny tendrils, cutting off the blood and leaving me bent over and stunned. I hardly recognize the face staring back at me. Fleur's light-brown hair whips in the raging winds, her mossy-green eyes are wide and wild. The ruddy pink of her skin is illuminated by the light of the moon. She swings her arms erratically from left to right. The terror in her gaze makes my stomach curdle and churn. *What is she afraid of?*

Snow swirls around her, blurring my view of her surroundings and making it difficult to pinpoint her location. The wind settles for a moment and her hair falls down around her face. She releases one gut-wrenching scream. Then I see them.

Wolves.

I drop to all fours, racing through the castle and barreling out the front door. Fear shreds my heart with claws of regret as I realize what a fool I was. I should never have left her alone. My thoughts were so wrapped up in the way I felt for her that I'd barely stopped to consider how she felt about me. My suspicions have been entirely focused on Gabriel and his possible attempts to flee. I trusted her to stay and she left. *They always leave.*

My paws pound past the front gate and I sniff the air, catching two familiar scents. One is horse, the other is human. A red mare barrels out from the tree line, racing past me and up toward the stables. Its whinnies of fear stab ice in my veins. The abandoned tracks lead me well past the castle grounds and deep into the forest.

How long has she been gone? Why didn't the mirror alert me to her absence? The snow is piled so thickly that it hits my chin with every lumbering stride. I'm grateful when it firms up and I'm able to pad across the top. What was she thinking, leaving during a storm like this?

A great howl snaps my focus forward. I'm close. I burst through a thicket of trees, landing in a clearing, and find Fleur fighting for her life as eight wolves prowl around her. They dive for her and she thrusts a broken stick out, using the pointed end to dissuade them with one hand while swinging a massive bundle of branches with the other. It's difficult to tell from this distance, but I don't scent any human blood in the air. Which is a miracle. It's also a miracle she's survived as long as she has under these harsh conditions.

The wolves stalk around her, believing themselves to be

the predators here. But these are my woods, and everything that resides within these trees is prey. I release a roar of sharp-toothed reckoning as I close the gap. Fleur spins, eyes growing wider as she spies me. My immediate sensation is relief, that she's still alive. It's followed shortly by fury, that she left in the first place. I'll deal with her punishment later. The priority now is her safety.

The glowing eyes of every wolf snap toward me. The hackles of their thick gray and white coats rise as they size me up. In a way, the wolves and I are so very alike. But where they're hunting for sport or food, I'm hunting in the name of love and a nameless desperation to keep it.

Despite being easily three times their size, they choose to take me on. I'm not surprised. They have the numbers, but I have the vengeful spirit. We shall see which is the greater advantage in the end.

The first one dives for me and I swing wide, slamming my right arm into the wolf's side and hearing a satisfying crack as it makes contact with his ribcage. The second wolf attacks from behind before the first has even hit the ground. It latches onto me, teeth driving into the curved flesh of my back and I howl as my skin is shredded. I reach around, gripping the wolf by its neck and hauling it off, wincing as the teeth tear through my hide and into the muscle as I pry the animal loose. It hits the ground hard and quickly scrambles to its feet.

Movement draws my attention back to Fleur. One of the wolves has refocused on her, stalking close. Before I can intervene, she swings the broken branch she's wielding, striking the wolf's gray muzzle and sending it sprawling several feet back. *That's my girl.* Two wolves flank me on either side, teaming up to take me down. My claws rake through the air, seeking purchase and I whirl, trying to map the pack's movements as each member plots their own attack.

My gaze again snaps toward Fleur. She slams her branch into the muzzle of another and pride swells in me. The feeling falters as I note the shaking of her arms, the chattering of her gritted teeth, the paleness of her flesh behind the wind rouge dotting her cheeks. She needs to get back inside or she'll freeze to death. I roar out a challenge, declaring my desire to end this quickly and save the girl I love. The wolves answer my challenge with howls of their own. And then they're upon me.

I'm struck by more teeth and claws than I can count as the pack assembles a coordinated strike in an effort to destroy me. This style of attack no doubt serves them well when taking down a bear, great elk, or a giant boar. They cling to my fur, driving their teeth into me, spilling my blood on the sparkling snow. *I've had enough of this.* Savagery splits my skull, allowing every trace of Renard to vanish, and releasing the Beast in its fullest, most barbaric form. I grip the wolves, one by one, stuffing them in my mouth, biting off heads, ripping through limbs, tearing into crunchy bone and chewy sinew. Crimson waterfalls from my lips, steaming as it hits the ground. The sensation leaves me hot and heady. I make a meal of the corpses, pulverizing every animal until each wolf is nothing but a furry sack of pulpy flesh and splintered bones. I unleash every ounce of rage on them, snapping the tether of tightly wound control I exhibit every day that I remain trapped in this beastly form. The howls, yelps, cries, and gurgles all fuel my bloodlust. I lap up the horror, savoring every moist, meaty pop. Flesh cakes beneath my claws. Meaty muscle lodges between my fangs.

The first few were brave, and their blood was metallic and musky. But the last few saw their deaths coming. Their blood tastes soured with fright and I laugh as the potent elixir of fear in the air and terror on my tongue pumps euphoria through my veins. Disappointment strikes me like a slap across my face when at last their mournful howls have fallen silent.

They're dead. Every last one of them.

My eyes snap to where Fleur is standing, frozen in shock, mouth agape. I must be a sight to her, fur dripping with sticky blood, eyes lacking any trace of the human within. She's afraid. She should be. But my bloodlust is not aimed in her direction.

I blink, drawing a bit of my human side forward, helping to ensure I won't devour her on the spot. I snatch up fistfuls of snow, using them to clean my face and paws as best I can. It's not much, but it removes the largest chunks of residual flesh and coagulated blood.

When I'm confident I can think clearly, I reach for Fleur, gripping her hard and tossing her over my shoulder. I move swiftly back the way I came, not bothering to start a conversation. She doesn't speak. Shock has likely stolen her tongue, locking it away with the dismembered carcasses freezing solid beneath the fresh snow.

My body throbs and aches as I trudge back to the castle with Fleur in tow. "You're bleeding." Fleur's voice draws my attention to the trail of blood tracking our path out of the forest. I peer back once. I don't have time to worry about my injuries right now. My main focus is getting Fleur inside before she freezes.

"You're hurt." Her observation comes out through chattering teeth.

"Yes," I snarl. "Injuries tend to happen when you take on an entire wolf pack, alone."

"You're angry."

"Angry?" The word does little to encompass the darkness battling within me in a constant effort to bring the full Beast and his bloodlust to the surface again. "You tried to run away, after I specifically told you not to. You nearly got yourself killed."

"I wasn't running away, I just wanted to check on Aida and the villagers. I was going to come back!" Her confession is genuine and yet, something feels off about her story.

"If you wanted to check on the old woman, why not ask me? I would have checked for you and saved you the trek through the snow." She's quiet and the silence settles an uneasiness atop the fragile shell of my hope. "Why didn't you ask me, Fleur?" Her heart rate picks up, its chaotic pace like the flapping of a wounded bird against my shoulder.

"I didn't think you would tell me the truth. Especially if you had already killed everyone."

"Already killed everyone?" My question is saturated in disbelief. "Why would you think that?"

She hesitates and I jostle her on my shoulder, shaking the answer out of her. "Someone told me. They said you've already killed Aida, and the other villagers too. That you've done things more horrible than I can imagine."

"Who?" My blood boils. "Who fed you these lies?"

"Are they lies?" Fleur pushes up on her forearms, glaring down at me.

"I did not kill Aida and the villagers," I irritably grunt.

"What of Gabriel's men?"

"Yes, I killed them." I mutter in frustration. "But that was a long time ago."

"A couple days is a long time ago?" She speaks the words with an eyebrow cocked and a sour tone.

I shove the castle doors open and lumber down the hall. "The point is, you ran away. I was worried you'd be killed before I arrived."

"Because then you wouldn't have a plaything anymore?" she mocks.

"Because then I would have lost the only woman I've ever loved!" I shout, then set Fleur on her feet in front of the bedroom door.

Shock is evident in her lovely features. "You... love me?" Fleur's brows are knitted together as she searches my eyes for the truth.

"Isn't it obvious?" My own voice is harsh and vexed. I expect Fleur to back away, but she doesn't.

"Obvious? No, Renard, it's not obvious. Kidnapping, threats, watching me fuck? That's infatuation, maybe."

Her accusation should cut cleanly through me, but the impact is dulled by the pounding in my head. My wounds are more pronounced now. I'm aware of the pool of red staining the pale-blue rug at my feet. A steady, pulsing throb hammers into most of my skin now that we're out of the cold. My flesh is torn most deeply at my nape. I can feel the wound splitting open, flesh separating and exposing muscle and fat to the air, each time I move my arms. A lengthy gash decorates my right forearm.

It's not a clean tear thanks to the wolves' many teeth. The flesh is ragged and maimed, as I suspect all my wounds to be after a fight like this. A sharp, slicing ache pounds in the meat of my upper left thigh, forcing me to bear most of my weight on the right side. Those are the worst of them, but I know dozens of smaller cuts and puncture wounds cover me from head to toe.

Fleur looks me over, studiously. "Come now, we need to stop the bleeding."

"I don't need—"

"Don't argue with me." She opens the bedroom door, dragging me in behind her. "Sit." She points to a large chair in the corner. Her assertiveness surprises me and the little blood that does remain in my body goes straight to my cock.

"What has happened?" A very startled Lucien stops

pushing the half-eaten dinner cart out of the room as we storm inside. Gabriel isn't here.

"We were attacked by wolves. Go get the doctor," Fleur instructs.

"We don't have a doctor in the castle anymore," I tell her. The corners of her shapely, pink lips turn down in a frown. A new hardness shines through her eyes, deepening the allure of those pale-green gems as they focus on me.

"Fine. Lucien, please get me a needle and thread."

"You're planning on sewing him up yourself?" asks Lucien.

"Yes, as a matter of fact I am, now move your ass. Find Mrs. Perle, I'm sure she'll have some." Lucien regards Fleur before turning to leave. "And bring me more towels!" she calls out to him.

I feel lightheaded. My tongue grows thicker by the moment, and there's a tenebrous echo of doom ringing in my ears. Wisps of mist and silken webs sweep across my consciousness as pain burrows deep into my tissues.

"Hey!" Fleur snaps, her tone commanding. "Open your eyes. I will not carry the guilt of your death on my soul, nor the stain of your blood on my hands." She glares up at me. "Now stay awake. You're the Beast. Don't you dare let a few wolves strip you of your spirit."

She shuffles around the room, making use of what she can find. Lucien returns quickly, his spindly, shaking frame crossing into my makeshift doctor's station. He carries towels under one arm and a tray of needles, thread, catgut, and wine.

"*Pardon, monsieur.*" He hands me the bottle. "You should probably drink the whole thing."

"Stop fussing, I cannot die, remember?"

"I wouldn't be so confident about that. Drink," Fleur

urges, snatching the bottle from the tray and shoving it into my hand.

I do as she says. Not because I care for being bossed around. But because the pain sizzling across my nerve endings is building to such an unbearable intensity that I can hardly breathe. Every movement, every expansion of my lungs, fuels the fiery knife-strikes stabbing into the raw open carnage the wolves left behind. The wine passes down my throat, prickling through my adrenaline and dumping a warm buzz into my trauma-numbed body.

Fleur threads her needle, opting for the catgut. The idea of being sewn up with sheep's intestines has never been appealing to me. At the moment I'm in no position to complain. A dark, shimmering veil creeps up around my field of vision.

"This one first." Fleur moves to the back of my neck. Her voice sounds echoey, muted, as if she's far away or underwater.

"I should go find someone to help," the male voice responds. Who is she talking to? I can no longer decipher if it's Lucien or one of the others

"There's no time for that. Pull the flesh together." I feel a deep pressure against my neck. There's a sigh of frustration. "It's too wide. There's not enough skin left to sew up." Her voice is slow and thick. "I think we're better off cauterizing it." *Cauterizing?* I wrack my brain, digging through the library of information housed inside my skull. The search is slow, painful, like trudging through quicksand laced with metal spikes. I've heard the word before, but every time I get close to its meaning the darkness spreads a little farther across my eyes. Feet are running around behind me as voices yell out at one another, the noises distorted, making them squeak like rats in a maze.

"You have done this before?" someone drones above me.

"I've read about it." Warmth hovers above my neck, slowly building in intensity.

"Hold him steady. This is going to hurt." *What is Fleur talking about?* A burning like the very surface of the sun sears into the tattered opening of my neck. I roar as hands steady my shoulders. The heat on my flesh intensifies until I'm being consumed by fire, by pain. I inhale deeply, preparing to scream, to beg for mercy. Singed fur and sickly charred flesh reach my nose. It's all too much. Too hot.

The creeping blackness rushes forward, extinguishing the flames of horror and shock as I'm swept into the darkest sleep of my life. Dreamless I fall, caring little if I awaken. In that second of silent peace I fall to the empty void, and all that keeps me from letting go completely is the pair of green eyes I can feel watching me from somewhere far, far away.

CHAPTER 13

RENARD

*M*y body feels like it's been run over by a carriage and then dropped off the side of a mountain. *What the hell happened?* Unwelcome sensations crawl along my skin. I was wounded and I didn't heal on my own. That's a horrific new development. The sounds of voices arguing reach my ears.

"There's a reason you were locked in here," Gabriel's deep voice accuses.

"He didn't do it on purpose," Fleur argues back. "It's an enchanted castle. Who knows what this kind of place is capable of?"

"Stop taking his side!" Gabriel yells loudly enough to make me wince. There's nothing to indicate how long I've been asleep. My eyes drift open to find the throbbing ache in my body has lessened. A tingling tightness across my skin is all I can feel now.

"Renard?" Fleur's voice is quiet, cautious. Her soft, heart-shaped face slides into focus. Her brow is creased and worry dots her green eyes.

"What happened?" I grumble, slowly sitting up.

"You blacked out and—"

"And this fucking castle went crazy. Then *shit for brains* Lucien left Fleur alone with you, and none of us could open the door." His body leers over mine.

"They should be open now," I murmur as my fuzzy mind continues to clear. I'm not sure how long it's been since Gabriel was able to enter the room, but Fleur appears to have washed in the meantime. Her hair is still damp and no blood covers her body or new maroon dress.

"No shit." Gabriel yanks the door wide and a trio of servants come tumbling in. "Jesus, have you been out here this whole time?"

A frazzled-looking Claude helps a weary Mrs. Perle to her feet. "*Oui*," he says. "Shortly after you summoned Mrs. Perle for supplies, the castle began to change. The walls shuddered, entire hallways vanished. The fires went out, the doors locked tight. We were worried."

Claude's words notch panic down my throat. *Was I truly that close to death?* Impossible. The witch cursed me to live forever, but I suppose that isn't the same as never dying. Surely I would have recovered on my own eventually.

A dark thought slithers into my mind, sparking my adrenaline. Can I truly be killed? Would the witch allow me to die now that I've found Fleur? Force me to live this long only to deprive me of the chance to break the curse as soon as the woman I love is finally in my grasp? The thought drops something slimy and raw in my gut, churning my stomach.

"I'm fine now and so is the castle." I stand, ignoring the pain of my scarred flesh and the tightness of my sewn skin. Gabriel is still glaring in the direction of a very nervous Lucien.

Mrs. Perle's frantic eyes score over my mended wounds.

"Is there anything we can get you, Master?" It could be my imagination, but Mrs. Perle seems paler, thinner, *older*.

"A bath."

"Right away. We'll head to your quarters at once—"

"Here," I cut her off. "A bath, here." I let my lip twitch up when she's slow to respond.

"At once." She nods quickly before running off. Gabriel and Fleur argue quietly in the corner. My eyes fixate on the tenseness in their postures, the closeness of their bodies. Anger heats my replenished blood as Claude returns with a fresh terrine of stew. Fleur hurries over, ladling the soup out and bringing a spoonful to my lips.

"Eat. You need to rebuild your strength."

I accept the food with a purr of contentment. Fleur's soft, floral scent mixes with the savory aroma of the stew as her hand brings the simmering liquid to my lips. I flinch as the over-hot liquid scalds my tongue.

"Too hot?" Fleur dips her spoon in again, but this time she blows on it first, rippling the surface of the soup with her breath. The rounded *o* her lips make as she cools the liquid makes my mouth water. If I were human, I'd have that perfect, plump o wrapped around my cock for breakfast, lunch, and dinner. The next spoonful passes my lips, and I resist the urge to pour the rest over Fleur's body, licking it off as it colors her skin pink from the heat. I swipe my tongue across my lips. A rosy hue dances across her cheeks. My desire for her must be less well disguised than I realized. In my periphery, I observe Gabriel. He paces the room like a caged animal.

"What are they doing?" Fleur asks. The servants scurry about, bringing hot water and towels. Fleur frowns at their efforts.

"Preparing the bath," I answer before taking another deliciously salty bite, sliding my lips farther down the spoon so they brush along Fleur's fingers. The rosy hue in her cheeks returns.

"You can't have a bath. Your wounds need time to heal." She gives me a stern expression, looking fiercely adorable.

"It's not for me." I glance between the two of them. Her mouth parts and Gabriel stops pacing.

"Now?" she whispers. "You need to rest."

"I *need* to see you, hear you," I growl into her ear. "Nothing would make me feel better." The blush deepens and spreads down her neck. The staff finishes their work and leaves us, their heads to the ground, eyes averting my stare. As soon as they exit, Fleur stands.

"After everything that happened tonight—" Her voice has a nervous edge to it.

"I want you both, in the tub." Fleur opens her mouth to protest. "After that, I will put your concerns to rest and prove to you that the townspeople are still safe."

"How?" The uncertainty and caution in Fleur's eyes sinks into my heart like my own sharpened claws. She doesn't trust me. It's time to change that. But first...

"In the tub." I drop my tone low. "Gabriel, drag a chair in there." Gabriel is staring after Fleur as she makes her way to the bathroom. "Gabriel?"

He turns to me with a smirk. "Yeah, yeah. A chair. You've got it, *your highness*." He locks eyes with me, waiting for a response. The phrase bristles my fur but I stifle my desired reaction, which would involve me smashing Gabriel's head against the golden wall sconces until his blood snuffed out the candles' flames. His icy eyes harbor no malice, though, only mischief. The realization that he's about to fuck Fleur again has lifted his spirits.

I show him where to leave the chair, keeping myself distanced enough to shroud my side of the room in darkness. Fleur stands by the large, steaming tub, her eyes sliding over Gabriel who's already begun to undress. Her tongue dips out, sweeping across her bottom lip as he drops his pants. She can fight it all she wants, but I can see the desire in her eyes as easily as I can feel it in my own blood. When her eyes turn to mine, they go wide for a moment. She knows I caught her ogling the man she still claims she can't stand. But how can she help herself? My eyes drink in Gabriel's impressive form. The raven-black hair paired with arctic-blue eyes, a strong jawline and deeply carved lips, a thick coating of dark hair that trails along the bulging muscles that dominate his entire body, and a cock that should be proof to most men that God has his favorites. I frown, remembering a time when I was God's favorite, too.

Fleur strips next and my attention hurries back to her flawless figure. Maple-brown hair frames her face, complementing the dewy green of her eyes and the pouty pink of her lips. It cascades along her body, barely covering the teardrop mounds and pert nipples of her tits. Her waist pulls in tight, leading to the area of her body that exhibits her love of sweet treats and fresh breads. Wide, goddess hips bow out on either side, giving her a bottom-heavy pear shape that makes my cock jump. A dark V of soft curls settles between thick thighs. My tongue flexes at the desire to be buried inside that hidden prize. The thought of that same luscious part of her dropped down on top of my face while she rides my tongue like a cock brings my dick to full attention. I dim the glow around me, extinguishing most of the candles and shielding myself from view.

"Gabriel first, then Fleur," I order. Gabriel enters the spacious tub, sighing as he sinks into the hot water. He settles back, draping his arms over the side and putting his muscles on display. "Step in, Fleur." She tentatively steps into the water, but before she can drop down into the warmth, I stop her. "Wait." She turns, seeking me out in my dark refuge. "Gabriel, use your tongue to ready her for your cock."

Fleur stands in the tub, stance wide. Gabriel surges forward without hesitation. I have to give him credit, the man loves to eat pussy and from the way Fleur's knees nearly buckle as he starts, he's damn good at it too. It's ironic really. I can count all the times I watched him eat out the other village girls on one hand. Perhaps he enjoys feasting on Fleur's pussy in particular. I can't blame him. I share the same affinity for our headstrong maiden. He braces his hands on her hips, supporting her weight. His mouth laps at every sacred part of her. Fleur's head rolls back, eyes falling shut.

"No," I bark. "Watch him as he devours your cunt."

Fleur looks toward me for a moment then drops her gaze to Gabriel. His icy-blue eyes ignite as they lock with hers and his fingers dig into the meat of her ass.

My cock is hard and needy but I don't touch it yet. My injuries are still tender and tight. If I'm going to aggravate Fleur's handywork, it will be for the main course, not the appetizer. Moans paint the air around me, echoing off the tiled walls and sinking into my ears like music. If I could capture that sound, I could bring the world to their knees. Gabriel is groaning, too, lost in the ecstasy of delivering plea-sure with such precision and ease. I envy him, and at the same time, I'm grateful. With him around I can guarantee Fleur will never go unsatisfied.

Fleur buries her fingers in his hair, driving him deeper. Her knees bend slightly as she grinds against his mouth, chasing her climax. I've watched her long enough to know when she's close and I want to see it—that look in her eyes as she comes undone.

"Now look at me." My speech is guttural, inhuman.

Jade irises flutter my way seconds before she cries out,

her eyes rolling back, body seizing up and then melting in Gabriel's hold. He grins up at her, messy-faced and victorious. I'm desperate to lick that shiny arousal off his chin, to know the way she tastes at this very moment. I bet she's sugary and sweet.

"Mount his cock." My words are gritty and rushed.

The water sloshes as Gabriel sinks back, splaying his arms over the edges once more and giving Fleur a filthy *come and get it* smirk. She braces herself on his shoulders before bending her knees and sinking all the way into the tub. Gabriel catches her by the back of the head, drawing her in and kissing her deeply. She doesn't push him away, just shifts her hands from his shoulders to his chest. His hands disappear in the water and she gasps into his mouth as I can only assume he's tipped his cock to her entrance. Curse the tub for obscuring my view.

One hand moves to her waist, gripping her hip as he pulls her down hard onto the length of him. Her mouth pops open in surprise and water rushes across the surface as he fills her. I allow my hand to drift to my cock, sliding over the fabric, tempting myself with partial relief.

"Ride him hard and fast," I demand. "You had plenty of practice riding earlier this evening when you stole a horse and attempted to run away." My words taste bitter. Fleur flicks her eyes to mine and opens her mouth to speak. Gabriel silences her when he thrusts upward, drawing her attention back to the stiff length currently filling her to the hilt. "I want to hear ecstasy, not excuses. Ride him."

She huffs out once, blowing a strand of wayward hair from her face, before reaching for the tub behind Gabriel. Her body rolls and a sigh of desire blows from my lips. Gabriel's tongue explores Fleur's face, neck, shoulders. His mouth lands on her nipple, and my eyes zero in on the way her flesh is sucked between his lips. She cries out in pleasure and his hands drop, gripping Fleur and working her hips faster.

A staccato rhythm of moans and grunts accompanies the splashing of hot water as both become lost in each other. Gabriel exposes Fleur's supple breasts to my viewing pleasure each time he bounces her up on his cock and they breach the water's surface. He knows exactly how to handle her, move her, how far he can push her limits. If he wants to take charge, then I might as well enjoy the show. I lean back, unbuttoning my trousers. I pull my cursed length free.

"Gabriel." His gaze is hooded as he turns to face me. "Dominate her."

Fleur's been flipped and stuffed again before she has time to voice her surprise. Gabriel has her back pressed against the tub while he drives into her. Water surges over the edges of the tub, flooding the floor below. Fleur's fingers grip the meat of his shoulders. I can see the crescent imprints from the biting sharpness of her nails on his flesh. At this rate he'll be coming before I can.

"Slowly, Gabriel," I urge, stroking my cock freely now. "Let's find out what our pet wants." He slows his pace and Fleur whimpers her disappointment. I chuckle darkly. "Not what you were hoping for, pet? Do you wish me to make him fuck you harder, faster?"

She moans and squirms beneath the languid rolls of his hips. "Yes, Renard."

"Yes, what?" I grin. I love the pouty expression on her face when she gets flustered and frustrated. "And I think it would be more appropriate if you referred to me as Master, while we're in here." Her hair is wet now. The dark length floats around her body like a living being.

"Yes, I want it harder, faster." She slides her eyes toward mine. "Master." I nearly come just from the sound of that word on her sultry lips.

"Give her what she wants."

Gabriel thrusts into her ferociously and her body slams against the tub. His muscles are on full display. I can see all the way down to the base of his abs as the water level drops with each powerful thrust.

"What else, pet?" I stroke myself more roughly, getting off on everything being said and done. "Do you want his tongue down your throat? His hand around your neck? Or perhaps his fingers in your ass?" I think back to their earlier encounter. Gabriel dabbled with that other part of her like he knew she would love it, and she came hard enough to prove him right. Watching that depravity only fueled my desire for Fleur. I want every part of her, ass, cunt, mouth, tits, all of it. Images of me covering her with my cum, watching it pour out from her holes and rain down her chest make my cock twitch and a feral noise escapes me. "Answer me."

"All of it," she pants out.

"All of it, what?" I bite back, enjoying the fearful expression my menacing tone draws out of her.

"All of it, Master." Her voice is as rich as honey. Holy fuck it sounds even hotter the second time.

"I'm sure Gabriel can accommodate you." I grip my dick hard enough to hurt and jerk it from tip to base, wincing as the wound on my forearm tests its sutures.

Gabriel's first hand drops below the water and I'm desperate to see where it's gone. Fleur's eyes go wide and she cries out as his fingers press into her. He quiets the sound with his mouth, snaking his tongue in between her lips and kissing her with a savage passion that leaves me practically wilting in my seat. His other hand wraps around her throat and I can't help but admire his skilled multitasking. All of this, and he's still pounding into her like it's his last day on Earth. Gabriel truly is a miraculous creature.

My cock swells as release breaks me open like a dam. My

cum spills out across the tile floor just as Fleur throws her head back, singing her orgasm to the heavens. Gabriel keeps his manic pace steady, refusing to succumb to the temptation of coming as well. "Another," he grunts out, biting into the flesh of Fleur's neck and making her whimper.

"Gabriel," she breathes behind the palm encompassing her throat. It cools my blood momentarily. I'd give anything to have her calling out my name while my cock is wringing every last ounce of pleasure from her body.

He snaps his hips hard enough to shake the tub. "Come on, Fleur, give me another." His tongue slides across her throat before he nips the skin on the other side of her neck. Her next climax is harder than the first, her body tenses, a silent scream shaping on her lips for several seconds before Gabriel releases his hold and a symphony of primal sounds rushes out of her. Gabriel's roar of release joins the music. I admire the way they can fuse together so seamlessly. *Someday, if I can break the curse, that will be me.*

The labored breathing of three bodies fills the humid room. Gabriel draws Fleur from beneath him, pulling her onto his lap. She presses her cheek to his chest with aching familiarity. His fingers glide through her wet hair in the way only lovers touch one another. I want that so badly, it's cleaving me apart.

"Bathe, then dress." I stow my cock and rise to my feet. "Then we will visit *the mirror.*"

CHAPTER 14

FLEUR

The castle is full of surprises. It's late by the time we dress and venture out of our room, though time doesn't merit quite the same effect here. My eyes wander over every inch of the enchanted space around me as we follow Renard. I'm quite certain the layout has changed since the last time I went exploring. The ceilings swoop lower, and a thick strip of gilded, thorny vines now runs corner to corner along both sides of the hallway. The impressive statues and armor displays have fallen victim to the winding golden bramble of the delicate, deadly vines, too. Even in my exhausted state, I am acutely aware of the ornate additions. "Things are changing in the castle," I note aloud, running my fingers across a dazzling sword that's now dripping in floral barbs.

"Indeed," Renard muses, his tone giving away none of his true feelings.

Gabriel moves closer to my side, placing his hand on my lower back. I peer up at him and find his dark brow furrowed and tense. Is he nervous? I think back to the events of the last few hours. Where was Gabriel when I returned with Renard? He didn't appear until hours later. "What's wrong?" I ask, sliding my hand into his. He visibly softens at the touch, squeezing my hand and locking our fingers together.

Here, in the castle, I find comfort in Gabriel's presence. That knowing drapes a satin shadow of uncertainty across my heart. Despite Gabriel's past actions, it's been almost too easy to dip back into our old familiarity and habits. I wonder how different things would be if I hadn't broken off our relationship those many years ago. Would we have settled down? Looking at the brawny, muscled spectacle of a man in front of me now, I find it hard to imagine the tall, thin boy who initially stole my heart. He peers down, the corner of his mouth hooking up in a roguish grin as he gazes at me.

"Always reminiscing," he teases.

"Why do you say that?" I frown, knowing he can't possibly read my mind well enough to know that is exactly what I'm doing.

"You get this dreamy look in your eyes when you're caught in memories." He shrugs. "Guess I've just seen you do it enough times to recognize it." Gabriel brushes a stray hair from my face, swiping his fingertips across my cheek and leaving heat in his wake.

"This way," Renard calls back to us in a gruff tone. A tinge of embarrassment washes over me as I remember Renard has been present throughout this entire conversation. It felt strangely intimate considering there was a third person present. Or maybe I'm just getting used to Renard's presence as part of our everyday lives.

That epiphany leaves me feeling both empty and full. Something prickles at the base of my tailbone, spinning a web of elated confusion and urgent mistruth up my spine and inside my gut. It's not just the castle that's changing.

Renard leads us up the main stairs and abruptly turns left,

walking us down the corridor that leads to his private quarters, the one place he told us never to venture into. The candles light as he passes, and a tingle of magic makes the hairs on my arms stand to attention. Gabriel rubs his own arm. He must be able to feel it too.

The temperature drops us into winter's icy clutches as we're guided into a bedroom. I suck in a breath as I look at the space. The room is in shambles. Snow is blowing in from an opened balcony with no door in sight. I shiver, and Gabriel takes me into his side. Broken furniture lies scattered across the floor. Shards of exotic wood and pulverized upholstery paint the room in a distinct air of dismal destruction. Tapestries hang in tattered ribbons. Each gust of wind whips through them, rattling their connection to the wall, the sound like a swan's song among stony crows. The material flows outward and the strips of hanging fabric claw out at us like ghosts. Shattered glass and bits of fine china crunch beneath my boots.

But even among such robust neglect, there is beauty.

Piles of blood-red petals haunt the forgotten room, forcing it to acknowledge the life it once knew. Even as I admire their lovely luster, a new batch is carried in on a frozen gust. Gabriel bends down, removing a petal from my hair and handing it to me. "Almost as beautiful as you," he whispers. The gesture lights a spark in my chest, illuminating my ribs.

"Thank you." I rub the petal between my fingers, noting the soft pliancy and warmth it has somehow retained during this difficult winter. "Enchanted?" I whisper up to Gabriel. His only response is a shrug.

"Everything here is enchanted." Renard turns to face us. "A *perk* of the curse." His tone is sarcastic and sad. It stirs in me a desire to move closer, to touch his face and wipe the sadness from his sapphire eyes. "This is the only item of

133

actual value here." He strides toward a massive wall-sized mirror. "The mirror is my window to the outside world. Through it, I can see anyone, anything." He turns to me with a flicker of magic in his gaze. "What would you like to see?"

"Aida. I wish to know if she is safe."

Renard nods once before pressing his palm to the glass. He flinches. It's subtle, but I don't miss it. The mirror swirls to life, bringing into view the inside of my childhood home. I move closer, needing a better look at this work of the occult. Everything in the cottage is exactly as I left it. The old, drafty cottage seems so small and bare in comparison to the castle. My heart lifts as I spy Aida, peeling potatoes on a small table by the fire. She appears well enough, humming a familiar tune as she works. Tears prick at the corners of my eyes as relief rushes down the carved path of concern etched along my heart.

I didn't want to believe Aida had been killed. And more than anything, I didn't want to believe Renard was responsible. A twinge of irritation lines my throat. The next time I see that lying little servant boy, I'm going to give him a piece of my mind. What kind of sick, twisted person makes up such a horrible story?

"Can we see the town square?"

"Of course." Renard's gaze fixes to the glass again and the image changes, bringing up a wide view of the center of town. The vendors have all gone home for the night. Disappointment settles in me.

"We can look again during the daytime, if you'd like?" he offers.

Gabriel moves in close. "Show me the tavern."

A warm, cozy light covers the mirror as the tavern comes into focus. There's a lively crowd tonight. Men laugh and drink, their bodies covering every stool, surface, and table in sight. Several women lounge on laps, giggling and leaning in close to the patrons. My eyes narrow when they settle on a trio of identical women. The triplets are as blonde and big-boobed as ever. An unwanted envy infects my blood, turning it green and making me wish I hadn't seen them at all. I know Gabriel kept them close while he and I were separate. Even though I didn't want him at the time, it still irks me that they had him for so long.

Jealousy is not a good look for you, Fleur.

I reach for Gabriel, taking his hand in a possessive move that has me cringing on the inside. It's not like me to feel possessive, but something ticks inside my bones when I think of either Gabriel or Renard with any other women. They've turned me into a creature of explosive feeling, doomed to inevitable destruction. I can't have them both. Hell, I can't have one of them at all. And do I really want to stake a claim on Gabriel now? After everything that's happened? Gabriel grips my hand tighter and whirls, dragging me out of the room behind him.

"Wait," I plead.

"I've seen all I need to see," he grits out. His tone is like flint, the sharpness surprising me. He's angry. I peer over my shoulder. Renard's eyes are on me, scorching with intensity. I expect him to follow, but he doesn't. Instead he watches me go, a wordless ache written plainly across his beastly face.

We round the corner, leaving the frigid bedroom behind. The mirror put some of my fears at ease, for now. But I have so many questions for Renard. Gabriel's strides never falter as his hand stays tightly clasped around mine. I guess my questions will have to wait for another time.

A yawn stretches through me as we approach the bedroom. Today was intense. It's hard to believe we're still walking through the same day as the wolf attack. I drop into bed, sinking into the soft sheets and letting my eyes close.

The last thing I see behind my eyelids are two pairs of

luminescent blue eyes. They're as pale as ice, and then as deep as the sea. Two sets of eyes. Two people so infinitely and unnervingly important. It's impossible to tell who is who in the end. Either way, they guide me into the darkness.

Sleep welcomes me.

* * *

Morning lifts my tired eyes, sparking my mind to life. The events of last night huddle fresh and weary in my thoughts. Memories of the wolves, frost, and the steady dripping as Renard bled out on the carpet. A shudder buckles through me. *He's safe now*, I remind myself. The rush of fresh oxygen as I breathe deeply settles my nerves and brings me back to the present. The room is quiet and still around me. I'll never get used to waking up here, beneath the gold and white canopy, atop this mass of fluffy pillows and thick blankets. I sneak out of bed, careful not to wake Gabriel. I don a simple lavender dress. Gabriel shifts and I peek back at him, sprawled out, gloriously naked, and fast asleep. Gabriel's cock rises earlier than he does.

I giggle, gazing down at the impressive appendage. It truly is a work of art, so wonderfully thick, veiny, and long. Desire dews along the insides of my thighs. I'm swarmed with the urge to climb onto him, mount that magnificent cock, and fuck Gabriel awake, watching the sleep flush from his eyes until they blaze with a need for reprieve that only I seem to be able to give him.

My thirst for power has grown since last night. Why has it taken me so long to realize I could be the one in control of both men? I am the one they both want, *need* even.

Renard enters my consciousness, giving me pause. What would he think if Gabriel and I were together without the scope of his piercing gaze? A flustered flutter of embarrassment and excitement pulses in my core at the realization that I like it when Renard is there.

I've never been considered a good girl. My propensity for independence, freedom, and the thrill of adventure has put me at odds with traditional ladylike propriety. Never has that been more clear than now. I want Renard to watch. I want even more than that…

A quick rapping of knuckles at the door alerts me to the arrival of our breakfast. I peel my eyes away from Gabriel and bury my lascivious thoughts behind a mask of pleasant control. Opening the door, I smile at Lucien and Claude who push our usual breakfast cart in, then slip past them.

"No breakfast for you, *mademoiselle*? Where are you headed so early?" Lucien asks, his worry barely hidden in the crease of his narrow features.

"I'm off to the library," I say cordially. Truthfully I don't know where Renard sleeps. It couldn't possibly be in the magic mirror's keep. I brush the thought aside. I don't wish to imagine him somewhere so cold and dark. The library is my best bet for finding him and checking to see how well his injuries are healing.

"Perhaps a tray of tea and scones then? I can have Mrs. Perle send one up," Lucien offers.

"That would be perfect. *Merci!*"

The two enter our room as I venture off. I can't help but grin when I hear Claude's shout of alarm, followed by a stunned, "*Sacré bleu! That thing is énorme!*" And I bury my giggle into the palm of my hand.

The castle halls are chilled from the storm outside, but the library is warm and welcoming. The fire is already gleaming vibrantly when I enter. The room seems to brighten as if it can sense my presence here. The cherry wood of the shelving shines and the dusty books hum with the anticipation of being chosen, read, appreciated. I pick through the unfinished pile from yesterday and settle into an armchair.

Time passes easily as I disappear among the pages of another book. Oh how I love to lose myself like this. Reading makes everything so simple. It's just me, the book in my hands, and the beautiful world my mind creates. Tea is served twice while I wait for Renard. Surely he's resting. It's good for recovery. Still, I miss his presence here.

"Fleur?" I nearly separate from my skin as Renard's voice whispers from merely two feet away. I was so engrossed in my poetry, I didn't even hear him enter. "Apologies," he offers quickly.

"It's fine." I chuckle lightly. "You just surprised me. You're awfully quiet for someone so large," I muse, raising an eyebrow in mock suspicion.

"I'll be sure to shake the doorknob or clear my throat next time." He gives me a soft smile.

"How are you feeling?" His bandages are still in place, though several are stained crimson.

"Nearly healed, thanks to you. You were quite brilliant." His eyes are so focused when they're on me. It makes something low and deep tighten in my stomach.

"It was nothing." A warmth creeps into my cheeks. Even as I flick my gaze away, I can feel those sapphire flames.

"Have you read anything new?" he asks, saving me from speaking next.

"Yes." I flip my book to the previous page. "This one is so lovely."

He moves gracefully to sit in his usual spot. The slight wince as his body bends and settles twists an ornate handle of solipsistic guilt, burying the feeling deeper into my gut. His injuries are my fault.

"Please don't look at me like that." He sighs heavily in his seat.

"Like what?" I protest.

"Like I'm a wounded animal. I told you I'm fine, I meant it." The bloodstains beneath his bandages tarnish my soul, sliding beneath my skin with their accusatory impermanence.

"Thank you." The edge of my teeth worry my bottom lip. "I'm glad you found me, even though it gave you those wounds. There was a moment last night when I thought you weren't going to make it. All that blood..."

Renard releases a low, mirthless chuckle. "I admit it was touch and go there for a bit." His stare locks onto mine again in that familiar way, like he's seeing past my eyes and into my soul. "But you saved me. You're everything I dreamt you would be and more."

Warmth simmers beneath my skin and it has nothing to do with the roaring fire behind me. The tingling ache that spreads through my body has become all too common when Renard is near. I soak up the sight of his pensive ocean gaze, the sharpness of his fangs as they peek out between his lips, the glint of his horns in the light of the fire. His massive frame shifts the energy in the room, tainting it with magic, spreading the flinty magnificence of stardust and charms. I scan down his body, dropping to the deep-blue trousers he always wears. What lies dormant beneath that rich cobalt fabric? What does he hide in the dark of the shadows when he watches me with Gabriel?

Renard clears his throat. "What did you want to read to me?"

My eyes pop up as embarrassment floods my cheeks with greater heat. Renard's mouth is turned up in a smirk that has me questioning if he can read minds.

"Read?" I ask, my eyes fixated on his mouth.

His smile widens. "The book in your hand."

"Oh, yes, the book." I flip through the pages, buying myself a moment while my brain unscrambles itself.

"The Wisteria Tree:

Standing in the forest on an open patch of ground
Surrounded by enormous trees, I'm never to be found
Until a drop from in the sky lands right upon my skin
The sun shines bright and opens up a shower to begin
My head tilts up, my eyes close tight, this beauty's pure and true
I open up, look straight ahead, and there I now find you
Walking forward, joining me, under the sun and rain
We laugh and take each other's hands, forgetting all past pain
Drenched and flushed and standing close, you plant on me a kiss
That sends a flash of warmth and light the forest does not miss
Now from our feet the roots begin to bury down below
Around our tangled bodies now, a trunk begins to grow
It wraps around us, keeping space, enough for just us two
Holes for sunbeams streaming in allow me to see you
Upon the top of this new tree the branches bud and bloom
Spilling purple petals down and filling our trunk room
Sealing us in floral grace for all eternity
Inside here we will remain, the wisteria, you, and me."

Something drips down, discoloring the paper and blurring the words. Another droplet hits the page, followed by another. I reach a hand up to my face, inhaling a sharp breath as hot tears greet my fingertips. When I read this poem alone and inside my mind, I found it beautiful and romantic.

Reading it aloud stirs up an unexpected cauldron of feeling inside me. Those whimsical words remind me of everyone I've ever loved and everything I've lost. Pain blooms in my chest, taking root and growing outward until the fibrous, memory-soaked chambers of my heart bleed each of their lost faces out onto a painted canvas of lifelong tragedy. I suck another tight breath between my teeth, praying to staunch the flow, but it merely deepens the wound. A chasmic, aching loneliness spills forward.

"Fleur?"

I tip my forehead up to find Renard kneeling in front of me. His vibrant eyes are a seaside mirror of concern. It's the closest he's ever been, face to face. Cinnamon fur serenades my senses. The warm, spicy scent swirls with a mix of pine trees and juniper. It's like a holiday, warm and comforting. But beneath the surface scents, there's something wild, something animal. It heats my blood as I inhale deep, wintery breaths of him.

His paw reaches toward my face, and I'm certain he's going to touch me. He hovers it there, and then drops it. "Wait." I reach out to grab him but he drifts away from me like mist on the wind, leaving a vacancy between us as he stands back up. "Please," I whisper. "I want to touch you. I want you to touch me."

He shakes his head, staring at the floor. When his eyes draw up to mine again, an endless pain flows freely from his irises. "If I could, I would brush the tears from your cheeks and kiss your sadness to the stars."

My lips part as the beautiful words draw pain from my wounds, exposing them to the air. "Why can't you?"

An unfathomable darkness stirs behind his eyes. In that look, I know whatever he's thinking of is more horrific than I can imagine. "I'll destroy you."

"From just a touch?" I rise, crossing the space to stand in

front of him. He watches my approach with an animalistic panic that sets my pulse ticking faster. "I don't believe that." He shifts his weight to step back. "Don't," I plead, inching closer. My fingertips stretch up above my head, reaching for his face. Renard has fallen so still that I'm certain he's not breathing. The moment my fingertips brush along the dense fur of his forehead, he releases a low, shuddering breath. His fur is soft and unusual. Up close I can see that it's not black, but a deep earthy shade of brown. Like soaked soil beneath a summer rain.

I bury my fingers deeper, running the tips down his long, wide snout. His eyes fall shut and he breathes my name on a sigh. *"Fleur."*

My hands dip lower, sliding over his nose and tracing the plush lips that surround a mouthful of sharpened fangs. He tenses as I press the pad of my thumb against one of his teeth. "Open your eyes." My voice is no more than a whisper as my fingertips coast back to his lips. His pupils are blown wide, eyelids hooded as he stares down at me.

"I have dreamt of you in this very room more times than I can count." His breath is hot on my palm.

"Tell me about your dreams," I urge, still stroking his fur.

"Fantasies," he corrects. The way he speaks the word sends a shiver down my spine. "I've pictured having you in so many ways." He leans into my touch. "Writhing in front of the fire while I feast between your thighs, tasting your sweet release until you beg me to come." My core clenches and my breathing quickens as his words skate across my skin. "Then fucking you, bent over the chaises, couches, tables, slamming into you until every piece breaks and this room is as ruined as my heart has been watching you from afar for all these years."

"Touch me." I grip fistfuls of his fur and he releases a hiss of frustration.

"I can't. My teeth would tear through your flesh." His eyes burn into mine as I take a step back. "My claws would shred your skin." He advances on me, sending me into a hasty retreat from the darkness blotting out the blue in his eyes. "My cock would split you in two."

My knees hit the wood frame of the chaise and I go boneless, dropping onto the velvety cushion. Renard is towering over me, glaring down with a hunger and intensity that rivals anything I've seen in him before—even the bloodlust I witnessed when he tore apart the wolf pack in the woods.

"So you see, my dear Fleur, I cannot touch you."

Power emanates from his pores, darkening the air around us, lacing my blood with fear and arousal. Now, more than ever, I believe the two emotions are completely interchangeable. "Then don't touch me." I lean back, drawing my skirts up and spreading my knees wide. "Just taste me."

Renard's gaze tracks to my bare pussy. The need in his eyes when he realizes I'm not wearing anything beneath my dress is more of a turn-on than I ever imagined. I'm wet, wanton, and waiting for him to make the first move.

"Fleur." His voice is husky. "I can't..." He never takes his eyes away from the dripping mess between my thighs.

"Just your tongue," I purr. Renard hasn't even touched me and I'm already mewling like a cat in heat. "Please." I slip two fingers inside myself and his blue eyes glow brightly. That's when I notice it, the hard ridge beneath his royal trousers. It's every bit as proportionate as one would imagine for a beast his size. The sheer length gives me pause. It's longer than my arm. I can't take my eyes away from it. There is no imaginable way that something nearly the thickness of my thigh could ever fit inside me. It truly would split me in two.

Renard's eyes follow mine and he licks his lips, dropping one hand to stroke his cock through the fabric. That one, quick sweep of his tongue catches my eye and I can't suppress the moan that pours out of me.

"Fleur, there are sides of me you haven't seen yet. Things I keep barely locked away."

Arousal leaks around my fingers as he steps closer, slow, controlled, a predator with his prey in sight. He lowers to his knees in front of me and my heart beats so fast it blurs my vision.

"If you get the part of me you want now, you'll end up getting the parts you don't want later." The dangerous edge in his voice makes me shiver.

"I want all of it." The words are a key that opens the floodgates of Renard's control. His posture stiffens, eyes taking on a new hardness.

"Remove your fingers," he commands in that same raspy tone. I obey, sliding them out. I tense when one of his massive paws wraps around my wrist. The contact is firm, but not painful. His palm is warm and rough against my skin. He raises my wrist to his face, and slowly lengthens his tongue. The long, wet flesh is rough as it glides up my fingers, tasting my cum and making me whimper. Renard's eyes roll back. "I knew you'd be sweet." He drops my wrist and dips low. His head is so large, I have to spread my knees almost painfully wide to accommodate him. My hands hover on my thighs, unsure where to touch. "Are you certain this is what you want?" He peers up from between my thighs.

Butterflies swarm my stomach and I swallow thickly. "You said you wanted to feast on me." I chew on my bottom lip. "Show me how starved you've been."

Renard groans at my words, gripping my thighs wide and burying his face in my cunt. His tongue is thick and powerful as it probes inside me, sinking so deeply and filling me so fully that I'm certain it could put most men's cocks to shame. My back arches off the chair as pleasure pulses through my core. He slides his tongue out, flicking up over my clit before lapping at my center. His tongue is flexible and muscular as it twists, turns, and swirls up, down, around, and inside every inch of me. If I had known he had this monstrously magical appendage before, I would have begged him to use it sooner. He thrusts back inside, fucking me with his tongue, making the chair jump with every rough, jerky movement from his head. I gasp, gripping his long, curved horns, needing something to steady myself. He freezes, mewling as my fingers wrap tightly around the vestigial features.

"Does that…feel good?" I pant out, acknowledging the way his entire demeanor has shifted.

"Yes," his breath hisses. "So. Fucking. Good." His reaction is unexpected. Perhaps no one has ever touched him here before? Maybe he's never been touched at all. I squeeze more firmly, gripping the thickest part of the base before slowly working my hands up and down. Renard's entire body shudders. His movements fuel my arousal and I squirm, eager to have his tongue back inside me.

He slides his tongue from the center of my ass to the base of my abdomen and I jerk, an involuntary spasm rattling through me at the contact. His tongue drives back inside me, forcing a choked sound from my throat. He flexes the slippery appendage, curling it upwards and making my toes curl along with it. "Ohhh yes," I moan. "Don't stop." I grip his horns hard enough to blanche my knuckles. His low growl sends vibrations rocking through my center. One of his massive paws drops from my thigh, dipping below the chair and toward his waistband. His tongue moves faster, harder, deeper. His body is writhing now, rutting forward in time with the devilish thrusts of his tongue, his hips and mouth timing up so perfectly. I can almost imagine him inside me like this. And he, no doubt, is fantasizing about being balls deep in my dripping snatch instead of pounding into his closed fist.

Grunts of desire fall out around his tongue as he chases his own pleasure along with mine. I peer down, desperate for a better view but can see nothing past his face and tongue as he eats my pussy with a reverence that has me shaking and simpering like it's my first time. The deep, uncontrollable wave of an orgasm is building to unimaginable heights within me, but I want more. I jerk on his horns, massaging my tightly closed hands up and down from base to tip, increasing my pressure and pace. The rhythm his tongue sets has my thighs quivering and my lungs panting in quick, shallow breaths. Something sharp brushes across my inner thigh as I grind my hips up, meeting his tongue. *His fangs.* He tenses and tries to pull back, but I squeeze his horns and ride his tongue.

"Don't stop, Renard. I'm so close." His free hand rocks my hips and the soft undulation sends the building pressure in my core skyward until I'm teetering on the very edge of madness. "Come with me, Master." I gasp as the orgasm detonates inside me. My walls clamp down around his tongue, and I scream out, the sound echoing off the walls of the vast library until they're swallowed by the stained glass above.

Renard releases a guttural roar with his tongue still inside me. The sound of his climax is so raw, so feral, so unbelievably sexy that I come again, muscles seizing, eyes blinded, hands gripping his horns for dear life. His thrusting movements slow and he draws his tongue out, following the emptiness with long, languid licks that have me jumping from sensitivity and pleasure. We're both breathing heavily, our lungs filled with ecstasy and disbelief. Renard slowly sits up, the fur of his chin dripping with my release. I move to draw my knees back together but he stops me, dropping his eyes to stare at my heated core, open and bare.

"Perfection." The word glides along my skin like velvet. It's another glimpse of the man beneath the monster. His deep gaze finds mine and I flush.

This changes things. The look in his eyes tells me he's come to the same consensus. *There's no going back now.*

CHAPTER 15

GABRIEL

How dare she. The image of Fleur's face contorting in pleasure as she let that monster tongue-fuck her ignites my blood. A sinister, harrowing heat courses along every tracing of veins in my being, dragging me into a depth of rage so shadow-filled it pumps a pitch-black hell into every dark vessel that bleeds through my heart. Those two were so wrapped up in each other they didn't even notice when I opened the doors. Watching that beast bury his distorted face between the exquisiteness of Fleur's creamy thighs made my gut twist and my heart plunge, leaving me with a pit of incredulity and utter shock. It was a wakeup call.

I need to get Fleur the hell out of here. She's lost her mind, fallen for her captor. Violence sparks in my chest, burning me alive from the inside. It's time to kill the Beast and move onto the next phase of our lives. My skin is raw with the need to put this behind us, to retell the story as a distant and unwanted memory.

Fleur's always had a proclivity for being different, sexual preferences included. I love that about her. When we were

younger, she would keep me constantly guessing with her evolving tastes and willingness to try anything once. My teeth grind in frustration. I knew she was getting off on the Beast watching us together, but I never thought…

Forget it. Everything's going to hell now. No wonder the servants believe he knows everything that happens within the castle walls. It appears the Beast need only seek a certain location and it will appear. I still don't understand how the mirror works. But I'm sure there are ways around it.

My own little look inside the magic mirror was most enlightening. I expected sorrow, worry, and uncertainty to be prevalent among the masses. Instead I found everyone existing as if nothing had changed. No search parties. No plans of action to save their old pal and fearless leader. Absolutely nothing. I can so clearly see them for the worthless bunch of drunks they really are. When I finish this, I'm taking control of the castle. I'll be so powerful, the villagers will be begging for a place by my side and in my closest confidence. I will take great pleasure in watching them beseech me and grovel at my feet.

I reach the servants' quarters. My voice rings out in the small, dimly lit corridors. "Elias!" Several startled faces peer out through doorways. "Where's Elias?"

"Here." The stocky young man saunters out. His chest is bare and the lack of clothing reveals a mashup of self-mutilation both old and new. Bizarre symbols and shapes have been carved into his chest, arms, and back. His left hand clutches a small dagger. The crooked metal drips with crimson. My eyes slide over his form until they reach a freshly carved X on his bicep. His mouth tips up, making his features more fit for a boy than man at the moment. The dichotomy feels all wrong. "Like my artwork?"

Something balloons in my chest, causing my thoughts to stagger and stall. The ability to read people has always been one of my strengths. A rocky pit sinks to the depths of my insides when I realize I may have misjudged this youth. His dark eyes are wild, ripe with the potential for danger. I'm suddenly aware of the delicate knife's edge, the fine line that keeps the boy sane and prevents the man from snapping, losing the small semblance of control he has left. Too many years in this cursed castle have unhinged him, turned him into something feral and insane.

I need to tread carefully. A loose cannon won't do me any good. I need malleable malevolence, not mindless vigilantes.

"Get your people together. It's time we made a plan."

A dozen haunted faces stare up at me. Physically, every member of the Beast's staff looks normal. If you passed one in the market on their way to buy a cut of meat or a dozen eggs, you'd never cast them a second glance. But from this vantage, with their eyes completely focused on mine, I see the truth. These people are shells, walking limbs and teeth, tragic puppets with vacant eyes and hopeless smiles. Being trapped in time may not be so bad for a King or his noble men and women, but for a servant, doomed to work under these deplorable and mysterious conditions, it seems a fate worse than death. They won't serve me well as soldiers, but they'll distract the Beast, and that will have to be enough.

"This is everyone?" I question Elias.

"There are others." He twirls the knife in his hand and I notice several of his fingernails are missing. "But their fear makes them untrustworthy. We can't have anyone running off and exposing our plan to the Beast, now can we?"

I know there are more servants in this castle, at least double the number present in this meeting. None of the usual three servants I'm used to seeing are here.

"There is a plan, *oui, monsieur?*" the blond man, Lyam, asks.

"I'm working on getting close to the Beast, learning his weaknesses and gaining his trust. When the right moment comes, when he's vulnerable and unaware, we'll strike."

"What happened last night?" Elias interrupts before I can finish properly motivating the masses—or dozen—fools at my feet. "We heard he was injured, practically bleeding to death. The castle locked us all down here, but you were in the same room. Why didn't you kill him then?"

My jaw ticks as I'm forced to confront this ugly truth. I take a moment to collect my thoughts. This is the question I've been avoiding answering in my own mind. From what I've pieced together, the two returned to the castle shortly after I left the room to search for her. Fleur was nearly frozen to death and the Beast was a charnel mountain of bloodied fur. Somehow, even without my help, Fleur saved his life. The Beast. *Renard*, as she calls him.

The truth is I wasn't in that room. After the Beast barged in, I went off to look for Fleur on my own. After checking the usual spots, things began to change. The castle became nearly unrecognizable. I wandered the halls for hours, unable to find my way back. The fear I felt when I realized I was lost is a sentiment I do not wish to repeat. When the castle shifted once more, I was spit out into the main entrance and foyer. Even after finding my room, I was trapped outside. I'd damn near dislocated my shoulder trying to get in.

It's only now that I see how deeply Fleur has her hooks in me. My fear for her safety turned me into a mindless, terrified brute. Relief spilled through my veins when I was finally allowed inside.

The opportunity for Renard's swift death at my hands passed by without even the smallest chance of success. The whole night seems like a blur of morbid panic and primal instincts. I love Fleur. She cares for Renard. And in that heightened state of adrenaline and carnage, my feelings for her were all I was able to think about.

A small bit of my gratitude floats unwillingly toward the Beast. If it weren't for him, Fleur would have died out there in the frozen woods, devoured by wolves until her delicate face and full frame were unrecognizable. She would have disappeared beneath the earth, a forgotten tragedy, a skeletal lullaby of woe. He saved her life, the woman I love, and I spared him. Even if it wasn't exactly by choice. Now we're even. Next time will be different.

Something mocking and sharp digs into my ribcage. I cannot let this plan fail. My, *our* future depends on it.

"You've been misinformed. The Beast was barely injured," I lie. Shame flavors my mouth.

"One of the maids saw Mrs. Perle with piles of bloodied—"

"I said you were misinformed." My voice cracks sharp as a whip. "Perhaps you'd like to send the maid my way, so she can be thoroughly punished for her lies." I rise to my full height, enjoying the way the staff cower beneath my influence. Elias glares at me, clearly unwilling to reveal his source. He's afraid of what I'll do to her. I smile inwardly. It feels good to be respected, but it feels better to be feared. "Scour the castle for weapons and keep them at the ready. When it's time, fight fearlessly and be swift with your justice."

The others cheer me on, all except Elias and a young maid whose eyes are glued to the floor. Our little informant, no doubt. I would very much like to make her swallow her story, rewriting the truth with my cock down her throat. But that won't do. I have a better target for my frustration.

I leave the servants' quarters without a backward glance. Fleur wants a beast in the bedroom? Fine, she'll get it. Hot anger pumps through my veins. My shaft strains against my pants. I am looking forward to reminding her who she truly belongs to.

* * *

I lounge in our bedroom, feet up, arms behind my head, adopting all the mannerisms of a man at ease. It's a farce of course. Inside, I'm brewing a storm so powerfully savage I'm surprised I don't drop fangs and sprout fur. Fleur hasn't returned since her library rendezvous. The longer she's gone, the more my desire to punish her, to prove how misplaced her feelings are, grows.

The doorknob turns and my muscles twitch in anticipation. Fleur flits into the bedroom, an airy grin on her face and a pile of books in her hands. She glides around the room, humming softly, seemingly unaware of my presence mere feet away. I watch her, allowing the light in her eyes and the soft smile on her lips to fuel my violent lust.

"Welcome back." The caught expression on her doe-like features makes me cluck my tongue.

"Gabriel." A hand moves to her chest. "I didn't realize you were here."

My eyes narrow. "Daydreaming? Or simply reliving the memory of recent events?"

Fleur's green eyes widen before she hides her emotion, stacking the books in a neat pile near the far wall. "Have you been in here all day? You really need to get out, take in some fresh air." She's acting casual but there's a ruddiness in her cheeks that I could never miss. She thinks she can hide things from me? I know her better than anyone. I know the way her body reacts to *everything*.

"No." I stand, casually advancing toward her. "I took a tour of the castle. Finally got to take in the sights of the magnificent library." My tone drips in sarcasm. Fleur stiffens, her eyes looking anywhere but into mine. "I was expecting some dusty, forgotten room with old books and crumpled parchments covering the walls." The pink in Fleur's cheeks is deeper now. "It turns out the library was even filthier than I imagined." I stop just in front of Fleur, pinching her chin between my thumb and forefinger and raising her eyes to meet mine. "Anything you wish to tell me?"

Embarrassment flashes in her eyes, but it's quickly replaced with defiance. "No." Her plump lips set tightly in a straight line.

"I thought we were always honest with each other, Fleur." I stroke my finger down the length of her neck, trailing it over one breast. "About our fantasies, our needs." I set both hands on her hips, kneading the flesh there, before pulling her roughly against me. She gasps as our bodies slam flush to one another.

"Gabriel." She pushes against me and I chuckle. The sound is void of joy, echoing the darkness filling me to the brim.

Fleur shivers beneath my hold, sensing the danger she's in. Her pupils are dilated as I lean close to her ear, hovering my lips just above her flesh. "And you should have told me if you wanted a beast..." My hand collars the back of her neck and I whirl her around, driving her forward and throwing her face-down on the bed before she has time to react. "I saw you together."

She struggles as I rip the clothes from her body, tearing the fabric to shreds and not giving a damn that she's begging me to stop.

"Isn't this what you want?" I bite the tender flesh beneath her ear. She cries out, her body squirming. I don't stop until her smooth flesh is fully bare beneath me. I pull both wrists behind her, pinning them against her lower back. She stills at the sound of my trousers coming undone and I grin. *You're in for it now, sweetheart.* My cock is painfully hard, desperate for Fleur's weeping cunt.

"Gabriel!" She thrashes on the bed. God, I love it when she fights. She kicks out a leg, trying to maim me, shatter my kneecap, or land a foot to my groin. I use the opportunity to hook my leg between hers, knocking her legs wide and planting myself between her splayed thighs. "Gabriel, please—"

"Uh-uh, sweetheart. A man might listen, might acknowledge your begging and pleading. But a beast takes what he wants." I thrust my cock inside her and she screams into the comforter. The sound shoots straight down to my shaft as I plow into her. Her wet pussy sucks me in with no resistance and the fact that she truly is turned on by this both fills me with anger and hardens my cock even more. "Vicious little flower"—I slam to the hilt—"so wet and willing, ready for a monster to destroy your tight cunt."

I rut into her, snapping my hips in rough, deep thrusts.

"Is this enough for you? Or do you need more?" I drag my fingers through her wetness before pressing three inside her stretched passage, right alongside my cock. She cries out, her body bucking beneath the overwhelming stretch of my thick shaft and large fingers all filling the same hole at once. "Does that hurt?" I grit out, working to pump my digits in tandem with my dick.

"Yes," she spits back, glaring over her shoulder.

"Good." I flex my fingers outwards, taking up even more precious space and relishing the way her body jerks and flails beneath mine. "A beast won't hesitate to rip you apart."

"Gabriel," she cries out, her face red and forehead beaded with sweat.

"Admit it." My pace is relentless. "Admit you want the Beast. Admit you desire his cock." My other hand claps hard across her ass and her pussy squeezes tight around my fingers and shaft. "I see the truth. You're filthy, Fleur, fantasizing about his monstrous form, claws, fangs, and all, ruining you while you scream for him." Her moans of pleasure spur me on, allowing me to entertain some feral animal part deep within me.

"Is that so?" The Beast's voice snaps my attention to where he now stands, directly behind me. My movements stutter to a halt. Fleur gasps with relief as I pull out, her face beet red. *How long has he been standing there?*

"What the fuck?" I rear to face him, unnerved by the fact he was able to sneak up on me, again.

"Please, don't stop on my account." His eyes glide down my body, sparing a few extra appreciative seconds when he reaches my cock. "By all means, continue."

"You're not mad?" Fleur asks breathlessly.

"Indeed, I would not usually condone you two together without my consent. It's not part of the *arrangement.*"

I balk at his words. The fucking arrangement? Does he really think he has the power to keep me from taking Fleur at my whim? He continues, "But I was on my way here to punish Fleur myself and I quite enjoy what you've started here."

"Punish?" Fleur pushes up to her feet, her hair mussed, face flushed.

"For trying to run away." The Beast's irises glow ever so slightly.

"But earlier—" Fleur starts.

"Earlier I warned you. There are many sides of me and if you want one, you get them all." His eyes rake across Fleur's flesh before flicking to mine. "And I'm quite certain Gabriel has more than a few reasons to want to help me punish you after all the years of dismissal and neglect." His words strike a poorly tended wound within me, digging up the past and sending long-repressed feelings bubbling to the surface. The sudden team effort raises my suspicion. Why is he acting like it's the two of us against Fleur? Like we have some bonded comradery over the way Fleur has treated us? Then again, this is exactly what I was hoping for. A chance to get closer to the Beast and ease him into trusting me. And if I get the chance to drive my dick inside Fleur in the process, well then it's a win-win.

My gaze falls on Fleur. Her eyes are wide with uncertainty, lips still parted with quick breaths. "Too many years." I glare at her. "What did you have in mind?" I ask the Beast.

He closes the space between us, forcing me to look up at him. I still, worried that if my cock hardens any more it will brush up against his thigh.

"If it were me"—his voice drops to a low, gravelly timbre —"I would tie her to the bedpost and fuck her against it until the wood cracks."

Behind me, Fleur gasps.

"Or until she apologizes and submits. Which we both know is unlikely." He smirks, bearing several sharpened teeth as he draws a length of rope from his pocket. My own smile mirrors his.

"I think that will do nicely." I take the rope and whirl on Fleur. She flicks her eyes between us and turns, scrambling across the bed in an attempt to escape the inevitable. I dive after her, gripping an ankle, and the little bitch actually kicks me in the face. It knocks me back, giving her time to run around the bed. A sharp, metallic tang fills my mouth. I probe my tongue around, seeking the source of the blood. My bottom lip is busted where my teeth cut it open on impact. Something boils deep in my stomach. If she wasn't in trouble before, she certainly is now. I launch from the bed, just as Fleur flings the bedroom door wide and bolts into the hallway.

"Catch her," the Beast commands, his hand rubbing across

the front of his trousers. I guess he likes it when she's feisty, too.

"With pleasure." I spit on the carpet, letting my blood mix with the ornate patterns of crimson and gold. I sprint through the doorway, not bothering to dress. Fleur is halfway down the hall, running as if her very life depends on it. Her bare ass bounces with every stride and I vow here and now to sink my teeth into the soft, round flesh as soon as she's back in my grasp. I lock my sight on her thick hips and take off in a dead sprint. "Fleur!"

She turns, fear flashing across her eyes as I swallow the distance between us. While Fleur's body is supple and curvy, the picture of womanly perfection, she's no athlete. My muscles have been trained near to breaking over the years. I was made for this.

She rounds the corner and I'm close behind, entering the spacious foyer. My feet skid to a halt when I find the room empty. Impossible. She didn't have time to make it up the stairs or to the far end of the room. I slow, picking up on the soft sound of swift footsteps nearby. My neck swivels to the left and I follow the echoing pattern. The footsteps are coming from behind the wall. The wood is cool and textured beneath my touch. I slide along, seeking a crack, indentation, anything that may lead me to an opening. My nails catch on a small gap and I push inwards. The panel creaks open, revealing a dark, stone hallway beyond.

Milky-white flesh glows in the low light. Fleur is nearly to the end of the corridor. My muscles coil and release as I spring forward, devouring the space in front of me with hungry, oversized strides. Fleur rounds a corner, but I'm close this time. I turn left, catching up to her in a matter of seconds. My arm reaches out, thrusting fingers into her dark hair and jerking backwards. Fleur screams out. She reaches for her scalp. I pull her body to mine and wrap both arms around her smaller stature, securing her tightly to my chest. Several worried staff members peek their heads out from doorways. Fleur's nakedness sends a torrent of blood rushing to my face.

"Avert your eyes or lose them," I snarl, watching the slowly gathering group quickly disband. The minacious threat serves its purpose, allowing me to drag Fleur back without the others interfering. Fleur kicks, thrashes, and eventually bites down hard on the back of my hand. Turning, I slam her against the wall and pin her body beneath mine.

"This is the last time I will chase you as some lover from the past. From this moment on, you belong to me. I own you. Nod that pretty little head if you understand."

"Fuck you." She spits in my face, catching me completely off guard. I grin wildly, unable to get enough of this raw, unhinged, adrenaline-fueled version of her. There's nothing she can do to me now that I won't like. Sooner or later she'll see that we're the perfect match.

"So eager to share spit, are you?" I grip her face, digging my thumb and forefinger into the soft flesh between her upper and lower jaw, squeezing until she winces. "Open your mouth." Defiance blazes behind her mossy eyes. I intensify the pressure until she opens her mouth, giving me the perfect view down her pretty pink throat. I spit, allowing every drop to pour into her mouth. She thrashes and I slam her jaw shut. "Swallow it."

She fights me and I cover her nose, giving her no other option. The second I feel her throat bob beneath my palm, I release her.

I can practically smell charred flesh as Fleur's glare sears two molten holes through my skull. But that green wildfire glossiness isn't all hate. I know that much. I reach between us, dropping my hand to her entrance. My fingertips trail across her lips and find them dripping with need. *She liked it.*

Little by little I'm breaking through that sweet, independent demeanor of hers and exposing the depravity within.

I toss her over my shoulder, ignoring the blows she's raining down on my back. My cock is aching, precum leaking from the tip when we reach the room. I drop her unceremoniously onto the bed and grin up at the Beast. I reach for the rope once more. I have her tied up and strung from the bedpost before she has a chance to run away again. Her arms are high above her head, toes barely touching the floor.

She looks stunning.

"Caught like a fly in a spider's web." I toss her a smirk, my hunger surging a rich tangy darkness through my veins. "How about a better look, Beast?"

I grab an ornate hand mirror off the dresser. The silver handle is etched with a winding array of roses and buds stretching up a mass of inlaid vines. Fleur's eyes track my every movement.

I press in close, whispering in her ear, "Give him a good show, *ma petite fleur.*" She yelps as I kick her feet wide, spreading her and dropping the mirror between her thighs. I soak up the plush, pink sight for a moment, my mouth watering with need, before angling the mirror toward the Beast. "So pretty, outside as well as in…" Grinning, I slide a finger up Fleur's thigh, using my feet to keep her stance open. I slip inside her easily, plunging into her depths, while Beast watches in the mirror's reflection.

"Use it," he demands, his voice deep and rough.

"The mirror?" I pause, my fingers still curled up inside Fleur's arousal.

"The handle. Fuck her with the handle."

Fleur's eyes drop down to the mirror then lurch back up to mine. There's a touch of fear buried beneath her arousal, but also a needy pleading look there, too. I'm liking this Beast more and more.

"As you wish. I'll have her cum dripping down until it coats the mirror, rendering it a dull, useless mess." I pump my fingers inside her a few more times, loving the way her eyes flutter. "And then fuck her until the wood cracks, isn't that what you said?"

The Beast exhales a rumble of acknowledgment. I drag my fingers out of her snatch and run them along the length of her body. Her alluring eyes fix on mine once more.

"All right, Beast. Let's see what we can do to make your fantasy come true."

CHAPTER 16

FLEUR

I can't tell what's more traitorous, my body or my heart. Gabriel manhandled me, humiliated me, dominated me, and dragged me back here kicking and screaming. The worst part of the whole experience? *I fucking liked it.* The effect his actions had on me were unexpected and darkly satisfying. I've always possessed a touch of darkness, but lately that small hidden bit of me seems to have forced its shadowy self to the forefront.

I don't think I've ever been as turned on as I am right now. Arousal drips down my inner thighs. I could probably come from sheer anticipation alone. Gabriel is pure masculine dominance and desire. There's something about him when he's like this, fully steeped in power, nearly as beastly as Renard himself. He's terrifying and yet, it's the one time I feel truly safe to be the one who's not in control. It's refreshing in a way I never thought feeling powerless could be. Why does it feel so perfect with Gabriel?

As much as I want to keep up my annoyance with him and the macho-bullshit attitude he's developed over the years, I trust him. I trust him with my body. I trust him with

my life. Little bits of the old Gabriel have been slowly resurfacing, chipping away at his faux exterior. And the way he enjoys making me scream, squirm, come, in front of Renard, is so damn arousing. Speaking of Renard…

I gaze up into those fierce blue eyes. This morning in the library the refined man in him was there, poetic and guiding, understanding and oh so giving. But now, the *Beast* is fully present.

Fibers bite into my wrists as I struggle, jerking at the tightly woven ropes, testing their strength. Gabriel and I have done many things, but he's never tied me up before. He moves forward, towering over me. When he's this close I have to tilt my head all the way back to see his face. The back of my skull bumps against the bedpost as I peer up at him. Cold metal brushes along my inner thigh. I try to look down, but Gabriel tips my chin up, capturing my lips in a devastating kiss. I cry out into his mouth as he presses the cool mirror handle deep inside me. The contrast between his feverish mouth and the chilled metal forces a shudder to race through me.

"Breathe," Gabriel whispers into my mouth as he glides the object in and out. My body heats the handle, bringing my attention to a new sensation. The carved ridges and ornate decor stroke firmly along my walls, sending tingles up my spine and making me roll my hips in time with Gabriel's movements. I release a gratified moan as the first satisfying traces of an orgasm build a deep heat within my core. Gabriel and Renard groan in unison as my cries of ecstasy grow louder. Gabriel's wrist bends and turns as he finds that perfect spot, increasing his pressure and dragging the textured metal across it again and again.

"Come on, Fleur. Give me every drop from that sweet wet cunt. Make a mess of my hand." His movements become rougher, deeper. "We can't disappoint the Beast, now can we?" His lips travel to my throat, sending heat sprawling down to my chest as he suckles on the flesh before biting down on my pulse. My body is shaking, hands jerking at my restraints. "Pull all you want, *ma petite fleur*. You're not getting out of those binds until I decide to let you out. You're completely at my mercy." He turns and gives Renard a roguish smile. "*Our* mercy." His mouth finds mine again and our tongues dance as the world grows blurry around me. "Now come for us."

My breaths come out in desperate pants as the over-whelming sensations build to an intolerable height before spilling over, hot and tense, into a dizzying orgasm that has my muscles gripping the handle as I scream into Gabriel's lips. Gabriel strokes me twice more, milking another smaller climax from my trembling body. He pulls the mirror out and holds it up for inspection. Shiny release covers it from top to bottom.

"Good girl," Gabriel purrs, dipping low to plant a soft kiss on my lips. I sag with relief and the ropes around my wrists pull tight.

"Give it to me." Renard's massive paw extends from his dark refuge. Gabriel drops the wet metal into his palm and it quickly retracts to the darkness.

"Did you enjoy that?" Gabriel grazes his nose along my cheek.

"Yes," I breathe out, still floating.

"Pity, it was meant to be a punishment." His tongue traces a hot line down my neck. "But I just can't help myself when it comes to you." His mouth finds my breast, and I arch into him as he licks and sucks the pebbled flesh. "It's time for the main attraction," he murmurs into my skin as his hands slide around the backs of my thighs. I gasp as he rights himself, picking my legs up and wrapping them around his waist in one, swift motion. "The more you scream, the harder I'll fuck. So give me everything you have."

His cock plunges into me, filling my overstimulated passage so full that I practically stop breathing. My back presses into the wooden bedpost behind me, eliminating any excess space as he thrusts into me with a ferocity that has my heart hammering against my ribs. He gazes down to where our bodies meet, watching himself disappear inside me with each hard snap of his hips. When his eyes meet mine again, there's something wild writhing beneath the great depths of that icy stare. Gabriel's fingers press into my hips, gripping me for dear life as he fucks me mercilessly. The bedpost creaks under the assault on its stature, its wooden ridges digging into my back.

"Harder," Renard urges from his hidden place among the shadows.

"Harder?" I gasp out, already feeling as though I may break in half from the mere intensity of Gabriel's thrusts.

"Show her what a fool she was to deny you all those years." Renard's words are taunting and breathy, and I'm certain he's touching himself now.

Gabriel's jaw ticks as he drives into me with a vicious dominance that's unlike anything I've ever felt before. "Every time I saw you, I wanted you." His cock buries into me so hard it hurts. "But you denied me. You pushed me away, talked down to me, made me chase you for years, forced me to the side while you had your dalliances with that feeble farrier."

"Gabriel—"

His hand flies to my mouth, his huge palm covering it. "Shut up and take my cock like the filthy little liar you are." My eyes roll back in my head as he changes the angle of his rough pounding. "That's what you are. A filthy liar who denied you wanted me for far too long." Despite the savageness of the sex, my body begins to swell. Pleasure crests like a wave, bringing me to the very brink of my sanity.

"Don't come until I tell you to," Renard commands from his side of the room. I flick my eyes toward him, mouth still covered, pleading as my body teeters so near to bliss. All I can see are those floating sapphire flames. "She's close. Back off."

Gabriel chuckles darkly as he slows his thrusts. I whimper in frustration behind his palm. His pace turns languid, casual, and my chance for bliss begins to slip away. I roll my hips, seeking the pleasure I'm so desperately close to.

Gabriel takes a step back, cutting off my ability to take him fully. His boisterous laughter grates on my nerves. I bite at the skin of his palm, savoring his angry curse as I break the skin. Warm metallic blood trickles to my mouth. He draws his hand back, glaring down at me with icy fire in his eyes. His thumb slides across my bottom lip. Crimson covers his finger as he pulls it away. But instead of scolding me as I expect, he admires the blood before diving in for a bruising kiss. It seems Gabriel has a beast in him that could rival Renard's.

"Faster, deeper," Renard orders. Gabriel gives me a crazed half smile before picking up his pace again. His cock fills me and I sigh with relief as my orgasm once again builds. I'm moaning, panting, jerking violently at my binds. "Slow down," Renard utters and I cry out.

"Maybe he wants you to beg." Gabriel cocks his eyebrow. His hips roll in a slow, sensual pattern that keeps my sweet release just out of reach.

"Please," I beg, willing to do anything at this point to come. "Please let me come, Gabriel."

"It's not me you need to get permission from." He glances back. I follow his gaze until I'm diving into the dark stormy depths of Renard's luminescent irises.

"Please let me come…Master."

Renard bellows his approval before uttering the sweetest words I've ever heard. "Finish her off."

Gabriel doesn't waste a second, driving into me and forcing the bedpost to screech once more in protest of his powerful thrusts. Our flesh claps together, my pussy dripping down his thighs as I slip and slide up and down his slick shaft. Pressure pulses inside me, tossing my vision into a blinding sea of white stars. We climax in unison, his groans and my screams filling our room with the lascivious symphony of sexual release. His cum fills me in hot, thick spurts. I love the feeling of being filled by Gabriel. There's something so primal about being owned in that way.

"Untie her." Renard's voice is raspy. Gabriel obeys, dropping my arms to my side after a few quick movements above. I rub my sore wrists. My legs feel like jelly as he sets me on the ground. "Now walk toward me," Renard purrs. My heart picks up, dragging me out of my haze. Finding my footing, I walk slowly in the direction of the invisible throne. "Stop at the edge of the darkness." I do as he says, standing just on the edge where the light meets the dark space beyond. "Turn around." A strange exhilarating freedom floods my veins as I turn my back on the darkness and the monster within it. "On your hands and knees."

I drop instantly. Two clawed hands wrap around my hips, making me jump, and drag me back until I'm half hidden in shadows. Only my shoulders and head remain in the light. Gabriel peers down at me uncertainly.

"What are you going to do?" I ask in a breathless whisper. Fear sends a rush of tingling warmth between my thighs. Renard's tongue answers for him as it slides up my seam, making me moan.

"I've tasted your arousal once before." His tongue swipes again and I dig my fingers into the rug beneath me. "Now I desire to know how you taste, freshly fucked and filled with his cum." His low voice vibrates against my pussy. His grip on my hips tightens. The next time his rough tongue connects with my skin, it's far from gentle. He plunges into me, and my hips buck as he invades my sensitive flesh. Pleasure spreads through me as his long, flexible tongue fucks into me with wild determination, lapping up every bit of my release mixed with Gabriel's spend. My eyes fall shut as I press my hips back, matching his pace and intensifying every wet, warm sensation. Heat rises to my cheeks as I listen to the sloppy, vulgar sounds he makes as he feasts on my cunt with the ferocity of a true beast. I pant and mewl, losing myself to the dangerous, forbidden feeling of giving myself to the Beast, and giving into those dark, unexplored parts of myself.

"Christ," Gabriel breathes, and I open my eyes. "You look so fucking sexy like this." He's dropped down to a crouch in front of me. His fingers run through my hair as he licks his lips. The Beast deepens his tongue on the next thrust, filling me nearly unbearably full and then flicking his tongue inside me. Gabriel steals my cry as he dips down, taking my lips in his. He swallows my whimpers with a fervent and passionate kiss. Gabriel's tongue snakes between my lips while Renard's tongue continues to lap and lathe me inside and out. The simultaneous sensations have me sweating, shaking, and barely able to hold myself up. Gabriel scoops his elbows beneath me, supporting my upper half just as my arms give way. Renard adopts a quick, rough pace that has me begging for more.

"Yes, don't stop…" I beg around Gabriel's eager lips. One of his hands trails around my ribs, rising up to toy with my nipple. He rolls it, pinching and kneading until I'm ready to burst from all the pleasurable sensations consuming my body. Gabriel bites down on my bottom lip, the sharp sting of pain driving me over the edge. My voice goes hoarse as I rasp Renard's name and clamp down around his tongue, riding out a devastating orgasm that has me forgetting my own damn name. The moment Renard pulls his tongue free from me, I collapse, falling into Gabriel's strong arms.

Voices murmur above me, but I'm so lost to the fog of lust and exhaustion that I can't decipher who's speaking or what they're saying. Time becomes a word on paper as the minutes brush by. I drift off, somewhere between consciousness and sleep.

"In we go…" a low voice speaks in my ear as warm water surrounds me. My eyes pop open as I realize I've just been set in the bath. How long was I out for?

Gabriel sits behind me, settling us into the relaxing heat. My tired limbs rejoice as the tension slips from my sore, achy muscles. I slide my eyes along the length of the room but Renard is not here.

"I've got you." Gabriel carefully washes me from head to toe. His movements are so gentle for someone his size. I practically purr as he washes my hair, massaging my scalp in soft circles.

"Thank you," I sigh, leaning back into his burly chest. Gabriel finishes cleaning us both before rising and toweling me off. He lays me down in the oversized bed and takes his place on the other side. This is how we've been sleeping since we arrived here. How strange to be so willing to connect sexually but not intimately.

I roll over, scooting close, and curl up to Gabriel's side.

"Fleur…" His breath hitches. I nuzzle into him, curling my fingers in his chest hair, and listen to the sound of his steady heartbeat until sleep casts its weary net upon me and I'm dragged off into my dreams.

CHAPTER 17

FLEUR

*T*he scones this morning were particularly delicious. Pistachio and rose if I'm not mistaken. I find myself hoping another tray will be delivered when Renard joins me here. I slept in later than normal. My body must have needed the rest after the evening's festivities. Just thinking of the time I split between Gabriel and Renard makes my toes curl. It was well past noon by the time I ventured off to the library. I discovered a new section full of fairy tales from around the world and the hours since then have flown by.

The library doors swing wide and a smile lights my face. It falters when Mrs. Perle enters. I had hoped Renard may join me. After spending more and more time in his company, the library seems rather lonely. He's educated and well-traveled. His mind is full of stories and knowledge, things my small-town spirit can only dream of hearing and seeing. I've loved learning and sharing my favorite things with him here. Of course, I've equally enjoyed the feeling of his tongue inside me as the books muse down upon us like paper gods trapped in time. Heat

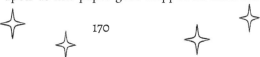

creeps into my cheeks when I remember Mrs. Perle is still standing in front of me.

"Sorry, what did you say?" I offer with an apologetic smile.

"Pardon my intrusion"—Mrs. Perle bows her head as she speaks—"will you be taking your dinner here, or back in your room?"

My stomach rumbles loudly, informing me that it truly is time for dinner.

"Oh my, I must have lost track of time. I'll have dinner in my room, Thank you." I move, quickly distributing the pile of books back to where they belong. When the door does not open again, I turn, finding Mrs. Perle still staring at me. "Can I help you with something else?" I ask.

The older woman removes her bonnet, wringing it nervously between her fingers. "What has the master told you about the curse?" Her voice is tired and laced with a terrible weight.

"He won't tell me anything." I move toward her, setting the rest of the books on an end table. "Only that it transformed him into the Beast."

"That, it did." Mrs. Perle nods. "But it is much more than that."

"Will you tell me?" I sit on one of the sofas, gently patting the space next to me.

Mrs. Perle appears both reluctant and relieved. She takes her seat and sighs. "The castle was not always like this. It was once vibrant, full of life." I can see the pain in her eyes as memories of older days sweep past. "But after the King and Queen died, things changed. Renard changed. He left with his hunting companions and when he returned, the prince we all knew and admired was gone."

"Where did he go? Why was he changed?" My need for answers coats my tongue in desperation.

"There was a woman, a beautiful healer. She tried to nurse the King and Queen back to health. After they died, Renard became blinded by grief. He convinced himself she murdered them. When the woman ran in fear, they hunted her down and killed her." My heart is pounding so loudly in my ears I can barely hear Mrs. Perle's next words. "That is when the curse began. And we've been trapped ever since."

"Trapped," I repeat as I try to wrap my head around this strange story.

"Trapped in the castle, and trapped in time. We cannot leave, Renard won't allow it." Tears trail down her face, catching in the wrinkles along her skin.

"Why?" My voice is a horrified whisper.

"He does not wish the world to know what is happening behind the castle walls. No one leaves, no one changes. We're trapped in time. Unless the curse is broken, we will remain doomed to never age, never grow, never change, never die. That is how it has been since the curse began. But since your arrival things have been different. We are fearful time is running out to break the curse." The darkness invading Mrs. Perle's usually cheerful demeanor makes me stiffen.

"Is there a way? To break the curse?"

Her sad eyes peer up at me. "Indeed. Love, my dear Fleur. Love is the only way to break the curse, and we're all praying you were sent here for that very reason."

"Love? The only way to break the spell is for me to fall in love with the Beast?" I push to my feet as heat and nausea send me swaying on wobbly legs.

"It's too much to ask, I know. But you are our only chance. The roses are wilting." Mrs. Perle stands. "Please, I don't know how much time we have left."

"Roses?" I mutter, unable to breach the ocean of tumultuous thoughts drowning me inside my mind. The library feels suddenly stifling. I need air. The older woman speaks frantically as I rush past. I can't hear her, my ears are unable to process sound around the monumental pressure that's just been forced into every open space inside me. My footsteps echo as I run, jogging down the first staircase. I hit the bottom and turn, sprinting down a hallway as the life-sized portraits of long-dead kings blur past. Their eyes stain my dress with accusatory glares. I round the corner and stop.

Two new hallways branch off in either direction. That's strange...I could have sworn this is where the second staircase is that leads to the foyer. Did I go the wrong way? Has the castle changed yet again? Teeth worry my bottom lip as I try to decide where to go next. The hallway on the left looks familiar, perhaps. I'm certain I went the right way. Which means the castle has shifted once more. I glance over my shoulder. I could retrace my steps back the way I came. The library is the most sensible place to wait. Renard or Gabriel will come looking for me if I don't return for dinner.

The hollow, hopeful light in Mrs. Perle's eyes flashes across my memory. Her sadness and desperation are too much to take. I need time and space to process her words. I opt to venture down the hallway on the left. I'll keep walking until I recognize something or run into someone who can point me in the right direction.

A muffled cry reaches my ears from somewhere up ahead. I hurry on, rushing to find the sound. It reaches its loudest and then quiets as I keep walking. It must have been behind me. But I didn't see anyone. I turn, moving back the way I came and the crying grows louder. Again, I spin around. There's no one here. A male voice speaks, delivering harsh words from somewhere nearby. I press my cheek to the wall and the voices reverberate through my ear. They must be behind the panel. Is it another secret corridor?

My fingernails scrape along the smooth ivory and forest green until I find what I'm looking for. A small crack reveals the edge of the hidden door. I push inwards, trusting this one to be similar to the hidden passage in the foyer, and am rewarded when the heavy piece of wall swings open.

Two figures are pressed against a wall just inside the opening. One is a young maid with curly blonde hair and a petite frame. A hand is wrapped tightly around her mouth, her wide eyes aimed in my direction. The other figure turns and I recognize Elias, the servant who told me the towns-people were dead. He has the frightened young woman in a position that's less than decorous. His head snaps my way as the panel opens fully, a twisted grin creeping along his features. "Look who it is"—his dark eyes crawl along my skin —"the monster's little whore."

The audible slap as my open hand connects with his face is highly satisfying. My palm tingles from the impact. "Get off her." My voice takes on an unrecognizable, venomous tone that tastes like sugared poison on my lips. The tang rolls across my tongue and squeezes into my throat as the words register in Elias's ears. I may not know their situation exactly, but I do know when a woman is in need of help. The way her eyes shine, wet and pleading, tells me everything I need to know.

Elias moves in slow motion as his chin tilts around to meet my gaze once more. The red strike on his cheek stands out brightly against the sallow cast of his skin. He pushes off the wall, releasing the maid. Her skirts rustle into place as she runs, looking back at me with the wide, sorrowful expression of a wounded deer, before disappearing into the shadowy depths of the corridor. Elias's dark gaze is pinned to me. There's something wild beneath the brown of his irises, like a marionette running around in circles with all the strings cut.

My heart drops and my courage recedes, dosing me with

a slap of nausea in its absence. Voices whisper words of warning as danger prickles up my spine.

Elias's words are low and cold. "You should have left this castle when you had the chance." The movement of his fist is so fast, so precise, that by the time I see it coming, I'm already falling. His laughter echoes in the distance. I sink down, down, *down*. A tangled web of gossamer stars floods my eyes, blinding me with seraphim light before rushing out like a wave and releasing me, mercilessly, into a floating field of nothingness.

* * *

"Pretty little lamb, fallen right in my hand. What song will you sing when your neck I do wring?"

Something cold presses flat to my cheek, jarring me from my pitch-black dreams and into the soft glow of a true nightmare. *Thump. Thump. Thump.* A slow, steady pounding taps a painful beat across my skull. My eyes are heavy. Attempting to peel back my eyelids brings awareness to a tender, bruising ache around my left eye. The world is blurry as I open one eye. The ache encompassing the left side of my face intensifies as I fight to open both. It's no use, the damn thing must be swollen shut.

My mouth tastes like ash as it hangs wide open. I'm slumped forward, held into place by some kind of rough binding. I wiggle my wrists, but they're secured so tightly behind me that the outer two fingers on both hands are completely numb. A violent trembling helps to clear my mind as I trudge through the fuzzy edges of unconsciousness. Again, the chill of a metal object presses against my cheek.

"Awake, little lamb?" Elias's voice finally reaches me through my muddled and morose train of thought. "Speak."

A muffled whine is all my paper-dry tongue can offer.

"Hmm." Elias looms over me, the nearness of his body offering the only warmth in this room. "Not good enough."

A sharp, slicing pain lights the soft flesh of my cheek on fire as he drags the cold metal object down the side of my face. I sit up with a start, crying out as the pain clears away any lingering vestiges of drowsiness and confusion.

"There she is." He grins down at me. Sticky, hot blood trickles down my face, collecting along my jawbone before dripping into my lap.

"What happened?" I croak, swallowing in an attempt to lubricate my throat.

"I knocked you out real good, didn't I?" He smirks in triumph. "You were out so long I was starting to get bored. Now that you're awake, the fun can begin."

My shoulders ache where they supported my body while I was tied, bent forward, and unconscious. He hit me, kidnapped me, tied me to a chair. Now he's mutilated my face. A crazed laugh escapes me, jarring my stiff body. "You're so fucked." The wound on my face turns fiery as I speak, revealing it's deeper than I initially suspected.

"What was that, little lamb?" Elias grips my chin, digging his thumb into the open cut, making me scream in pain and forcing me to look up at him.

"I said, you're fucked. Renard knows everything that happens in this castle. He'll use the mirror and when he finds me, you are going to wish you'd never been born."

A strange, manic confidence slithers through me, chilling my fearful blood and pasting on a thick face of bravery that's so close to real, even I believe it. Elias slams the bottom of his boot into my ribs, forcing the breath from my lungs and making me buckle as much as the restraints will allow. It takes what feels like forever before I'm able to catch my breath again. When I do suck in air, it hurts.

Elias's lips peel back in a snarl. "*Renard*? You mean the Beast? Oh, he may have this rumored mirror, but he'll never find us."

I grit my teeth against the pain in my body, refusing to cower beneath this psychopath. "Idiot. He can simply ask the mirror where I am and it will show him this exact part of the castle. You don't have a chance." I expect this to have some semblance of an impact on him, but it doesn't. Instead, the backside of his hand claps across my face, sending fresh pain radiating across the gash. Tears pour down my cheeks in hot, desperate streams. Elias draws his hand away and sneers. His skin has a freshly painted coat of crimson. He stares down at it before sliding his tongue out to taste the sanguine spread.

"He can ask all he wants. This isn't part of the castle. As far as he's concerned, it doesn't even exist." He paces the small room then, sliding his hands along the dark, earthy walls, affectionately. "I built this with my own hands. It's amazing what you can do when the days have no purpose and you never age." He flexes his dirty fingers and sighs. "I started this project with my brother. You haven't met him"— Elias pulls at his hair, screaming and kicking out at the small wooden table in the corner—"because your boyfriend crushed his fucking skull."

His actions are deranged, driven by grief and lunacy. I take a closer look at my surroundings. It's not a room at all. More like a nine-by-nine hole hollowed out of the ground. A misshapen, rectangular panel is the only identifying feature in this simple space. We must be beneath the castle. *Did he burrow into the walls? Underground?*

"He will still be able to see this in the mirror," I argue, ignoring the growing number of excruciating aches across my face and side.

He laughs darkly. "Don't you see? It doesn't matter if he can see where you are. He doesn't know where this place is.

All he'll know is that you're somewhere dark and completely out of reach. He won't be able to find something he never knew existed." His words hook sharpened talons of fear into the rapidly beating lining of my heart. Surely Renard will find us. He'll be able to see me. But if it is a place he's never been before, will he be able to find his way here? "There it is." Elias steps back, framing my face with his fingers and peering through. "Fear is very fucking sexy on you, little lamb."

His boot flies toward my stomach, hitting me hard enough to tip my chair. It crashes backwards to the ground. With my hands tied behind my back I can do nothing to brace my fall. I wail on impact, feeling the delicate bones of my hands and fingers pop and twist as the weight of my body and the chair crush them against the hard, frozen ground.

"There they are." Elias grips me by the front of my dress, dragging me upright. "Your screams are probably even sweeter than your snatch." His hand drops to his pants and he strokes himself, closing his eyes.

"You're sick," I spit out. "Renard and Gabriel will find me—"

"Shh." He presses his fingers against my lips. The scent of dirt and metallic rot fill my nostrils. I jerk my head back and away from him. His hand fists in my hair, yanking my head back to look at him. "We're going to be spending a lot of time together, so don't talk." He leans in close enough I can feel his breath on my face. "Just scream."

CHAPTER 18

RENARD

*T*he rose gardens are nearly empty. The magic of the castle is waning. *Time is running out.*

I was on my way to the library, eager to see Fleur again, when a trail of wilted red caught my eye. I followed it, gut tightening and heart racing until I found my way to the east gardens. The sight of the once-majestic gardens makes my blood run cold. Piles of petals cover the ground, their vibrant hues darkening to a brownish red. With Fleur around, it's been easy to distract myself from the signs of change that I'm not ready to face. What will happen when the last petal falls? I used to curse this never-ending cycle of days passing by as time stood still within the castle walls. Now, I find myself more desperate than ever for time—to fix things, to try to break the curse, to be with Fleur.

A noxious fear keeps me trapped, gazing out along the floral tragedy with a lost hopelessness that drowns me in a regret so potent, I nearly give up. The hours pass and the petals fall. No one comes to find me. No servants check to see if I need food or tea. The staff has been avoiding me. No

doubt they've noticed the changes. I pity them, trapped in a loveless castle with a monster as their master.

When the sky grows dark, I force myself indoors. Numb paws brush piles of settled snow from my fur and face. I'm cold inside, and it's not just the winter weather. I crave the warmth that ignites within me when Fleur is around. She's the only thing that makes me feel alive in this endless torment of immortality. Her presence is a light, a star among the vast haunted darkness of regret and loneliness that has filled my days for far too long. Her face shines in my mind and before I realize it, I've already walked halfway across the castle and toward her room. It's past dinner now. She and Gabriel may already be in their room for the night.

I grab a quick snack from the kitchens and swing by the library. She's already gone. I sigh, knowing my catatonic contemplative state cost me my alone time with Fleur. It's not all bad though. Things are changing, and it seems relations between Gabriel and I may be changing too. Last night was new, unexpected, and more pleasurable than anything I've experienced before. Taking Fleur for myself in front of Gabriel was a gamble. He's possessive—that much was obvious from the way he had her pinned down, forcing confessions of our time together in the library—when I entered their room. But after I watched her take the mirror, and then Gabriel, so flushed and wet, I couldn't help myself. I needed to do more than watch. Her cunt in my mouth was pure heaven. Gabriel's encouragement and participation only made me harder for the both of them.

Their bedroom door approaches like a promise. Giddy anticipation shivers awake inside me. I knock, turning the knob before they can respond, too eager to get my fill of Fleur for the evening. Gabriel stares up at me from his chair. I scan the room, a sharp feeling welling in my throat. "Where is she?"

He shrugs. "She was already gone when I woke up this morning. I figured she was with you?"

I shake my head. Worry flutters to life like a nocturnal moth in my stomach.

"Well then, my money's on the library. Fleur would read all day and night if no one forced her to eat, drink, or sleep."

The oxygen thickens in my lungs. He hasn't seen her all day. I haven't seen her all day. Memories of the night she ran away send fear and doubt traipsing through my veins like weeds. "I stopped by the library on my way here."

"Maybe the kitchen? She didn't join me for dinner, and we both know how much Fleur loves to eat. And be eaten," he adds with a filthy grin, winking a pale-blue eye at me.

"She isn't in the kitchen." My mouth is dry, papery. I don't like this.

Gabriel's smile fades. He jumps to his feet. "You think something happened? She wouldn't run away again. She has no reason to." His jaw flexes as he opens himself to the possibility. "If she didn't run away, and she's not in her usual spots in the castle, then where is she?"

"I'll consult the mirror. You—"

"No." Gabriel steps close. "I'm not going off alone and getting lost in this freezing enchanted castle for hours on end again."

"When did that happen?" I frown.

"The night you were attacked by wolves. I went to find Fleur, but the castle kept rearranging itself. None of the doors or hallways were the same. It took me hours to find my way back." His gaze drops to the floor as he relives the memory. I didn't realize just how severe the changes had been that night.

"Fine. Come with me."

His long strides keep up easily with my fast pace. The castle does feel colder, darker too. The corners that usually house carvings of cherubs and harps are now home to gargoyles and creatures of the night. How recently did that happen? The more I look around, the more unnerving changes I notice. The edges of every railing seem to have sharpened. The colors in the sky painted above appear dull and lifeless. This is not good.

The castle is a whirlwind as I hurry toward the mirror, my unease growing by the minute. I'm practically choking on the roots of my fear by the time the mirror comes into view. I slam my paw against the glass.

"Show me the girl." I need not say her name this time. The mirror knows things, feels things. The quick bite of pain hits my palm as the blood toll is extracted, and the mirror swirls its silvery-black magic, drawing a sickening picture into view.

Fleur is someplace dark. She's being restrained. Through the flicker of candles I can just make out the ropes binding her to the rickety chair. Next to me, Gabriel sucks in a breath as we take in her brutalized state. One of her eyes is swollen shut and badly bruised. A deep red gash weeps down the side of her flawless face. Her lip is split and bloody. A toxic rage like nothing I've ever known burns molten and deadly beneath my calm exterior.

She peers up at something and defiance shines in the jade of her unharmed eye. "Renard and Gabriel will find me. They'll figure out we're still in the castle—"

"Shut up!" a deep, wild voice shouts from somewhere out of sight. "Why do you keep saying that? You've said it fifty times, again and again, and again."

Fleur smirks. "I'll say it until they hear it. Renard and Gabriel will find me. They'll figure out we're still in the castle and when they do—"

A hand claps hard across Fleur's wounded cheek and she

screams. An eerie laugh echoes through the space they're hidden in.

"No one knows about this place, little lamb. They won't find you until I dump your mangled, gaping body in the castle foyer. Then that monster will know what it feels like to lose the only thing he cares about. Your death will make him realize what a big mistake it was to take someone so precious from me with such little thought or care. My brother will be avenged and then I'll slaughter the Beast as he weeps over your corpse." *His brother?* The voice is so familiar and yet, I cannot place it.

"Oh, fuck," Gabriel hisses. "It's Elias." I wrack the seeded depths of my brain, searching for the faces of all I've deemed insignificant over my years trapped in the castle.

"Renard and Gabriel will find me. They'll figure out we're—"

A dark-haired boy ducks into view, bending low and pressing something shiny and sharp near Fleur's mouth. "One more time, and I'll cut your tongue out." The dark hair and feral eyes of Elias sear into my sockets. He slides the knife to her pursed lips, pressing until dark liquid pools against the metal and Fleur winces in pain. I bellow a roar so loud and filled with such white-hot fury that the castle's walls shiver and shake. Both Fleur and Elias look up suddenly. *They can hear me.* Elias takes a quick step back, paranoia flashing over his features as his eyes shift around the room.

Fleur grins, showing bloodstained teeth. "You're in trouble now."

The mirror shimmers as the image fades away, revealing my reflection alongside Gabriel's. How envious I am of that roguish face in the mirror. What I wouldn't give to see myself in the same way once more.

Gabriel whirls to face me. "Where are they?"

"I don't know," I grouse.

"Fleur kept repeating that we would find her and figure out they were still in the castle—"

"Because she knew we would use the mirror." I look at him. "She was giving us clues, hoping we would be watching."

"Well based on the way they both reacted when you roared and blew my fucking eardrums out, I think it's safe to say they're most definitely still in the castle. Did you recognize the room?"

"No. It didn't look like any room here." I shake my head as frustration brews a storm in my soul.

"It was dark. No windows, no doors that I could see." His pale eyes sparkle in the inky shadows of my quarters. "Could they be underground?"

"It's possible." I take a deep breath, trying to stop my mind from the horrific spiral of thoughts giving me glimpses of what Fleur will have to endure until we find her. Or what she's already endured.

"Someone knows where Elias is." Gabriel turns, and quickly strides out of the room.

"Where are you going?"

"The servants' quarters." He flicks his gaze to me. "I doubt you know the way."

I bare my teeth but he ignores my threat. "No."

"Lucky for you, I do. That's where we're headed. Someone knows something and they're going to tell us." The gleam in his eye goes dark. "We're going to make them."

* * *

I'm not sure I've ever ventured into the servants' quarters. I've never needed to. This part of the castle is not fit for royalty, whether it be foolish princes or regretful beasts. I still feel the differences in status, upbringing, and bloodlines each time a servant passes me in the hall or cowers before me when they enter a room I'm occupying. That same fresh twinge of guilt wriggles into my stomach. I haven't been a prince for so many years. It's easy to forget the staff is trapped here, too.

As we pass the meager accommodations and cold, bare rooms, the guilt in me blossoms into something I'm unable to ignore. Had I known the deplorable conditions down here, I would have…what exactly? Moved them all into royal rooms? Given them freedom to roam the castle without fear of being murdered in one of my heated rages? Allowed them to leave this place? I swallow the lump in my throat. I didn't possess these feelings then. Not before Fleur.

As much as I hate to admit it, she's softening me. The warm, fuzzy feelings are more akin to scabs across my skin than they are burdens lifted from my matted heart. I roll my shoulders back, eager to shake off these sensations and focus on the task at hand.

"What happened to his brother?" Gabriel asks, mercifully jostling me from my thoughts.

"Who?"

"Elias. He said he took Fleur to make you pay, for taking his brother." He quirks a dark eyebrow. I'm hit with the too-vibrant flash of an unwanted memory. The stable boy stares up at me, his dark hair and wild eyes the same as Elias's, pleading with me just before his head bursts between my fingers. "I killed him."

"Why?" Gabriel gives me a sideways glance but never slows his pace. What was the reason? I was enraged, storming across the castle after my meeting with Fleur and Gabriel. They were being obstinate, and my fury flowed over. In the end, the stable boy's death was pointless. A worthless attempt to quell my anger.

"Because I'm every bit the monster they believe me to be." Grinding my jaw, I stare straight ahead. Gabriel stops in front of a room near the end of the hall. The door is ragged and wooden with a knob too new to have been part of the original decor. He grips the handle, jerking on it. A stiff rattling fills the space where a twisting click should have been.

Gabriel's jaw flexes in irritation. He kicks out with one powerful leg, sending the door collapsing inward. Shouts of alarm pour from the room. He stalks forward and I follow, ducking to avoid hitting the top of the doorway.

Nine servants huddle near the far wall, their eyes going wide with terror as they lock onto mine. Gabriel closes in on them, his body coiled for a fight.

His words are deadly cold. "Where are they? Elias and Fleur?"

No one speaks, they all just stare, quivering like a flock of sheep up against two murderous wolves. It's a fight they know they can't win, and they seem to have given up already.

"Answer me!" Gabriel roars, making everyone jump. The dangerous desperation and intensity in his voice sparks electricity up my spine. Gabriel is willing to do anything to find her. So am I.

I step forward and the group releases a round of whimpers. "Elias has taken something precious to us," I say. Wide, watery eyes lock onto mine. "And we'll do whatever it takes to get her back."

I nod toward Gabriel. He grabs a tall, thin man, dragging him to a nearby table, and bends him over it until his cheek is pressed against the rough wood. He draws an ornamental knife from his pocket and I pause, curious as to when he got ahold of it. Was he planning on using it to harm me? His gaze meets mine and I refocus, addressing the current and most pressing threat.

That psychopath has Fleur in his filthy clutches. I snarl. An agonizing rage claws through me all over again. "So if you're not going to give us information willingly"—I set my jaw, settling into a calculated state of deranged determination—"then we will extract it, piece by piece."

CHAPTER 19

RENARD

Six fingers and two ears later, we begin to make headway. "He goes somewhere at night." The older man trembles beneath Gabriel's hold. Gabriel tosses the severed ear down. It hits the wooden table with a soft, wet splat. Four others sit gripping their mangled hands or clutching their heads in the corner. The old man is our fifth attempt at gleaning some insight into Elias. Thus far it's been nothing more than the repetitive, "He's changed," and, "We avoid him as much as we can."

"Where?" asks Gabriel, his voice filled with an icy detachment that has me questioning who the monster in this room truly is.

"Down an abandoned tunnel where they used to store wood. He comes back with bloodied fingers and filthy clothes." The old man's face is whiter than a ghost as the space where his ear should be continues to seep metallic red all over the table.

"Why didn't you tell us before?" I don't even bother to hide my irritation. Bloody fingers and filthy clothes? What has he been doing down there?

188

"I forgot, honest! It's been months since I've seen him down there. Please, we all just do our best to stay out of his way. He does things to the other servants, the maids—"

"Monsieur!" Lucien's voice breaks across the room as he and Claude shuffle inside. "The castle is in an uproar. What has happened?" His horrified eyes flit from one injured servant to the next. His hand shoots out, stopping Claude in his path as he slowly backs the two of them away and toward the doorway they just came through.

I turn slowly, glaring at the two of them, and they freeze. "Elias has taken Fleur. So unless you have information about his whereabouts, this does not concern you."

"Oui, monsieur." Lucien tosses the other servants a pitying glance before gripping Claude by the collar and running them both out of sight. I don't know all of the staff members in the castle, but I do know Lucien and Claude. They would never allow anyone to treat a woman the way Elias has treated Fleur. If I can count on nothing else, I know those two and Mrs. Perle would have stopped him if they'd known. Kidnapping, torture...the mere thought of what's happening to Fleur in this exact moment makes bile climb up my throat.

"Take us to the tunnel," I snap, my jaws frothing. It's been hours since we last peered into the mirror. We don't have any more time to waste.

Gripping the man by the back of his loose shirt, Gabriel walks him out of the room and tosses him into the hallway. "Walk," he bites out. The man clutches his maimed ear but moves with quick steps. It takes us another ten minutes of winding hallways beneath the castle until we come to the tunnel.

"I saw him come from here. Please, that's all I know," he simpers, pitifully.

"Fine." Gabriel releases the man. He scampers back the way we came. The tunnel is dark and damp with the scent of noxious mildew and putrid decay. The candlesticks we hold in front of us are the only light in this part of the castle. "You take that side, search for anything unusual." Gabriel seems to think he's in charge now. While I don't appreciate being ordered around, I do understand the time for fighting over dominance will have to come later.

I comb over every inch of my side of the tunnel, candle-flame in front of my face, searching, seeking, needing to find the woman who soothes my soul and heats my heart. "Fleur!" I roar as I reach the end of the tunnel. Desperation feeds me flavorful fear that has my mouth sticky and deathly sweet. My head snaps around at the sound of a muffled cry. "Gabriel?"

"I heard it." His candle moves quickly in the distance, signaling his approach. "Fleur!" Another muted cry. This time I have a better idea of the direction.

"This way." I stalk toward the sound. We walk along the same wall, searching again and again.

"Wait," Gabriel says. I follow his gaze to the ground. A small pile of dense dirt and gravelly rubble cakes beneath his boot. I swing my flame from left to right. There are no other piles nearby. "The entrance." He passes me his candle and drives his fingers into the wall, searching for anything that could signify the edge of a door. He sucks in a breath and jerks his whole body weight back. "It's stuck!" he cries out, and then pulls his hand back to reveal two bloodied finger-tips with empty nailbeds.

"Show me." I place one of the candles down and reach my hand toward the wall. Gabriel's own hand wraps around mine, guiding me to a small hole among the thick earth. His palm is warm on mine, his fingers so callused I can feel it through my fur.

"Here." He presses my finger in more deeply. "I think this is the way to open it." He drops his grip on me and I wince at the loss of physical contact. How long has it been since someone willingly touched my hand?

I pass the remaining candle his way, and then pull on the small space with all my beastly strength. A loud pop hits my ears as a makeshift door hinges open. The entrance is small, but there's a light glowing within.

Gabriel ducks through instantly, and I follow, working to contort my massive frame to push through the opening. The room on the other side is even smaller than it appeared through the mirror. My eyes snap to the center—and there she is, bloody and battered, and as beautiful as ever.

Fleur.

* * *

Gabriel

I enter the tiny space before the Beast, plunging into the near darkness with Fleur's cries echoing through my thoughts. The scent of blood and filth hits me in the nose, making my stomach clench. I'm a hunter, and I'm all too familiar with the smells of massive blood loss and trauma.

My eyes find Fleur in an instant. She looks even worse than the last time we saw her through the mirror. She gives me a weak smile when she sees me. How she's able to smile under these horrific circumstances is beyond me. My gaze drops lower to the blade at the base of her throat and the dirty hand holding it there. Elias is huddled behind Fleur, his eyes bulging and arm shaky.

"Don't come near me." He glances toward the hole in the wall where the master of the castle has just entered. The Beast looks even larger than normal in the cramped space.

He snarls and Elias seizes up. I take advantage of the moment of pure fear and launch myself at Elias. His focus shifts to me a second before I hit him and he falls back with a scream. Fleur's chair flips with the force and she cries out. The sound of her pain forges a fresh path of bloodlust through my very being. I slam my fist into Elias's face over and over, ignoring the sound of bone and cartilage crunching and popping beneath my knuckles and the blood spraying up into my face.

As soon as Elias stops moving, I wheel around, finding Fleur free from her bindings and swept up in the Beast's arms.

"She needs medical attention, now." His deep-blue eyes settle on mine and I'm certain they reflect my own relief and fear. We communicate through silence. *We cannot lose her.*

Elias sputters at my feet and I glare down at the pulpy mess of his face. I haul him up, slamming him into the chair he had Fleur secured in, unable to ignore the blood covering most of the wood. *Her blood.* I snatch up the stained remnants of the ropes. The ends are cleanly cut thanks to the skilled precision of the Beast's wicked claws, making it easy for me to reuse the pieces to tie up Elias. Fleur whines in pain and I glance back worriedly.

"Take her," the Beast urges me.

"But—" I protest, looking back at Elias.

"I'll take care of him." There's a darkness in the Beast's gaze that sends a literal shudder through me. I don't know if there ever truly was a man in the monster, but if there was, he's long gone right now.

"Just one thing first." I pick up the discarded knife and kick Elias hard enough to rouse him. Brown eyes flutter and then open fully in shock. He whimpers, his crushed face weeping blood and bits of bone. I turn the crude knife handle over in my palm, the sight of Fleur's blood and suffering fueling my actions. "What did you threaten to do to Fleur?

Cut her tongue out?" I reach for his chin, my fingers dipping into shattered spaces, and his eyes practically spew from their sockets. "It's got to be here somewhere."

I fish around some more until I recognize what must have once been his lips. I peel the mangled flesh back and find the wriggling pink tongue within. Using the knife blade to prop his mouth open, I grab hold of the slimy, thrashing meat. I pull it far enough out to see it properly.

I grin down at Elias. "You never should have touched my girl."

The rough blade saws through his tongue in three strokes. Elias shrieks and gurgles as blood rushes over his chin and down his throat. His screams become sobs and I nod, satisfied. I drop the tongue, watching it flop onto the floor, then stomp it with the sole of my boot.

Elias is still crying when I turn away from him, gently taking Fleur from the Beast and cradling her to my chest.

"You'll take care of her?" The Beast gazes down at Fleur, and my chest tightens.

"Don't worry about her. You'll make him suffer?" I tick my chin at the slobbering, bloody mess that is currently Elias.

The Beast stares at him and the sobs go silent. "He'll be begging for death before I give it to him."

I smirk, ducking through the hole and hurrying out of the tunnel. The first, blood-curdling, tongueless scream reaches me as I round the corner. A genuine smile pulls at the corners of my mouth. "Music to my ears."

CHAPTER 20

GABRIEL

The first few hours after Fleur's rescue were more intense than anything I've ever experienced. Finding each wound, stopping the bleeding, setting her bones. Mrs. Perle was more than helpful, hurrying around me in a fluster, offering up clean towels and fresh supplies. Some injuries were stitched up, others had to be cauterized. Thankfully Fleur passed out almost as soon as the first hot iron kissed her skin. I'm no doctor, but two years on a hunting expedition exposed me and the other hunters to all manner of horrific attacks and injuries. We all picked up a few things for the sake of survival.

"You need to eat, sir." Mrs. Perle holds a bowl of soup out to me. My body is stiff and achy after watching Fleur for hours. "We've done all we can. She'll need sleep and you need to eat and rest yourself if you're going to be of any help to her."

I accept the soup with a sigh. She's right. The hot, salty liquid warms me from the inside out. Mrs. Perle refills the bowl twice more before I wave her off. My eyes drift closed as the comfort of a full belly and warm blood sinks me into a

deep sleep. A knock at the door drags me back to consciousness and I turn to find the Beast musing down at me. I have no clue how long I was asleep. The Beast is in fresh clothing, with no signs of torture and spilled blood.

"Is it done?" I ask, sleep coloring my words. He nods and I release a sigh, sitting up from my bedside chair to stretch. "And did you make him pay?"

"Any remaining pieces of him have been nailed above the main entrance to the servants' quarters with strict instructions not to remove them for a week." *Fuck*. His brutality and cool demeanor contradict each other, reminding me there's much to fear from the Beast. If it ever comes down to a fight, I'll need to be clever, quick, and guided by God's own damn hand. "How is she?" He looks longingly to the spot where Fleur is fast asleep.

"Resting. She has a long recovery ahead of her." I grimace, glancing down at the bluish purple covering her face and the line of stitches that runs down her cheek. Whatever the Beast did to Elias, it wasn't nearly enough. He pulls a chair up next to mine. The wood creaks as his excessive weight tests its craftsmanship. He hands me a glass before procuring a bottle from within his clothing.

"I think we could both use a drink." He fills my glass with a rich, burgundy liquid and the scent of fermented fruit floats around me. "We haven't had much of a chance to talk since you arrived at the castle."

"You mean since you kidnapped me. And no, we don't do much *talking* when you come for your evening visits." I raise an eyebrow.

He chuckles. "I suppose I shouldn't have expected delightful conversation and access to a deeper understanding of others when I had them prisoner. It appears my social manners are even more outdated than I realized." He shrugs his great shoulders.

I laugh, a real, boisterous laugh. "No, I think it would be wise to leave social manners off your list of accomplishments completely."

He grins back at me, revealing those gleaming, sharpened fangs. "I suppose my list of accomplishments has grown thin over the years. At some point I was considered quite the accomplished gentleman." He smirks, a mischievous glint sparkling across the sapphire of his eyes. "Well accomplished at least. I've never been considered a gentleman."

"Gentleman has never been on my list of accomplishments, either," I add with a knowing smile.

"Good thing Fleur seems to overlook that one." He drains his glass and refills both. I stare at him, observing the contradictions that make him who he is. His form is truly monstrous. There's no denying he is a beast, as wild and savage as an animal when he needs to be. But he's also so uniquely refined on occasion. From his tailored clothing to the way he sips priceless wine, even his ability to discuss literature and great works of art with Fleur. There is more to this monster than meets the eye.

Uncomfortable stirrings trickle through me as I begin to see him as someone who was quite possibly once a man, now trapped in a monster's body. I down my second glass, already feeling the heady buzz draping my thoughts with a film of fuzzy, warm carelessness.

"She calls you Renard." He stills when I say the word. "Is that your name?"

"It was." He sighs, sinking deeper into his seat. The chair's shuddering protests grow louder. "But that was another lifetime."

"So you really are the prince? Cursed to be a beast?" His eyes are sad as he nods. "The rumors are true," I realize aloud, thinking back to the ghost stories told to scare children and keep villagers in their homes at night.

"Fleur is lucky to have you." His words surprise me and the wine burns down my throat as I swallow thickly.

"She doesn't… Things aren't really… Or they haven't been for a long time…" I trail off, unable to find the right words to express the strain I've felt having to live all these years without Fleur by my side.

"Perhaps things were different for a while. But I believe she's always cared. I could see it in the way she glanced at you when she knew you weren't watching, or the jealous expression when she saw you out with another woman, or two, or three—"

"Yeah, yeah I get it. But even if I could secure a dozen women, they'd never measure up to just one Fleur." It's hard to remember now why I ever wanted things with Fleur to be different than they were. She's unconventional, that's for certain. Maybe that's what I love most about her, the way she walks her own path without a single care as to what others think. I could have had her as a partner, but instead I wanted to control her, tame her. I shake my head in disgust, finally seeing what an arrogant fool I've been for all these years. So much time wasted.

We sit in silence, abandoning small talk in the midst of melancholy. Renard appears as lost in thought as I am. Perhaps he's reliving his own regrets. Fleur stirs and we both move to our feet, ready to tend to her every whim. She breathes something unintelligible before falling back to sleep. We look at one another before sitting again. Renard fills our glasses a third time and I nod my gratitude.

"Are you hungry? Have you eaten?" he asks, his deep voice somehow smoother than normal.

"The old broad brought some soup. I have no clue how long ago that was." My stomach gurgles loudly and Renard chuckles.

"I'll have a proper dinner sent in." He stands to leave but

pauses. "Perhaps I could dine in here as well, in case Fleur wakes up."

I stare at him in confused silence for a moment. Is he asking for my permission?

"Sure." I nod, unable to do much more after the events of the day, or night, have rendered my body exhausted and my brain muddled. "I'm sure she will be glad to see you when she wakes up."

"Do you think so?" His voice lifts to a hopeful tone.

"Yeah. I think she likes spending time with you. She's always smiling when she comes back from the library."

"Perhaps that's just because my tongue makes her moan with—"

"Yeah, yeah I'm trying to block that out. Let me at least pretend it's for the books." I take a long swig from my glass.

Renard chuckles as he leaves the room. "I shall return shortly."

* * *

Two weeks have passed since Fleur was kidnapped. Two long weeks spent taking care of her and putting off this visit entirely. My stomach twists as I travel through the servants' quarters. The last time I was here was a true nightmare. I can't imagine what the staff are feeling after Renard and I unceremoniously began cutting off fingers and ears. Probably wasn't the smartest move, but it got the job done. I'm also grateful the servants feared for their lives enough in the moment not to disclose my plans to kill the Beast while Renard was present. And with their fearless Elias gone and many members injured, I had little to no fear that they would unite and rise up before I got a chance to speak to them.

That being said, there's always a chance. Waiting any longer than two weeks felt too risky.

I locate several servants lounging in a laundry room. They freeze upon seeing me, eyes welling with fear. "It's all right." I hold my hands up in a gesture of peace. "I wish to call a long-overdue meeting."

One of the girls hurries off to locate more staff and I wait, suffering the tense silence as she gathers the group. One of the men left behind clutches a bandaged hand. It's hard to differentiate between the faces from such a heated night, but I have to assume he's one of the servants who had a few fingers removed in our quest for information.

The others file in and I spy more and more bandaged hands and missing ears. The eyes that once looked to me as a hero now glower and glare. This is far more awkward than I anticipated. "Welcome, friends."

"Friends?" an older man with a missing ear spits out. "This is how you treat friends?" He points to his mutilated head.

"That was a necessary evil to gain the Beast's trust and keep our plan from being revealed too early," I offer.

The man spits on the floor. "Lies. All you two care about is the girl. We shouldn't trust him." He turns to the others. "He'll kill us if he gets the chance." Murmurs run through the room and I grind my teeth in annoyance.

"Why would I kill you when I need your help to take down the Beast?" My irritation flows freely and I allow them to feel the power in my tone as I speak. "Think for a minute. We're all in this together."

"When is it then?" a nervous-looking woman asks. "When will we kill him?"

A lump forms in my throat. In the last two weeks I've spent nearly every waking minute with Rena—the Beast. We have more in common than I could have imagined. In that time I've seen his true personality and observed how deeply he cares for Fleur. Maybe even loves her in a way I didn't believe him to be capable of. At this moment he's the closest thing to a friend I've got and that slight notion is messing with my head.

"Soon," I promise them. "The girl needs to heal first. It will be too hard to get him alone and vulnerable before then." Yeah, we'll wait until Fleur is fully mended before striking. It's necessary to wait. Or at least, that's what I'm telling myself.

"Why not kill him now?" another pipes up.

"Because I said so," I snap, allowing my tone to darken and my eyes to drive the point home. The room falls silent and several of the wounded cradle their injuries as I lock eyes with every person here. "Until then, keep on as normal. I'll have some extra food and wine sent down here," I offer, hoping to win a bit of their good graces back. The people only nod, but I can feel their distrust like a dozen knives in my back as I take my leave. Things have gotten complicated in ways I didn't anticipate. Time. I just need time to sort things out.

I forget their glares and accusatory stares the moment I enter the foyer. Renard is waiting for me. We're venturing into the forest for a hunt. It's the sixth time since Fleur was attacked. I have missed hunting like a hole in the soul. The moment Fleur was well enough to be let out of our sight, Renard invited me out of the castle. Mrs. Perle will stay with Fleur while we're away for a few hours. She's been instructed not to open the door unless it's Renard or myself, and mark my words, if she lets anyone else in I'll have her wrinkly, gray head on a tea tray.

"Where were you?" Renard gives me a questioning look.

"I just like to pay the servants a visit every now and then to keep them in line." It's not a complete lie. He cocks his head to the side but doesn't question me further. "Ready to go?"

He nods, leading me out. "Fleur seems much more alert today."

"She does. It won't be long now." And when she's healed, will my time be up? Will I have to face the truth of my circumstances? I push the thought aside as I mount my horse and Renard ventures ahead on foot.

Surely I have a few more weeks left to decide. Those are worries for another day. Today I'll enjoy hunting the King's land like royalty and ignore the future leering its ugly head around the corner. My stomach twists in knots as the wind rushes through my hair. Everything will reveal itself in time.

CHAPTER 21

FLEUR

Six miserable weeks and these two are still fussing over me. "I don't know how many more times I need to tell you, I am perfectly capable of dressing, feeding, and bathing myself." I glare at Gabriel as he dries me off with one of the castle's fluffy cloud towels.

"Perhaps, but it's all the more fun to let me do those things. I get to see you naked, put things in your mouth, touch every inch of your body…"

"Pervert." I giggle, swatting him in the chest. "You have to let me do things for myself now. Enough is enough."

"Fine," Gabriel relents. "I suppose you can start to do a few things yourself."

A triumphant grin spreads across my face. In the last six weeks all of my wounds have healed nearly completely. The bruises have vanished, the stitches have mended and been removed, and the fractured bones of my hand and wrist are nearly one hundred percent better.

"And you have to let me go to the library," I toss back over my shoulder as I make my way to the bedroom.

"You have books in here," he argues.

"It's not the same," I pout.

Gabriel wraps his arms around me. "I know it isn't. I just want to make sure you're fully healed and safe." His light eyes flash with a torment that convinces me he's seeing that horrible day all over again.

"I will be safe. And I am healed. I've had six weeks of doing nothing while you've been off riding horses and playing hunting buddies with Renard." I drop down into one of the chairs with an exasperated sigh.

"Come now, that's not all true," he says, suddenly looking cagey and antsy. "It's not all been horses and hunting."

"What else?" I sit forward in my chair, suddenly desperate to know more. Gabriel paces a few times, and my nerves prickle. "Gabriel, what's wrong?" He gives me the strangest look, and for a moment I fear something terrible has happened. I've never known him to act so anxious and unsure of himself. He picks up a book and sits in the chair across from mine. "What are you doing?" I ask, totally at a loss for why he would want anything to do with a book. He cracks open the first page and clears his throat.

"Once up-pon a time, in a land ac-cross the sea, was a magnif-magnificent castle. Every atem, attempt to—"

"Wait." I move forward, placing my hand on the book. "You learned to read?" A deep blush I'm not used to creeps along Gabriel's cheeks.

"I'm learning. Renard, he's teaching me…" He trails off, appearing embarrassed.

"You did this for me?" I place my hands on his cheeks, searching the icy blue of his eyes for the truth.

"Yes. I thought it would make you happy," he says in a soft voice.

An excited giggle bubbles out of me. "It does! I can't believe this. I've always wanted to share things with you." I toss the book aside, enjoying the startled sound he makes as I jump into his lap. "Thank you." I kiss him, pressing my lips to his and holding them there for a long moment before drawing back. "This means more to me than you know."

His eyes shine in a way that makes me believe he does know how much this means to me. "I love you, Fleur. I would learn anything, do anything for you. I love everything about you. Every wild, infuriating, beautiful part of you. I'm sorry it took me so long to figure that out." His voice is so steady, so real.

My lips part but no words come out. *Love*. Can I return the sentiment? Am I in love with Gabriel? Maybe I never really stopped loving him. I certainly love this version of him. The one I always knew was the real version. I dip down to kiss him again, moving to straddle his lap. He groans as I drop my towel, trailing my lips lower to kiss his neck.

"Fleur"—his voice is strained—"you need to rest and heal."

"I've rested long enough. I need you, Gabriel. I need this," I whisper into his skin as I grind my hips against his lap. "Stop treating me like a broken doll and give me what I need." I bite his bottom lip, eliciting a throaty growl. Gabriel's eyes darken as he claims my mouth with a series of deep, sensual kisses. His hands roam over my body, pushing the towel to the floor so he can run his warm fingers along my skin.

"Well." Renard's voice makes us both jump. "It seems I've arrived just in time. Don't push yourself, though, you need rest—"

"I need to be fucked. *Thoroughly*."

I swear the ridge in his trousers engorges almost instantly.

"Well then, by all means, Gabriel. *Fuck. Her. Thoroughly*." His words send heat rushing between my thighs and I moan as his sapphire gaze hooks into me.

Gabriel's mouth finds mine once more, his tongue driving between my lips. His hand traces down my stomach, landing between my thighs where he toys with the sensitive flesh. I throw my head back in relief. It's been so long since I've been touched. His finger slips lower, probing into the wetness and plunging into my needy depths. I grasp his shoulders, grinding against his fingers and seeking the release that's been denied to me for so long.

Gabriel slows the pumping of his fingers and I grit my teeth, releasing a sound of impatience. "What's your hurry, *ma petite fleur?*" I glare at him and his grin widens. His fingers up their pace again and my head falls back with a deep moan. He slows again just as quickly and I practically snarl at him. The next time he starts to move, it's rough, practiced, and with clear intent. My body reacts with a rush of arousal as my walls flutter in anticipation around his fingers. Gabriel has always known how to work my body. Always been able to drive me crazy.

A whimper pours out of me as my climax swells. I grip him, afraid he'll stop again when I'm so close.

"I've got you," he purrs in my ear. "Let me feel how badly you needed this." His thumb presses down on my clit and a sharp tightening of muscles sends me careening into a desperately needed orgasm. I cry out, releasing a guttural sound of need and gratitude. Gabriel sucks on the delicate skin beneath my ear as I come, dragging every bit of pleasure from me. Oh how I've missed this euphoric, post-orgasmic haze. My forehead drops to his shoulder as I pant. One hand strokes softly up my spine while the other slips out of me.

"You know, Fleur"—I lean back, taking in the sparkle of mischief in his crystal-blue eyes—"I think things have been a little one-sided between you and our new friend here." He glances up at Renard. Renard's eyes are fixed on Gabriel, curiosity growing behind them. I'm staring between the two of them, wondering what the hell is going on. I yelp as Gabriel gets to his feet, dragging me up with him. "Get on your back, Beast, and we'll see what we can do to remedy this."

"What?" I whisper as shock sends my heart thumping wildly. Renard says nothing, but his eyes darken with a hunger that makes me want to feed every starved part of both the monster and man. Renard remains frozen.

"Clothes off. To the bed. On your back." Gabriel's alpha tone sends fresh arousal dripping from my core. Renard looks at me, uncertainty in his eyes. Is he awaiting my permission? I take a few steps closer, reaching out my fingers, and pop the first button on his trousers. His massive paws wrap around my wrists.

"Wait…" he protests.

"I want to see you, all of you." I reach a hand up, stroking his fur and his eyes fall shut. "Let me have you, like this," I beg.

Renard's broad chest rises and falls as he gazes down at me. "I can't…" His eyes lower to the floor. "I can't be with you in that way."

"I have an idea of how we can work around your differences," Gabriel assures him. My eyes narrow as I size up Gabriel. *What is he up to?* I can't figure out why he would offer to help Renard. It seems genuine, which is even more confusing. Sure, the two of them spent a lot of time together while I slept an entire month away, but could they possibly be *this* close?

"I don't know." Renard shifts uncomfortably.

"What have you got to lose?" Gabriel claps him on the shoulder.

"Let's just try." I offer up an encouraging smile. "Do it for me?" I gaze up at him hopefully, chewing my bottom lip until he sighs, giving in.

"Very well. But I want the lights low." The room plunges into near darkness before we have a chance to argue. Several candles remain lit near the bedside tables and in the far corners of the room. Renard strips off his clothes, his deep sea eyes locked onto mine the entire time. I allow my vision to adjust to the low light. When he finishes, my gaze sweeps over every part of him, landing on the monstrosity between his thighs. It was more difficult to get a true size estimate of him through the fabric of his clothing, but now...

The sheer size of the practical tree branch between his thighs is almost laughable. It's as wide as the thinnest part of my thigh, and as long as my torso. Any deeply hidden fantasies I had that we would find a way to be together skitter away, melting back into the shadows. His cock is as dark as his fur, with velvety skin and a tracing of purplish, pulsating veins that rival even Gabriel's. Thick, white precum collects on the bulbous tip before dripping to the floor.

"Are you disgusted?" he asks, his hand moving to cover the gargantuan appendage. I place my hand on his, moving it away. The deep, warm tingle sparking within my core brings a flurry of muddled emotions to the surface. Fear, shame, desire. I raise my eyes from his hard length and lick my lips.

"Not at all." I speak in a tone so honest and genuine there's no chance of it being misconstrued for anything else. His expression lightens and he expels a heavy breath.

"You heard her, Beast. Now on the bed." Gabriel's eyes betray none of his true feelings. Renard moves to the bed, his massive cock bobbing as he walks. He lays on his back, his face a mask of uncertainty and nerves. "Fleur." He gestures for me to head to the bed. I perch on the edge, uncertain of what to do next. My stomach is a blizzard of butterflies as I wait. Gabriel's voice is heavy with lust. "I'll need her dripping wet for what I have in mind." He smiles at me with a depraved hunger. "Ride his face, Fleur. That ought to do the trick."

Nerves coil in my belly, stiffening my movements. Gabriel's eyes darken as he approaches me. His fingers settle on my chin as he tilts it up.

"Ride. His. Face."

I turn away from him, crawling toward Renard's face. I swing my knees wide as I straddle his head, peering down with a flush of embarrassment. Renard is as stiff as a board, arms by his sides as he stares up at me, unblinking. "If this is too much or if you're uncomfortable, we don't have to... "

"You want this?" Renard asks in a quiet voice meant just for me.

"I do." I nod, a blush lining my cheeks once more. Renard closes his eyes and inhales deeply. The silence surrounding us is damn near suffocating. *Well, if he doesn't want to do this.* I slide one knee back, lifting it to move away from him. Renard grasps the backs of my thighs before I make it off, pulling me down practically on top of his mouth. The first stroke of his tongue is long and soft as it snakes out, sliding over every part of me and focusing a few tantalizing swirls around my clit.

"Renard," I gasp. His tongue cups my sex, pressing against it with the wet warmth of his mouth. The tip of his tongue dips between my folds and I tense. It buries deeper inside me, inch by inch. Having him from this angle gives Renard the ability to go as deep as he wants. His tongue writhes inside me as it settles and my hips jerk in reaction.

"Ride his tongue," Gabriel commands from somewhere nearby. This twisted game feels even more intense when Gabriel is at the helm. There's a thin thread tying the two of them together. They're both alpha male, both used to getting what they want, and both experiencing something completely new when they bend to each other's wills. I imagine the two of them, galivanting around on their adventures, growing closer.

Closer. A lewd grin pulls at the corners of my mouth and I bite down to lock it out of sight. Thoughts of those two possibly together gets me far more excited than is appropriate.

Renard's horns glint in the candlelight, their sleek, curved shapes begging to be touched. My hands grip their bases, squeezing firmly, using them to gain some stability over my body and the delicious torture sweeping between my thighs. I'm rewarded with a growl of pleasure from Renard. It spurs me on. My fingers knead the smooth horns, sliding up and down and delivering as much pressure as I'm able. Renard growls again and his tongue fucks me rougher, faster. My body rocks up and down automatically, treating the tongue like a wetter, more flexible cock with a range of motion that's driving me near to madness already. My motions are awkward at first, but the more Renard explores me on the inside, the faster I bounce on the outside.

My hips are already burning from the stretch of being planted on either side of his head and repetitive clenching of muscles that have been dormant these past six weeks. My legs tremble with the strain. I continue on, stroking his horns and riding his tongue despite the discomfort. My hips seize up as a moment approaches when I feel I can take no more.

Before I can voice my concerns, Renard's hands are sliding up my hips, gripping my waist and taking over the pace. I sigh in relief as the discomfort subsides and I relax into his hold. Renard drags me up higher and down even farther than I dared go before. His tongue writhes inside me, massaging my walls and forcing a steadily building heat to simmer within my depths.

Gabriel's fingers thread through my hair, pulling my

head back until I'm looking into his crystal eyes. His lips crash down on mine, his hand keeping hold in my hair, pressing our mouths together while Renard bounces me harder. The first scorching eruption of my orgasm ricochets through me and I moan into Gabriel's eager mouth, loving the way his groans swallow the sound. He drinks me in, kissing me with the passion of a lover who's sacrificed too many lifetimes apart. I tense, back arching, toes curling as I tighten around Renard's devilish tongue. When my screams quiet, and my panting breaths slow, Gabriel pulls away from me, hungry, hooded eyes devouring me on the spot.

Renard's tongue retracts and Gabriel dips his fingers between my thighs. "Well done, Beast. She's dripping." He skims his knuckles along my freshly devoured cunt and I whimper when he pulls away. "Straddle his cock," Gabriel commands.

Adrenaline zaps me to a new level of alertness. Gabriel gives me a glare that puts an end to my protests before I can even open my mouth. I carefully move my knees past Renard's shoulders, working my way down his chest. Gabriel mounts the bed behind me. His hands clutch my waist, dragging me farther until I'm straddling the base of Renard's cock. His massive, hard length lays flat against his stomach and I gaze down, uncertainly.

How on Earth is Gabriel planning to include him?

He slides my knees wider, until my pussy is flat to Renard's shaft. "How does she feel, Beast?" He uses his hold on my hips to slide me forward before dragging me back, using the slickness of my arousal to coat Renard's cock. Renard tenses, releasing a low, needy moan. Gabriel moves his fingers lower, digging them into the meat of my ass. He pulls, gently spreading my cheeks. The sound of him spitting reaches my ears, followed by the slick sensation as it drips down, wetting me and preparing my body for what's coming next.

Nerves rocket through me. I've never let anyone else do this, not since Gabriel. His throbbing, blunt head presses against the tight ring of flesh, and I tense in anticipation. "Breathe, Fleur. Let me in."

I cry out as the first inch presses in, my lungs tightening as he carefully works his way deeper.

"That's my good girl." He starts to move and the breath whooshes out of me. Relief spreads through me as pain blurs with pleasure, and my body welcomes the thick intrusion.

Renard's cock remains pressed to his stomach as I slip and slide along his shaft, coating the underside of his impressive cock in my cum. Every thrust of Gabriel's hips causes a deep, delicious friction as my clit rubs against Renard's length, sending pleasure skittering through every nerve ending. The intricate pattern of pulsing veins on the underside of Renard's shaft provides the perfect texture as I grind against every bit of him.

Renard's howls of pleasure grow louder as Gabriel picks up his cadence. A moment of clarity has me acknowledging just how unusual this situation is. Gabriel is fucking me, delivering unimaginable pleasure while at the same time, using my body to work Renard's oversized cock. Renard's chest rises and falls, his hips rocking ever so slightly to meet the rolling movements of Gabriel's hips. I have no doubt the slick feeling of my wet cunt on his aching length is far superior to his rough hand in the dark.

My body shakes, overstimulated by the fullness of Gabriel in my ass and the raw pleasure of Renard against my needy pussy. Heat engulfs me and a simpering whine works from my lungs as pleasure spirals out from my center, making my muscles tighten as an orgasm so uniquely devastating and altogether new utterly destroys me.

My pleasure loosens the last of Renard's control and he roars loudly enough to shake the room as his thick spend paints his stomach white.

"Fuck," Gabriel grits out behind me, his movements erratic and rough. Warm release rushes out of him, filling me as his cock thrusts in one final time, deeper than ever before. I gasp as the lewd sensation sends a shudder up my spine, triggering another orgasm deep down in my core.

My mouth hangs wide, my mind a mess of lust and exhaustion. The three of us bask in the silence, all bathing in the glow of our earth-shattering orgasms. Gabriel's lips fall to my shoulder, kissing softly as he pulls out of me. My body jerks with tenderness as he empties me. His arm wraps around my waist, dragging me into his chest as he pulls us off of Renard's body and drops onto the bed beside him.

As soon as my mind clears enough for me to gain some semblance of normal thought, I freeze. *Holy shit. Did that really just happen?* I chance a glance in Renard's direction as shame and desire fight for control of my emotions. Renard's eyes are closed, and he looks more peaceful than I've ever seen him.

As if he can sense my stare, his eyes open. The heat that burns through my cheeks could rival that of the largest roaring fireplace in the castle. The dynamic of our group has shifted in a way that cannot be ignored.

I bite back a smile. That was one of the filthiest sexual experiences of my life, and one I'm already fantasizing about recreating.

I shift in Gabriel's arms, wincing a little at the soreness enveloping the majority of my body. Okay, maybe not recreate right this minute. But I have a feeling there's a lot more where that came from and I am very much looking forward to what the future has in store for our unusual trio.

CHAPTER 22

RENARD

Fleur pushes through the library doors, pausing in surprise when she spots me seated on a nearby couch with a book in my hands. A tray of warm scones and steaming tea sits on the table in front of me. "You're here early!" she says, brightly. The way her eyes light up when she sees me makes a deep purr of contentment reverberate through my being. In truth, I've hardly slept. I laid in bed, replaying our erotic encounter from the night before.

She drops down next to me, her eyes sparkling as she spies the tea tray. "Those smell practically sinful." She breathes in deeply, her eyes falling shut. I chuckle as I watch her. She's got a taste for sweets, and I've got a taste for her. "Have you eaten?" she asks and I shake my head.

Fleur grins as she makes two plates, handing the first to me before making us both a cup of tea. She adds cream and sugar to both. I don't have the heart to remind her I usually enjoy my tea with neither. Instead I sip at the sweet, creamy liquid and gaze down at the beauty that I'm lucky enough to have in my presence.

My eyes fix on the pink scar that lines the left side of her

face from the top of her cheekbone to the edge of her chin. Guilt gnaws away at me, crumbling bits of my pride and tossing them like rotten wood into my ever-growing pile of regrets. I should have sensed her distress. How long was she trapped in Elias's cruel clutches before Gabriel and I rescued her?

She's been so terribly brave about the whole situation. The fact that she's handled it with such grace and dignity brings me little comfort. It only deepens the clawed fingers of inadequacy that drive deeper into the part of my brain that fears losing Fleur above all else.

She's oblivious to my concerns as she munches happily on her breakfast. When her eyes flit to mine they're bright, mossy, filled with joy and a need for adventure. I try to shift my focus away from the scar before she notices, but the damage is done. Her eyes dull and sadden as she sweeps her hair forward, covering her face. She looks away from me.

"I understand you may find it distasteful to look at," she whispers, placing her scones back on the table. "But there's nothing that will change the past."

The melancholy tugs between us like a tattered thread with its web of strings tangled deep in the meat of my heart. I reach forward, drawing her hair back and tucking it behind her ear. The pad of one finger traces down the raised flesh and Fleur sighs, leaning her cheek into the palm of my paw. Every moment of contact with Fleur brings a little more of me back to life. Her soft, green eyes peer up at me as I stroke her cheek.

"You've never been more beautiful."

She gives me a deflated giggle. "Somehow I doubt that."

"It's the truth. In that scar I see the brave, defiant woman who was clever enough to lead us to her location, and who never backed down or lost faith despite how abhorrent the situation seemed." Her lips part as she listens to me. "In that scar I see your strength."

"Still"—she blushes—"I just wish it wasn't on my face." She reaches her own delicate fingers up to trace the mark.

I tilt her chin up, prompting her to meet my gaze. "My love for you is not measured by the smoothness of your skin, nor the color of your eyes." I run my gaze along her body. "Not even by the roundness of your ass or the thickness of your thighs, which are both quite perfect, by the way. No, my love for you stems from your kindness, your resilience, and your adventurous spirit. There's no one else quite like you, Fleur." This draws a soft smile to her lips and a cheer of victory sounds within me.

"You better cut back on the gratuitous flattery or I'll get a big head." Her voice has its usual stubborn, sassy tone back.

"Don't worry, your large hips will balance you out."

Her mouth drops open and her face turns adorably red. She smacks me on the arm with a horrified giggle. "Renard!"

I just grin. "It's a compliment. I love the way you're built. I wouldn't have you any other way."

"Thank you." She twirls a strand of soft brown hair between her fingers.

"You're welcome. Now finish your scones, I have something to show you."

Our trip through the castle is pleasant and filled with conversation. My eyes drift to the darker and more concerning changes in the castle's interior. Are the walls closing in? Has the room gotten smaller? I watch as Fleur's eyes catch on a new pair of stone gargoyles stationed at the base of the stairwell.

"The castle is still changing," she observes, quietly.

Neither of us seem to want to dive deeper into the *why*. The rest of our journey passes in silence. The garden I'm taking Fleur to today is all the way at the back of the castle. I grab a heavy sack from a closet nearby and she eyes me suspiciously.

"What is that for?"

"You'll see." I smirk, enjoying her sound of frustration at being left in the dark. I take her out back, pushing open the doors and revealing the small, hidden garden. This particular space has been left free of the abominable rose vines. It's the only place I can go without staring the curse and my impending demise in the face. Perhaps that's why I protect this sacred space so fervently.

Fleur gasps as she steps into the snowy wonderland. Birds flit about, squirrels scamper across the fresh powder. I open the sack, tossing several handfuls of seed to the ground and the animals descend on it, flapping and chirping happily.

"You come out here to feed the birds?" Fleur looks stunned.

I savor the purity of her shocked expression. "It was something I used to do with my mother." I shrug. "And it's cold out here. This time of year is the most difficult for them to find food on their own." I toss another few handfuls out before offering it to Fleur. She dips her hands in the bag and scatters the seeds around us.

"I hadn't noticed hardly any animals around the castle grounds. I guess they've all been back here, waiting for snacks." She giggles, dipping her hands in and dropping a small pile of food in front of a curious red squirrel.

"I told Gabriel he's strictly forbidden from hunting any of the animals that come to this garden."

"You brought Gabriel here?" she asks, surprised.

"He was less keen on feeding the birds as a pastime." I shake my head, remembering Gabriel's utter confusion at why I would spend my time watching birds peck up seeds from the snow. "If I ever need to, I may be able to use feeding the birds as some sort of punishment for him." I smile mischievously and Fleur bursts out laughing.

"Do they ever eat from your hand?" she asks.

"I've never tried." I'm not sure if the animals are more comfortable with me because I'm closer to an animal than a man or if they're terrified of my predator size and menacing energy.

"Let's give it a try. Hold your hands out."

I do as she says, stretching my arms out, palms facing up toward the billowy gray sky. Fleur dumps a pile of feed in both hands. I give her a half-hearted growl when she sprinkles a bit on my head too before quickly backing away.

"Hold still or you'll scare them away." Fleur can barely contain her laughter as she presses her lips together, eyes dancing with amusement. Nothing approaches me at first and I sigh.

"They're scared of me, just like everyone else."

"Patience," she whispers.

I turn my attention back to the birds. Memories of my mother fill my mind. The sounds of spring, the scent of flowers, the feeling that I was happy, safe. I wasn't always the cruel and heartless prince I became. In my early years, my fondness for creatures great and small led to many unusual animals ending up inside the castle. My father would be furious, ranting and raving about wild beasts remaining outdoors where they belong. But my mother understood. She helped me nurse them back to health, joining me each time I released a fully mended rabbit, crow, or deer back into the forest.

Even as a hunter I've always taken great care to ensure the animal's suffering is at a minimum and that every part of them, from the meat to the skin, bones, and fur gets used in

217

one way or another. There's a great balance in nature that demands respect. It's a lesson I learned right here, feeding birds with my mother. The only woman to ever love me. *Possibly the only one who ever will.*

At some point I'd gotten too old to accompany her to feed the birds. I was too busy hunting, chasing girls, and finding my way as a young man in the world. I wish now that I'd stretched my desire for adulthood out a few years longer. My mother was kind, fair, and beautiful. Her death devastated me, and before I knew it I was deep in the woods, chasing after that witch.

The familiar regret that so often clings to me like a shadow presses in close. There are so many things I would do differently...

A small brown bird with red and white feathers on the tips of its wings lands on my left palm. I suck in a breath as it pecks seeds directly from my paw. A giddy excitement stitches against my stomach. I slant my eyes toward Fleur. She's smiling, her fair skin tinted rosy from the cold. Another bird lands in my palm, this one is pure black with a yellow beak. The brown bird chirps something, and before I know it my hands and head are inundated with feathery creatures of all sizes. I bask in the contented feeling of their lack of fear. Even one of the larger squirrels makes his way up. His tiny feet pad through my fur, reaching the seed pile before biting down on my hand and forcing a roar from my chest. "That hurt," I bellyache as the animals scatter.

Fleur is still laughing as she approaches me, taking my hand in hers and looking it over. "Did he bite you?" Fleur nibbles her lip, suppressing another bout of giggles.

"He did, and it hurt," I grunt, my surprise and embarrassment getting the best of me. She wraps her fingers in mine, sending a surge of tingling energy through my palm and guiding me back toward the castle.

"I think that's enough for the birds and squirrels today."
She glances back at me over her shoulder. She radiates
happiness and my heart lightens. We take a new path back
through the castle and Fleur stops, mouth dropping wide as
we pass by the dining room. "It's so beautiful. Why on Earth
do you have us eating in our rooms each night?" She wanders
around the impressive room, gaze fixed to the massive chandeliers above.

"Would you like to have dinner with me?" I blurt out.

"Here?" Fleur asks.

"Yes, a formal dinner, here. Just the two of us." Nerves
squeeze along my insides as I await her response. *Why does it
feel like I'm asking for so much more than one dinner?*

"I would love to." The genuine warmth in her tone melts
away my anxiety. "Tonight?" she asks, her green eyes brim-
ming with excitement.

"I need a few days to get things in order," I say apolo-
getically.

"I understand." Fleur gives me a bashful grin. I love how
easily she gets swept up in the thrill of the moment.

I escort her back to the library. My thoughts are glued to
our date and all the possibilities that an evening with Fleur
promise. There are many preparations needed in such a
short amount of time. Things have to be perfect. I fight the
urge to rush off and prepare, making sure to give my girl
what she deserves first.

Fleur's eyes are hooded as I lay her back, propping her up
on the stacks of books, giving her a dozen or so mouthwa-
tering orgasms with my tongue, before hurrying off to
prepare for our soon-to-be date. The sounds of her screaming, "More, Master," to the sun and stars above as I brought
her pleasure until she fell limp and hoarse will never cease to
make me harder than stone. She was a sweaty mess when I

left her, barely able to raise a hand to acknowledge my departure.

A smug smirk graces my face. I'm just as capable of making her come with my mouth as Gabriel. One small step toward humanity.

I send Mrs. Perle up with tea and sandwiches, quite certain Fleur is more than famished by now. I, myself am full, having feasted on her pussy to my heart's content.

The castle breezes by, blowing a sense of dread across my fur. Something dark is settling over this place. I pause, swallowing the lump in my throat and turning toward the nearest rose garden. Petals are piled all around, some plump and red, others shriveled and brown. The barest handful still remain attached to the bushes and vines. *How am I to know what will happen when the last petal falls?*

Again, the witch's laughter echoes in my mind, taunting me. I know she's dead. I watched the life drain from her eyes. But sometimes I wonder if the curse keeps her tethered to this world somehow, allowing her to spy on me and mock my every moment of pain and suffering.

A small glint of satisfaction sparks in my chest at the realization that things have gone even better with Fleur than I could have imagined. I bet the witch didn't see that one coming. Or maybe she did. The curse will only break once I gain the love of another. My heart stutters as a new fear sprouts within the weed-filled garden of my heart. Would the witch allow me to find true happiness? What if the curse makes me unlovable in a way that will never allow me a chance to be human again?

I can sense Fleur's feelings have grown for me in the way she gazes at me, seeks out my company, and trusts me with her body and thoughts. But is that enough? My insecurities writhe, alive and ever present in the deep, scarred shadows of my soul. I take a steadying breath, hating the way my thoughts have gotten the better of me and soured my mood. All I can do is show Fleur how much she means to me and pray for a miracle.

* * *

It's been a long time since I've cared for anything enough to feel a tremor of excitement in my bones. But the days pass more swiftly when you have something to look forward to. This dinner, this *date* with Fleur has enlivened me in a way that I had long since thought impossible. I set the staff on their individual tasks right away. Three days later, everything is completed.

The magic mirror feeds me my own reflection for a change. No spying, no eavesdropping, just the hard-edged face of a monster playing the part of a man in love. The dark suit and gilded accompaniments that wrap around my hideous body were designed for a prince. Such a pity they had to be tailored to the form of a beast. I long for my old body. I yearn for it with every ounce of yearning I possess. I'm screaming inside this grotesque outer shell.

I'm convinced now more than ever that hell is a life spent watching the world continue to change while you stay trapped in the mistakes of your past. There was never a single moment in the cushiony royal entitlement of my youth that hinted at the barest whisper of the forlorn future I was cast into. I desire the life I had before the witch's wrath. My greatest desire was to change the past. Or so I thought. The past is where my thoughts have dwelt all these long years since my curse began. But some small part of me questions how my future would have been shaped regardless of the sins I committed. Would I have ever met Fleur?

Surely, the Renard of the past would not have lowered himself to mingle with commoners. In fact, I'd never even been to the village before the Beast's curse drove me to that town square, my loneliness stripping me of my royal privileges and antiquated beliefs. As a monster, I no longer had the luxury to look down my nose at others as I did before.

This curse has tormented me in ways too horrific for most to endure. But if I'd known this was the only way to find Fleur, to win her favor, have her wild spirit and soft body close by, I'd suffer the curse all over again without a moment's hesitation. The world is changed by her beauty, by her laughter. She's all that matters in this lonely life.

I push the past away, burying it alongside the other dark pillars of my soul. Tonight, I have a date with the woman of my dreams. Her presence lifts my spirit, filling me with a light and joy that I do not deserve. Tonight I'll allow it. Tonight I'll bask in her affections and pretend the horrors of the past were all just some bad dream.

CHAPTER 23

FLEUR

*M*y hands drift along the exquisite, gold fabric as it shimmers beneath my fingertips. In all my years I could never have dreamed of wearing something as elegant and beautiful as this dress. The skirt falls down around me in layers so lovely and perfectly stitched that it hurts my heart to envision ever taking it off again.

The bottom layer is a sparkling soiree of golden roses that have been carefully embroidered across the entirety of the base. A decadent ivory layer of gossamer that shines like starlight sits pinned in cascading waves above the rose-filled layer. It leads to a fitted golden bodice with a single vine of roses stretching out across each side of my waist. The blossoming vines curl upwards, landing just beneath my breasts. The sweetheart neckline is held in place by two ivory sleeves that drape daintily across my upper arms. I've pinned my hair up and out of my face, exposing my neck and shoulders.

I gaze into the mirror, unbelieving of the figure peering back at me. *Who is the woman behind the glassy green eyes?*

A crazed giggle colors the air around me as I take in my current situation. I'm in a castle, heading to dinner with a

prince cursed to be a beast, wearing a piece of clothing so breathtakingly beautiful I couldn't have imagined it even in my wildest dreams. Every inch of the dress shimmers like moonlight and gold dust. It's deserving of nothing short of a fairy tale.

The gown arrived shortly after six o'clock with a hand-written note.

My dearest Fleur,
Your radiant beauty shines more brightly than the stars. This gift is but an impossible attempt to capture that same gilded glimmer in the seams and folds of a dress. Wear it for me tonight and know that I would happily give my sight throughout the vast eternity of my immortal life just to be blinded by your beauty for one unforgettable moment. I count the seconds until I'm by your side once more.
Renard

It's easy to believe that I'm floating through a dream, lost by the fireside with a fairy tale in my hand and forbidden romance on my mind. This is by far the most romantic thing anyone has ever done for me. I swish my hips back and forth, admiring the way the golden fabric glints against the flicker of candlelight. The bedroom door opens and Gabriel trudges in, sweat upon his brow and mud on his boots. He's been hunting again. He kicks his shoes off and is halfway done sliding his shirt over his head when he spots me. The way his eyes grow wide and his mouth drops open makes me blush despite myself.

"Fleur…" He steps closer, his icy eyes drinking in every inch of the decorous dress. I expect a mocking grin or dirty quip about ripping it off of me later. Instead he gawks at me with unshielded wonder in his gaze. "You look like the sun, the stars, and everything in between."

His sincerity has me stumbling over my words. "Thank you. It's the dress." I smile sheepishly and give him a twirl. Warm contentment settles inside me.

"No, it's you. You're beautiful." There's a sadness in Gabriel's expression that has me moving toward him. My fingertips graze his stubble and he exhales. "I'll get your dress dirty." He takes a step back but I press forward, leaning up on my tiptoes. I plant a kiss on his lips. Something unspoken and carved deeply within our hearts passes between us as our eyes meet.

A knock on the door breaks the tender silence, locking all of the things left unsaid even deeper away.

Renard enters, looking more dashing than ever. His attire is midnight blue, with gold embroidery along the edges. Ornately carved rose buttons line the front of his vest. The patterns along his sleeves match my dress and I marvel at the careful thought and planning that went into this evening. His hair is combed back, gifting me unobstructed access to the depths of his eyes. Those sapphire irises shimmer as they look me up and down. His footsteps are quiet as he glides toward me. Gabriel backs away then, and heads into the bathroom without a word. My heart stings at the sight of him walking away.

"You're sad," Renard notes. He slides the back of his hand down my cheek.

"No," I lie. I'm not entirely certain of the origin of this tumultuous emotional undercurrent. My eyes again follow Gabriel. The feeling of losing something precious pulls tightly in my chest.

"Do you want him to come with us?" Renard whispers, watching Gabriel shut the bathroom door behind him. My lips hover momentarily on a *yes*, but one deep look into Renard's dark eyes brings me back to the present moment. He's put so much work into this. So much effort and thought. He deserves this night with me, alone.

"No." I smile, allowing Gabriel to slip from my thoughts. "I want to spend the evening with you, good sir."

He grins and I know I've made the right decision. "Shall we?" He offers his massive arm and I take it willingly. The hallway outside our room seems brighter, as if the castle is alight with magic and love. I inhale a sharp breath as the hem of my dress brushes over the first red rose petal among a trail of what must be a hundred petals or more. They line the hall, guiding us toward the dining room. I peer up at Renard with a smile as a wistful sense of pride warms my heart. He's using the fallen petals, the symbol of his curse and the dark memories of his past, to make something beautiful here, now.

"What is it?" he asks.

"You've changed." I smile, warmly. "You're a different Renard than the one I first met all those months ago."

Emotion flickers across his starstruck gaze. "You've changed me, Fleur." His words are steady and sincere. There's something there, something behind that dark demeanor and cursed form that I hadn't noticed until tonight. I stroke my fingers deep in his fur as he escorts us to the dining hall and ballroom. A deep vibration that sounds an awful lot like a purr rumbles from his chest.

"Are you purring?" I grin up at him.

"I'm a beast, not a house cat," he huffs, then a short growl. That elicits a bout of giggling from me. Even Renard cracks a smile.

The sight that greets me as we step into the ballroom steals the breath from my lungs. The room has been transformed. Candlesticks and candelabras line the walls, filling the room with a twinkling golden glow that has me feeling like I'm walking among the heavens. Dark bowls of varying sizes sit scattered throughout the space, their wide mouths filled to the brim with water. As we move closer, I realize the surfaces reflect the dancing flames from above, casting even more light around us and adding a magical touch with their shimmering pools of illumination. Renard flicks his wrist, sending a soft current through the room. Every candle flickers, casting us into a twinkling version of the starry night sky itself.

"It's magical." I breathe in, emotions welling within me.

"I tried to capture your bright spirit and the way you make me feel inside," Renard admits, adorably.

"I love it. It's absolutely perfect." I lean in, resting my head on his stomach. His hands press gently against my upper back, warming the exposed flesh there.

"Welcome, Master." Lucien materializes from the direction of the kitchens. "I'm afraid we need a few minutes longer to prepare your meal. I will do my best to get it out as quickly as possible."

"No need to rush," I say before Renard can scold him. "I quite like the idea of this evening lasting forever."

Renard's eyes flick down to mine, and a smile softens his features. Lucien gives us an over-the-top bow before hurrying back out of the room.

"How shall we pass the time?" Renard asks, his tone dropping low. A wave of warmth creeps up my neck and I bite my lip. "Fleur, Fleur, Fleur," he tsks. "Your mind has gone straight to the gutter."

My mouth pops open, caught. "Well what did you have in mind?" I glare back at him.

"How about a dance?" He extends his hand to me. The gesture is so gentlemanly, so different from the Beast that stands before me.

"It would be my honor." I take his hand and he pulls me in

close. He leads us in a waltz, ignoring the lack of music. I can't suppress my giggle as Renard stumbles over my dress, cursing.

"I was once quite good at this." His tone is clipped and brusque but I can sense the shame beneath.

"Well I'm quite certain you had smaller feet back then," I point out. He sighs just as his toes catch the hem of my dress once more.

"This is far from romantic." He releases his hold on me, stepping back. I rush toward him, wrapping my arms around his waist and squeezing him tightly.

"It's the most romantic evening of my life." I slide my hands beneath his jacket, stroking the dense fur of his back. My arms grip him tightly, willing the unhappiness to rush from his body. I look up into his eyes as he towers over me, my beast. Something has changed between us. Sometime in the past few months, a light dusting of affection settled its seeds into my heart without my knowing and grew into something real. "Renard, I—"

"Master!" Lucien's panicked voice snaps through the air and he and Claude sprint into the ballroom. The unmistakable fear and alarm in his tone sink beneath my skin. Dread floods my blood as Renard whirls, hiding my body behind his. Claude gurgles and spits something dark across the floor before collapsing. Lucien looks back at him with terror in his eyes. "We're under attack! The staff—"

I peek around Renard's large frame just in time to see something shiny come spinning through the air. The mystery object hits Lucien square in the back and I scream as his body slams into the floor. The wooden handle of a hatchet protrudes from between his shoulder blades, blood spilling from around the blade and pooling on the floor.

"Stay behind me." Renard's tone makes my spine stiffen. Bodies spill from every hall, doorway, and servants' panel until the room is teeming with more than two dozen servants. Their stares are darkened with an unhinged malice that makes bile rise in my throat. Something's wrong with their faces and the color of their skin. Each one clutches a weapon of sorts. Decorative swords from the artwork vaulted to the walls, maces from the metallic arms of the armored sculptures that line the halls, kitchen knives, pitchforks, and even a few hunting guns. They come from everywhere at once, closing in on us with revenge in their eyes and death in their hearts.

I clutch the back of Renard's coat, my fright reaching unparalleled heights. A pair of doors leading in from an outdoor balcony burst inward, and my pulse lurches as Gabriel tumbles through. My heart clinches as he stands, raising a musket to eye level and pointing it our way. *No.* Time stands still, the horror and beauty of the scene before us swirling together in an unsettling cocktail of tragic opposites.

Gabriel's eyes harden. And then he pulls the trigger.

CHAPTER 24

GABRIEL

*M*rs. Perle serves me dinner in our room, bringing one place setting instead of two. The sight of my solitary meal brings pain to my chest. Fleur looked so unbelievably beautiful before she left for dinner with his royal highness, Renard. I read the note he sent when Mrs. Perle delivered Fleur's dress. My stomach twists. How can a beast of a man make me feel so inferior? He's a literal monster and yet, there's more refinement in his little finger than in my entire being. The way he's able to so eloquently lace together words and compliments enrages me. I've never had a problem attracting girls. Back in the village they fell on me like flies to honey. No wooing necessary. If only I had tried harder to expand my knowledge of things outside Montrésor. Learning to read is a step in that direction but each lesson has me feeling more matched to a stumbling, illiterate child and further from the suave refinement of cursed royalty.

This castle has brought to the surface all manner of inse-curities I never knew existed in me. I was happy enough in the village, idolized by my men, getting my cock sucked by

the triplets on command, hunting whenever I pleased. Or at least that seemed like happiness then. Now I realize I can never know true happiness without Fleur by my side. She's all I desire in the world and I'm forced to share her with Renard on a daily basis. The way her eyes light when she sees him. I never feared she would care for him more than me, but lately…

The door to our room opens without so much as a courteous knock and I frown. Surely Fleur and Renard haven't finished their extravagant solo dinner so soon. I wait, staring at the doorway, but no one enters. "Spooky fucking enchanted castle," I mutter irritably.

I stomp to the bedroom door, poking my head through the doorway and preparing to rant about how tired I am of the changes in this place, when a wild cry and the sound of something whooshing through the air have me stopping short. I jerk my body back just as a brawny redheaded servant finishes swinging an oversized sword at the spot where my neck was just craned into the hall.

"What the hell?"

Another battle cry resounds from outside the door and two men rush inside. The first is the sword-wielding man, a larger servant I'm unfamiliar with. He holds the ornate sword out in front of him, jabbing it in my direction with the jerky, graceless motions of someone who possesses little to no swordsmanship skills.

The second man wields a broken pitchfork with just three prongs instead of four. I recognize him as the older man who led us to Elias's secret tunnel. The right side of his head has healed poorly, leaving the flesh where his ear should have been a bumpy, deformed mess.

Both men are sweaty and dirty, with dark circles beneath their eyes and a blotchy, sallow cast to their crepey skin. *Are they sick?*

The two charge as one, releasing feral screams and revealing bloodied gums and throats. I set my sights on the larger man, quite certain he can still manage a decent amount of damage with a sword that size even with his lack of skill. He swings the sword down in a chopping motion and I dodge, bringing my left elbow up to slam hard into the side of his face. Blood flings from his lips along with a few rotted teeth. The man drops bone over bone, knocked out cold from the blow.

I whirl as the older man thrusts his pitchfork forward. My body twists and bends to avoid the rusty metal but one of the prongs catches me, spearing into the left side of my ribs.

"Fuck," I grit out, jerking the pitchfork loose and spinning it around before plunging it straight through the disfigured man's chest. His mouth gapes before he falls to the ground clutching the deeply buried prongs. Blood pours from between his lips as he babbles the incoherent and all-too-familiar sounds of death.

I survey the two, wondering what in the hell just took place. My side aches where that motherfucker stabbed me. It's bleeding, but doesn't look too deep. The torn pieces of a spare towel serve as a compression wrap for my ribs.

My steps are determined as I march across the castle. I need to know if this was an isolated incident. Was it revenge for torturing the servants for information? Or is something far more nefarious in the works? My path takes me past the den where I keep my favorite musket. Luckily the piece is buried behind a dark wooden chest, just where I left it. I've stashed several such items over the past few months, the idea of a fight to the death with the Beast kept fresh at the forefront of my mind.

If the castle hasn't rearranged itself again, my quickest path to the ballroom should be straight past the kitchens and down the hallway to the left. I make my way past the kitchens, fear notching down my spine as I glance inside. Pots bubble over, sizzling as their contents land on the flames below. Black smoke billows from the oven with what I can only assume is food that was never removed and served. Who is cooking the meal for Fleur and Renard? I don't see a single person anywhere.

A putrid stench slams into me as I reach the end of the hall. My hand instinctively covers my nose and mouth. What is that godawful smell? My boots skid to a halt as I round the corner and duck back behind the nearest wall. A mass of chambermaids, cooks, laundresses, and other servants huddle together, meandering at a queasy pace toward the rear entrance of the ballroom. Each one appears armed with both decorative and makeshift weapons at the ready. My stomach roils as their fetid stench seeps into my nostrils. Something is very wrong with the staff. I think back to my last few encounters. Everyone did appear weaker, more tired, and infinitely more unhappy the last time I visited. Since then I've seen almost no one. Just the three from Renard's trusted inner circle.

Now the signs are more obvious. The wrinkles in Mrs. Perle's face appeared deeper than before, Lucien's spindly body having thinned out even more, even Claude with his nervous habits seemed to sweat and stutter to a degree that would have been worrisome had I paid closer attention. Something bad is happening to the servants. It's been happening for a while.

A throng of dark, angry voices whisper hateful words as the horde moves closer to the ballroom doors. My gut tenses. *They're after Renard and Fleur.*

It would be foolish to fight my way through the mass. Even a dozen untrained servants can land blows when the odds are twelve to one. I need to find another way inside. I tread silently through the maze of archways and halls, begging the castle to retain its shape long enough for me to find a new way inside. Rot fills my nostrils as I reach the doors that open to the far end of the ballroom. Another dozen or so sickly servants push and shove their way to the second set of doors. I curse as my second attempt to break into the ballroom is thwarted. Think, Gabriel.

Bang! A loud, repetitive slamming draws my attention behind me to where the castle is rearranging itself. The archways are sealing up one by one, blocking my retreat. I'm not getting trapped in here with those half-dead psychos and their revenge plots. I run, breaking cover and sprinting straight past them, barreling out a massive set of doors and into the snowy garden beyond. I spin on my heels, checking to see if anyone followed me. My muscles are coiled and stiff as I listen. A bitter wind singes my skin with its frosted touch. No one follows and I breathe deeply, fucking finally.

The garden I landed in when the castle practically spit me out has positioned me near the front gate. I turn away from it, knowing if I run along the far wall, I'll eventually find the outer windows of the ballroom.

My heart beats a violent rhythm in my chest. Those things have probably already made it inside. Fear grips me, its frigid fingers latching onto my ankles, trying to drag me into the desolation of despair and surrender. I'll never give up, not when there's a chance to save the woman I love.

There's the glow of candlelight as the first of the windows comes into view. There are four monumental arched windows along the ballroom's main wall, and nestled right in the middle is an extravagant balcony that juts out and into the elements. *That's my way in.*

I sling the blunderbuss over my shoulder and start the steep climb to the top of the balcony's railing. Thorny vines slither across the stone surface, burying into my palms and making it difficult to find traction as I ascend the wall. I could swear the vines themselves are moving, sliding into the vacant spaces just before my fingers grab hold. This fucking castle has a mind of its own, and right now it feels an awful lot like keeping me away from Fleur is on the top of its list of priorities. The pain fuels my rage and I push through, ignoring the way my palms sting and bleed.

Nothing can stop me now. I'm love embodied in a weaponized fury. My only mission is to save Fleur, and I'll suffer the pain of a million sharp thorns to reach her and ensure she's safe.

I grip the top of the railing and a rush of relief grants me a featherlight kiss of hope. Grabbing hold, I pull my body up, resting my chin on my arms as I drag the rest of my weight up higher. *It shouldn't be this difficult, something is slowing me down.* I pull with all my might, gasping as I feel the pressure of a thick vine wrapping tightly around my boot.

"Son of a bitch." My right arm latches onto the balcony with all the strength I possess as my left hand reaches into my pocket for the hunting knife I have hidden there. "Fucking roses," I curse as I hack away at the invasive vine, slashing it to bits and finally hauling myself over the railing and onto the balcony.

I land on my back, the blunderbuss digging painfully into my flesh and pushing the air from my lungs. *Fucking move.* My body fights to ignore the freezing air, the stinging punctures from the thorns, and the consistent throbbing of the wound against my sore ribs.

By some miracle that can only be attributed to the power of my love for Fleur, I push to my feet, slamming my body against the balcony doors several times before they splinter and give way. The sight that confronts me is more gruesome than I'd imagined. Servants have poured in from every direction, even more than I saw stalking through the hallways. The fetid stench of the ballroom is unbearable. My eyes water as the first wave of noxious rot hits me full force. My gaze fixes on Fleur as she peers out from behind Renard's broad frame. Her eyes are wide with alarm as they catch on mine.

Movement to their left draws my gaze. A dark-haired woman with bleeding eyes and mottled skin lunges from the shadows behind them, a butcher knife clutched in her hand. There's no time to warn them. I raise my gun, firing with the practiced confidence of a skilled hunter. The attacker drops to the ground with a satisfying thud and lays there unmoving. Renard and Fleur whirl, shock slowing their movements as they take in the dead woman who landed so close to their feet.

Fleur wheels back toward me, opening her mouth to speak. Then the room ruptures into chaos, and the horde descends as one.

The crowd parts, splitting their attention between us. Everything happens so fast. Fleur is blocked from my view and a suffocating panic pounds through my blood like poison. There's no time to reload my blunderbuss. The swarm of bodies comes stabbing and swinging every weapon imaginable. My gun becomes a blunt-force weapon. I loosen the strap from my shoulder, yanking it free. My movements are primitive and crude as I bash in the skulls of anyone who dares come within four feet of me. Blood flies and bones crunch beneath the metal butt of the gun. The servants outnumber us, but they have no experience fighting. Their movements are driven solely by instinct and the desire to kill.

A vicious roar rattles the room. *Renard.* I steal a sword from a dead man's hands and swing it violently, spinning and thrusting so that one hand is swinging the heft of the gun and the other is wielding my newly acquired sword. Both arms thrust, chop, smash, bury, slice, break, *destroy* everything in my path that breathes. The new level of savagery works to my benefit and within moments I'm back within eyesight of Fleur and Renard.

Fleur spins in circles, swinging an oversized ax in every direction. Her face is smattered with blood. I can't tell if it's hers or one of the damned dead at our feet. My heart beats painfully hard. Renard is making quick work of any servants foolish enough to have chosen him as their target. Stringy lumps of flesh hang from his jaw and buckets of blood pool around him on the floor. I have to step over a growing pile of bodies to get to her. His ferocious eyes cut toward me and the sight stops me dead in my tracks.

Renard's monster is fully present.

"Get the girl," he bellows. I shove my sword through the chest of an old man with a gaping wound on his cheek. The number of servants is noticeably thinning out, finally. I reach Fleur, swiftly decapitating a tall, thin man who dared point a rifle at her in that moment.

"Gabriel!" she cries out in relief. I massacre the remaining servants, finding a second wind in my close proximity to Fleur. The room falls quiet and the next time I look around, all of the servants are dead at our feet. Renard is breathing heavily, dark fur dripping with crimson. The three of us look to one another, checking in and assessing wounds.

"What the fuck was that all about?" I pant.

"Something's wrong with them," Fleur breathes out, a tremor in her tone. "Look at their faces."

"The curse"—Renard wipes a massive paw across his gore-streaked face—"it's done something to them, infected them, made them sick."

"Is this all of them?" I ask, optimistically. Renard shakes his head and my stomach drops. "Where are the rest?"

"I don't know but we need to—" A sudden rumbling all around us stops Renard. Fleur screams as a chandelier falls from the ceiling, sending pieces of shattered glass flying our way. Another hits the floor, and another. The doors to the balcony slam shut before transforming into a solid wall of wood.

"The castle is rearranging. We need to move." I drop the sword, gripping Fleur's hand and running for the closest exit. Renard is right beside us, ducking and dodging the debris crumbling all around. We surge through the doorway and find ourselves in the center of the library.

"The library?" Fleur whirls around, confusion and fear comingling on her breath. Books fly from the shelves and we duck to shield our heads.

"Keep moving," Renard commands. A new archway has opened up on the far end of the library where the fireplace was. We hurry through it, plunging into the darkness beyond. Screams echo off the stone walls as we fall face-first down an unseen stairwell. I try to hang onto Fleur but she's ripped from me as we tumble head over feet down the stairs.

I hit the bottom, stunned, breathless. A roaring from above rushes me back to reality and I grab Fleur, rolling us both out of the way before Renard's mountainous form can crush us. The Beast hits the bottom hard and bellows in pain. The unwelcome sounds of deep, earthly tremors resonate through the castle. Light blazes behind us, and a new candlelit hallway appears before our eyes.

"On your feet, Beast." I reach for his blood-soaked arm, hauling him up as best I can. We limp down the hallways, each of us injured in a dozen ways or more but unable to stop and assess the damage. There's a single ornate door beckoning us from just beyond the last candelabra. It swings in automatically upon our approach and we rush inside. The temperature plummets and the second the three of us are through the doorway, the door slams shut.

Renard's private quarters are a mess of broken furniture

and snowdrifts. My eyes dart around but no other doorways appear. Fleur gasps and I follow her gaze to where the dead form of Mrs. Perle lies crumpled in the corner. Her neck has been slit, draining the color from her frail face. Poor old woman. She must have come to find Renard or seek shelter and been killed by the crazed servants. Her sallow skin and hollow eyes reveal the sickness she was suffering from, just like the others.

"What now?" Fleur buries her face in my side. Her teeth are chattering from the cold.

"We've got to get out of this castle," Renard says. "We'll use the balcony, move to the stables and then—" His words are cut short as the pointed head of a spear bursts out the front of his chest cavity. Blood spews from his mouth and his eyes triple in size. Renard drops to his knees and it's only then that I'm able to see Elias's companion, Lyam, standing behind him, eyes sunken and face oozing blood.

"Nooo!" Fleur rushes to Renard as he collapses. Lyam grins at me, revealing a rotted mess in his mouth.

"We've done it, Gabriel. We've killed the Beast."

CHAPTER 25

FLEUR

$\mathcal{M}$y hands press in around the pointed protrusion sticking out of Renard's chest. There's so much blood. *So much blood.*

"Renard," I whimper, shaking him as his eyelids droop shut. "Wake up, Renard!" The blue in his eyes begins to fade and my heart shatters as I beg him to wake up. "Gabriel!" I turn to him for help but he's not looking at me. Gabriel stands eye to eye with the servant that just stabbed Renard.

"Finish him," the pale man cries out. "This was your plan from the start. Finish him, and set us free."

What? Gabriel doesn't move, doesn't speak, and fear spikes adrenaline through my blood.

"What are you waiting for? Can't you see? We will all die if he continues to live!" Blood drips from Lyam's nose, eyes, and ears. Gabriel shifts his gaze to Renard and the uncertainty I see there chills me to the bone.

"Gabriel!" I urge, commanding his attention back to me. Elegant words won't come. Fear swallows them up, leaving me nothing more than a shivering, fearful mess with desperate, pleading eyes. *"Please."*

Renard's breathing is so shallow now. I can barely feel the rise and fall of his chest. Tears waterfall down my cheeks, and my cries seem to shake Gabriel from his stupor.

He snatches a broken teapot from the floor, whipping it forward and jamming the sharp edge deep into Lyam's face. The man screams in agony as he clutches the porcelain buried in his flesh. He drops to his knees, wailing in horror, and I cover my ears. Gabriel kicks out hard, striking the teapot and forcing it even deeper into Lyam's face. The screaming abruptly ends. Gabriel drops down beside me, removing my hands from my ears.

"It's over," he soothes.

"But Renard." I look down at his still form. The wind gusts through the room, blowing snow in our faces. As it settles, I notice a single red rose petal floating through the air. It swirls up above before softly landing on Renard's chest. Everything around us grows dark and silent. *The last rose petal.* "No!" I yell, slamming my hands against Renard's chest. "Don't you dare die. I need you." I fall across his body, my tears spilling into his dark fur. "I love you," I whisper, already knowing it's too late. I should have uttered those words while he was alive, should have told him the moment I—

A blinding light beams from Renard's chest, knocking me backward and bathing the room in a glow so devastatingly bright, we have to shield our eyes from it. When it finally dims enough for me to blink up, my mouth hinges open at the sight.

The Beast is a mere pile of fur, emptied and settled on the bedroom floor. And where his monstrous body once lay, now stands a man. Renard's human form towers over us, several inches taller than Gabriel. My eyes trail up, sliding along the length of his golden skin. Thick, sinewy muscles coat every inch of Renard's body. There's something inhuman about the way he's shaped. His body is closer to that of a mythical god than of a man.

My gaze lifts higher, coasting his broad chest and wide-set shoulders. Pale hair so blond it's nearly white whips its long strands wildly in the wind. The man's head is turned down at the floor. When he raises his chin, my heart stills. Sapphire eyes burn fiercely, pinning me, holding me. Even set within a human face, the eyes glow in that same unnatural, luminescent way. *Renard?*

The room trembles moments before a powerful shockwave pulses out from beneath his body, throwing us back. My spine slams into the wall and the world grows hazy and dark.

I sit up, gasping, the Beast's bloody death still fresh in my mind. "Renard!"

"I'm here."

My eyes blink incessantly, trying to focus on the man who spoke. Renard's angelic face floats into view, gazing down at me before he kneels at my feet.

"Renard?" I reach out a hand, brushing my fingertips across the bridge of his sharp nose and down the hard edge of his jaw.

"But how?" asks Gabriel, getting to his feet.

"You broke the curse." Renard moves a strand of hair from my face before leaning down and brushing his lips against mine. "And now I can be with you the way I've always dreamed." I lean forward to deepen the kiss, but he's gone. Renard moves to his feet, pressing in closer to Gabriel.

"Wait," I beg, a sickly feeling settling in my stomach.

"Gabriel," he purrs, dragging his hand down Gabriel's chest. He trails his fingertips to Gabriel's waistband, toying with the fabric there before sliding them back up again. "You've taken such good care of Fleur for me." Renard dips lower, ghosting his lips across Gabriel's throat. "But I'm afraid I just don't want to share anymore…"

Renard's jaw opens wide before latching onto Gabriel's throat. Gabriel screams, fighting to free himself from Renard's hold. Renard only bites harder, sinking his teeth into the front of Gabriel's neck until blood pours out from around his lips. With one swift jerk of his head, Renard wrenches backwards, ripping Gabriel's throat out and killing him on the spot.

Terror seeps into me, rendering me unable to move, speak, think. Gabriel drops to the floor, the gaping hole in his neck spurting blood across the room. *No no no!* The light from Gabriel's icy-blue eyes extinguishes and the scream I've been holding in comes tearing out. Renard spits out the slack lump of flesh and turns to me. My screams shift to sobs as he sinks to his knees before me.

"Don't cry, Fleur." He leans in, pressing a bloody kiss to my lips. "Now we can be together, forever."

I sit up, gasping and screaming, tears falling freely from my eyes. "Woah." Renard's deep voice reaches me through my panicked haze. "You're okay, just breathe." The brightness of the room stuns my vision momentarily. It takes several long blinks to focus on my surroundings. We're in the library. The chaos from earlier is no longer visible. The books have returned to their designated spots on the shelves and the familiar fire roars brightly behind the chair I'm seated in. A shadow looms above me before Renard bends down low, taking my hand. His eyes still shimmer like blue flames, but his face is clean and unsullied. "There she is." He smiles warmly, his teeth triggering memories of Gabriel's tattered throat.

"Gabriel," I start, looking around.

"I'm here." He strides through the doorway, dropping down beside me. "How are you feeling? Whatever the hell that burst of energy was, it sent you on a collision course with the wall. You've been out for hours." He reaches out, brushing his fingers against a sensitive spot on the side of my head. I wince and he pulls back. "Sorry. Does it hurt?"

My eyes drink him in, instinctively dropping to his throat. It bobs as he swallows. There are no markings on his neck. The whole thing is intact. I look back and forth between the two men, willing my present situation to somehow line up with my memories.

Renard cuts his eyes to Gabriel. "Maybe she hit her head harder than we thought."

"I thought..." I reach out, stroking Gabriel's face. "...I saw you die." Tears well in my eyes at the horrible sight of his gruesome death at Renard's hands. "Renard killed you. He didn't want to share me, he said—"

"Must have been a bad dream." Gabriel draws me into his arms and moves to the couch. His fingertips run along my back in a soothing manner. I'm surprised he can hold me this way given the size of my extravagant gown. The lovely golden dress is ruined. Bloodstains cover the shimmery fabric and entire sections of material are missing.

I shift uncomfortably. Next time I have to run for my life, I'll be sure to choose a simpler outfit.

It takes several long minutes with my face buried in Gabriel's chest, breathing in his unique, masculine scent, to convince me he's really here. Dawn peeks its warm face in through the windows, washing away the dark of the night and the shadowy terrors along with it. I lean back, finally able to look at Renard again. His body is covered in a loose white shirt and dark trousers, likely Gabriel's, based on the fit. A stiffness hovers between us. Renard's posture is tense as he studies me intently. Guilt gnaws away at me as I realize this interaction is far from the celebratory experience Renard was expecting when he broke the witch's curse and gained his human shape again. The vicious nightmare still clings to me and I suck in a fresh lungful of air, willing myself to think clearly.

"You really broke the curse?" I ask. Renard nods slowly, a smile turning up at the corners of his mouth.

"Technically you broke the curse, Fleur. Your love for me was able to bring me back from the brink of death." Renard's voice is tight with emotion as he speaks.

"So you're human again?" I take in the way his eyes still flicker, and the inhuman shape of his massive, chiseled body.

"The curse is broken. I'm no longer the Beast, but things aren't exactly the way they were before." He and Gabriel exchange a look that insinuates they know something I don't.

"How do you mean?" I ask, not enjoying the feeling of being left in the dark. Renard flicks his wrist and the library plunges into darkness. A moment later, the candles reignite and the fireplace roars to life. "Magic? But how, the curse..."

"That's not the only thing. I'm larger, nearly a foot taller, and much stronger than I was before the curse."

I study him, observing the mountain of muscle that rests on his tall frame.

"Also this." He opens his mouth and a pair of gleaming white fangs lengthen, sharpening as they descend. Renard grins and the teeth retract just as quickly. He's as beastly a human as I've ever seen, minus the fur, claws, and horns.

"So, you're a hybrid? But why? To break the curse, you needed love." I frown.

"Perhaps because I gained your love, Fleur, but not your entire heart." He glances past me at Gabriel. "I've managed to steal half your heart and so half my curse was broken."

"It's the only conclusion we could agree upon. And if you

think about it, it makes sense," Gabriel chimes in. My stomach sinks. It's true. I love both of them. *Need* both of them.

"What happens now?" Nerves flap in my unsettled stomach, stuffing me with an airy fullness that makes me ache inside. The fireplace roars and cracks, chewing through the wood and coloring our silence with sound.

"Now we find a way to make this work," Renard offers. My spirit lifts. "We just need a story that makes all of this make sense." A story. My mind clears and our future flashes before my eyes.

"The Beast has been slain and the prince returned. Take back your throne," I offer. "Blame it on magic. Tell the people you were imprisoned by a monster. Enough people have seen the Beast to make the story as real as it needs to be." I take Gabriel's hand in mine. "Tell them the Beast captured Gabriel and me and that Gabriel killed him and freed you. Gabriel is one of the best hunters around, and the people look up to him. They will believe it to be true."

"And what of the three of us?" Gabriel asks, his jaw tightening.

"Since neither of us is willing to give up Fleur..." Renard thoughtfully strokes his chin. "...the prince would surely offer the hero a place among his court to show his gratitude. Possibly even a permanent residence here."

"We would *all* live here? In the castle?" I can't contain the spark of excitement that's quickly overtaking the fears and doubts in my chest.

"Would that make you happy?" Renard's eyes are piercing as he awaits my response.

"I want the two of you more than anything. Whether it's in a castle or an old farmhouse, as long as I can have you, the both of you, I'll be happy." Warmth tugs at my heart, spilling over and bleeding heat and happiness into my veins.

"What of the remaining staff?" Gabriel asks, bursting the fragile moment of happiness. "They know too much. They know what goes on between the three of us." His words drape a somber air around us.

"Purge them," Renard growls, and I sense the familiar dark energy of the Beast in his words. "There can't be many left. Any who survived will be purged. We will hire an entirely new staff, one that is completely unaware of the history of the castle. *Our* history."

I think of the way the servants attacked us, their dark eyes and bloodied faces contorted in hate and disgust. A shiver ripples through me and Gabriel squeezes me more tightly.

"I'll do it." Gabriel moves me off of his lap and stands. "It's what's best, for all of us," he adds, softening a bit.

Renard rises to his feet. "I can help—"

"No. We can't leave Fleur alone. We don't know how many of those bastards are left or where they are. You will stay and protect her." Gabriel strides purposefully to the library doors. He casts a look over his shoulder. "It will give you time to catch up. Things are different now. I'm sure you two could use a private moment to talk." He gives us a smirk before heading out of the library and closing the doors firmly behind him.

Silence feeds the nervous energy trickling through me. I turn my gaze to Renard and find him already watching me. He moves silently, walking slowly to the couch. My heart races as I remain statuesque and still. His approach is cautious, a hunter fearful of scaring his prey away. The couch dips as he sits beside me.

"Fleur." He calls my name and I turn my eyes up to his handsome face. "It's me," he soothes, caressing his hand down my cheek. The feeling of his skin on mine makes me shiver. I raise my own fingers, tracing the lines of his face. Renard's dark eyes fall shut at my touch. When they open again, they're as endlessly blue as ever.

"It is, isn't it?" I whisper, trailing my fingers along his lips. Renard dips down, moving closer until our faces are just inches apart. The scents of cinnamon and pine wrap around me. I breathe deeply, inhaling spicy lungfuls of the familiar scent. My hands move down, tracing his neck and landing on the firm shoulders below. "Kiss me," I breathe and Renard obeys. His lips find mine, soft but firm, giving but demanding. We both sigh as the beastly wall that separated us for so long crumbles away, disappearing beneath that one searing kiss. I move to climb into Renard's lap, but the damn gown stops me before I can get as close as I need to. "Undress me," I beg, turning my back toward him. Strong fingers make quick work of the uppermost bindings of my dress, but when he struggles to undo the last of the laces, I sigh in frustration.

"You try unlacing something as complex as a woman's dress after years of having claws instead of fingertips," he grumbles in response.

"Rip it," I urge. The sounds of the dress tearing apart send a rush of arousal between my thighs. I stand, shimmying out of the torn remnants until I'm bare before him. Renard's hands reach out to me, gripping my waist and hoisting me onto his lap. I moan at the feel of a thick, hard cock beneath his trousers. This one belongs to a man, not a monster.

Our lips clash together as months of unmet need catches fire between us. His tongue snakes into my mouth as he deepens our kiss, drawing another moan from my lips. I rock my hips, grinding against the hard ridge. Renard's hands are all over me, exploring every inch of heated flesh. I reach between us, jerking the trousers open and dipping my hand beneath the waistband. My hand grips his cock and he pants with relief.

"Renard." I devour his mouth as my hand pumps his length. "I need you."

He howls, flipping me over and pinning me down in the blink of an eye. He rips his shirt over his head, revealing the vast expanse of his knotted muscles. I reach between us again but he catches my wrist, pinning it above my head and snarling in a way that proves there's still some part of a beast beneath this new guise of a man. His hand dips between my thighs, parting me as he slides the first finger through my wetness.

"You have no idea how hard it was to resist touching you like this, to resist ruining you." He plunges two fingers inside me, making my body arch in pleasure. His fingers are rough, pumping in and out of me in deep, desperate strokes. I rock my hips, meeting his touch with a desperate need of my own. I've had so many fantasies, so many wanton daydreams about Renard. They all seemed impossible, until now.

Renard's thumb dips forward, circling my clit with the perfect pressure. My toes curl as my body tightens. I cry out his name as my body comes undone and my release floods his hand. He growls, never stopping, gripping my wrists harder as he works me toward another climax.

"Renard," I gasp out as I wriggle in his grip. My sensitive body fights to break free of his merciless assault.

"Again," he urges. "I need to know this is real. That you're truly mine."

"I'm yours," I pant out, the sensitivity in my body reaching its unbearable peak before plunging me into something savory and deep.

"Then give me what I need. Come again, for me." His dominant tone sends my heart stuttering as his fingers force another bout of pleasure from my writhing body.

The second climax is brutal and unforgiving, sucking the air from my lungs and forcing a silent scream from my trembling lips. A deep, clenching heat races through me and the second my muscles relax, his fingers are gone. I whimper at the loss of contact, my empty, heated core weeping with need. Renard doesn't make me wait long. He lines his engorged tip against my entrance and I suck in a breath of anticipation. He may be human now, but his cock is still massive.

He teases the first inch in and we both groan. I've needed his cock for so long. I wrap my heels around his muscular back, urging him on. Renard thrusts fully into me with no warning, forcing my body to take him all the way in. I yelp out as he fills me, my body struggling to accommodate his size, buckling beneath that first demanding thrust. The animalistic sounds of pleasure that pour from his perfect mouth have me close to another climax before he's hardly begun. The next snap of his rough hips has me seeing stars.

There's something feral about the way he's fucking me. My body is completely at his mercy as he pins me beneath him. It's beastly, unhinged, almost too much to take. Which is why I'm as surprised as anyone when I hear myself begging, "More. Give me all of you."

Renard rolls us off the couch and we hit the ground below. His muscles are coiled and tense as he flips me on my stomach, jerking my hips back until I'm spread out before him on my hands and knees, panting in front of the roaring fire. His cock plunges back into me and I choke on a grateful sob. His body moves faster, harder, more savagely than ever before. He tilts my hips up and the next climax bursts through me as his cock slams into the perfect spot again and again. Renard snarls, his beastly side taking control. His fingers are bruising on my hips and I love it. I've wanted him this way all along. I never desired him to turn back into a human so that he could be gentle with me. No, I desired him in human form so that our bodies would fit together in a way that allowed me to take everything the Beast has to offer.

His hand claps down hard on my ass, making me yelp. Renard howls in response, the beast in him driving his hips forward, spearing into me at an unrelenting pace. He slaps my ass again, hard enough to leave a welt. I open my lips to cry out just as his hand clamps around my mouth and his fangs bury straight into the side of my neck. The unexpected and inhuman gesture sends my next climax crashing down around us, dragging me into a near-delirious state of dark pleasure.

Renard groans in ecstasy as my blood drips down his lips and my pussy grips his length, squeezing him tightly and demanding he come with me. The first rope of his hot cum spurts into me and I moan, coming one last time and milking every bit of spend from his monstrous cock. He roars, and there's nothing resembling a human in the sound. He fills me up, thrusting and growling until we both collapse into a heap of sweaty, satisfied limbs.

Minutes pass in silence, our orgasms rendering us unable to speak or think. My legs are jelly, my throat raw, and my body so deliciously sore I can hardly move. Renard rolls me over. Drawing me into his chest, he devours me in a possessive kiss. We stare at each other, drinking in the feeling of being close in a way that, until tonight, seemed so completely far-fetched it could never happen.

Renard's broad chest rumbles, that same unusual purr emanating. "How's your first day back as a human?" I tease, finally finding my voice. The words come out gravelly, hoarse.

"I can't complain," he purrs, grinning wickedly down at me. "Though there were a few things I wanted to try with my new body that I didn't get a chance to explore just now." He nips at my lower lip, rolling me onto my back and pressing his hips against mine. His cock hardens as he circles his hips. My eyes go wide.

"Again, already?" I squirm beneath him.

He smirks. "I told you all the ways I would have you in here once you were mine." He swirls his hips again and my breath catches as arousal dews between my already-sticky thighs. "I want you every second of every day for always." *God, does that sound good.* Between Renard and Gabriel, I doubt I'll be getting much sleep in the near future.

I drag him down, pressing a loving kiss to his swollen lips. "Lucky for you, we have all the time in the world now."

"You're right." He peers down at me, eyes filled with wonder. He nuzzles into my neck, breathing in my scent. He murmurs into my skin, "I love you, Fleur."

Wrapping my arms around him, I pull him close. "I love you, Renard. My prince, my beast, *mine.*"

EPILOGUE

Fleur

Seven Years Later

The sound of silver clinking on glass stops me mid-mouthful of pot de crème. "I would like to raise a toast." Old man Dupont rises, addressing everyone seated at the oversized dining table before turning his attention to Renard and I. Dupont is one of Renard's largest trading partners now that the castle has reopened its walls to the world. He has an affinity for too much wine and long-winded speeches. "To the King and Queen of Montrésor," he says. I quickly swallow the sweet vanilla custard as all eyes swivel toward me. "May your reign long endure and flourish in this time of great peace and prosperity."

"Here, here," Gabriel agrees, raising his glass and flashing me a grin.

"And to the Lord of the Realm," Renard adds, turning to

253

Gabriel. "For uniting us with the people, and sharing with me the most beautiful woman in the world."

I smile, warmth creeping along my cheeks. In the end it had been Renard's idea to make our relationship public. He said he'd spent too long living in the shadows and wanted his life to be free of secrets. He came up with the plan to elevate Gabriel to Lord of the Realm, claiming Gabriel was discovered to be part of a lineage of royalty that was long since gone. In the name of the kingdom, and good relations with the people of his realm, he and Gabriel tied themselves together through union, with me as their shared bride. It's an unorthodox relationship, and one that took a bit of convincing with some of the old-fashioned nobles. But with a lot of effort, and a little bit of magic, we made it work.

Nothing like this has ever been done here before. But with Montrésor restored to its former power, the others have made the choice to accept our differences and rally beside us. Renard stopped the pointless wars, the infighting and land squabbles, when he took up his throne. Having him as the one true King has brought peace to the people.

Another round of applause fills the dining hall and wine is passed around, topping off any glass that needs it. The castle is all but unrecognizable like this. Every corner illuminated, every room filled with laughter and joy. It is easy to forget the darkness and horrors that once roamed these halls. Sometimes I sense it, in the deepest parts of the castle, lurking in the darkness. Memories of Renard's time as the Beast push to the forefront, quickening my pulse. I could have never known then, the future I would have now.

"Pardon my intrusion, Your Majesty," my lady's maid, Anette, whispers behind me. "But the princes refuse to go to bed. We've tried everything—"

"I'll handle it." I rise from the table, grateful for the opportunity to excuse myself from dinner. These affairs tend to drone on long after the last plate has been cleared away. Renard kisses my hand before I go, leaving my skin tingling. My journey through the castle is quiet and contemplative. The sleek fabric of my sky-blue gown rustles as I make my way to the boys' room. Voices reach me a few feet away and I peer inside.

"Back, Beast, or I shall slay you where you stand," Bastien commands, raising his wooden sword high in the air.

"No fair, you always make me play the Beast. I want to be the hero," Noé protests, crossing his arms and pushing out his bottom lip.

"That's because I'm older," Bastien boasts. I chuckle and their eyes turn to the door, lighting as they catch sight of me.

"Mama!" they shout in unison, running to greet me. I take a moment to admire my little warriors, staring lovingly down at them. Bastien is my strong, brave boy, with his raven hair and soft-blue eyes. At only six he already believes himself a grown man. While Noé, at four, is my sensitive son. His fair blond hair and deep-blue eyes are so like Renard's. Both boys are blessings, and Gabriel and Renard have treated them as such. Despite their looks or lineage. They treat the boys equally, loving and spoiling them both to bits. The boys in return practically worship their papa Gabriel and papa Renard.

"You two are meant to be fast asleep by now." I raise an eyebrow and they both frown up at me.

"We never get to come to the parties. We want to be eating, drinking, and dancing! It is boring playing in our rooms," Bastien says, dropping to the floor dramatically.

"Yes!" Noé joins in. "We want to come to the party." He drops down next to Bastien, peeking over to see what he's doing and mimicking the same over-the-top theatrics.

"How about this?" I offer and they both sit up, eyeing me excitedly. "If you two hurry off to bed and promise to go right to sleep, I'll sneak two pots de crème from the party and let you have them for breakfast tomorrow." Both boys grin up at me. "Do we have a deal?" They nod, rushing away and diving into their beds. I give each a quick kiss and tuck them in.

"Will you be returning to dinner, ma'am?" Anette asks as I emerge from their room.

"No, I think I've had enough fun for one evening. I'll take a bath in my quarters. Oh, and please set aside two pots de crème for the princes."

"A bargain was struck?" She smiles.

"Indeed." I giggle. Anette has become my closest confidant in the castle. She's the friend I always wanted. She's honest, kind, and doesn't find me the least bit odd despite knowing all my quirky and curious ways.

"I'll arrange for both at once, ma'am." Anette curtsies before hurrying away. I take my time wandering back to my room, stopping to peer inside the library. Memories of my time here bring a sultry smile to my face. It's still one of my favorite places to spend time with Renard, reading and enjoying tea, among other things…

A blush crawls across my cheeks and I grin widely. Perhaps dinner won't last too terribly long. I'm missing my loves already.

The bath does wonders for my achy muscles and tired feet. When the water is good and cold, I slip out, drying off and donning one of the many beautiful dressing gowns that fill my wardrobe. I'm just preparing to tuck into bed when the door to my room opens wide and Renard and Gabriel enter together.

"Is dinner already over?" I ask. The two share a look, and a shiver of anticipation dances up my spine.

"Hunt or be hunted?" Renard asks, making my pulse tick faster. *Hunt or be hunted?* My favorite game to play. Both are thrilling in their own ways. But tonight, I crave the danger, the chase, the feeling of the two of them tracking me through the forest before devouring me beneath the moon.

"Be hunted," I answer in a flushed whisper. They grin and the hunger in their gazes sends arousal flooding between my thighs.

"You have ten minutes." Renard's eyes rake along my body, his gaze practically melting the thin fabric of my night-gown. "Then the hunt will begin."

"Run, *ma petite fleur*." Gabriel smirks, his eyes darkening.

I spring to my feet, rushing to the tapestry that covers the hidden door in the corner of my room. My fingers slip easily past the fabric and into the discreet handle of my secret panel. I wrench it open, slipping through and barring the door behind me. *That will slow them down a bit.*

My bare feet fly as I rush down the stairs. I take a quick left and run blindly through the darkness. I've taken this path enough times to know where the corridor ends. My fingers hit the wooden door and I fumble for the handle. Warm summer air spills into the open doorway and I inhale the sweet scent of honeysuckle before dashing out into the night.

The moon is nearly full tonight. It casts a luminescent glow on everything beneath its sway, bathing the castle and surrounding forest in silvery moonlight. I race down the small garden path. The flat, worn stones are cool and smooth against the soles of my feet.

Red honeysuckle vines rush across the top of my hair as I duck through the overgrown archway. Leaving the garden, I step into the open meadow. The second my feet dip into the soft, twisted grass, I run, sprinting full speed across the open ground, testing my muscles as I cross the clearing. My sights are set on the dense thicket of woods just beyond.

A howl echoes through the still night air the moment I reach the forest's edge. My pace quickens, anticipation hums in my veins. Those howls are not the song of a wild wolf or some creature of the dark. They're the warnings of the Beast. *They're coming for me.*

Time always passes so quickly when the hunt is afoot. I break into a small clearing, spying the tiny pond that helps me keep track of how far I've traveled. Another howl spills out into the night.

My heart beats out a wild lover's tune as a plan forms in my mind. Renard hunts me by scent, the lingering beast within him granting him the keen senses of his inner animal. Gabriel tracks me by the trail I leave. He follows my footprints, checking for broken twigs, damaged foliage, or pieces of clothing caught amidst the clawing fingers of the towering trees. If I want to prolong this game, I need to fool them both. Renard first.

I ditch my nightgown, rubbing it along several tree trunks adjacent to each other. The soft ribbons that decorate the neck of the dress release easily from their bindings. I tie the first to a low tree branch to the right of the pond, the second to a higher branch in the middle, and finally toss the dress deep in the woods to the left of the water. That should provide enough decoys to buy me some time.

Now to fool Gabriel. I tiptoe to the edge of the pond, lightening my footfalls to minimize the markings left in the grass. The pond is warm and welcoming as I dip my feet in, keeping close to the edges so the water never rises above my ankles. Frogs leap away, croaking out their unhappiness as I slosh through the lily pads, following the pond's outermost shallows until I reach the far end. Water splashes around me as I jump the last few feet out. I land on the forest floor and run into the dense woods.

A grin tugs at the corners of my lips. I'm confident I'll throw them off my trail this time. I'm getting quite good at this game. My pace slows as my adrenaline dips low and the burning in my muscles finally warrants my full attention. I press my back against the trunk of a great oak tree, breathing deeply. A soft crack in the distance has my breath halting. I freeze, peering into the darkness. A second crack follows and my adrenaline spikes again. I turn, fleeing deeper into the woods just as something huge slams into me, sending us both crashing to the ground. My stomach hits the damp earth below and knocks the wind from my lungs.

"Using the pond to hide your tracks? Did you think I wouldn't see through that in an instant, *ma petite fleur*?" Gabriel's body is hot on top of mine, his weight keeping me pinned to the forest floor.

"You were slower than last time." I grin victoriously.

"I still caught you first." His voice is low in my ear. Gabriel's grip is unyielding as his fingers dig into my hips. He pulls me back, forcing me onto my hands and knees. There's a few seconds' delay as he frees himself from his trousers. The blunt head of his cock presses against my dripping entrance. The hunt always has me drenched and begging to be taken. "Now it's time for my prize."

He thrusts into me hard enough to knock me forward, his hands on my waist the only things keeping me from falling flat on my face. Gabriel's hips pump into me, slamming his cock to the hilt as our wet flesh claps loudly together. Arousal drips down my thighs and a heady moan slips out, no doubt betraying our location. Pleasure spreads through me, tingling up my spine. A fresh flood of warmth spreads between my thighs.

"Yes," I cry out as Gabriel fucks the soul from my body. He always knows what I need. Some days it's gentle, loving, safe. Other days, it's positively fucking feral. "That feels so good, Gabriel, please—" His weight abruptly shifts as he's pulled off of me and I find myself empty and desperate to be filled once more. Turning, I gasp as I spot Renard there, his hand clasped around my lover's throat.

Renard stands several inches above Gabriel's massive frame. They both pant heavily, their bodies bare, ropey muscles on full display. Gabriel's flesh is lean and deeply chiseled. Dark, dense hair covers his chest before narrowing into a thin line that descends to his cock. His skin is pale in the moonlight, and I can't help but appreciate every hard-earned ounce of muscle on his tall frame. Renard, on the other hand, is covered in bronzed skin and golden-blond hair. His body is stacked with veiny, thick muscles that fill out every inch of his mountainous form.

Their bodies are so different and yet I could never choose which I prefer. I know now, after all these years, I can't live without them both. Choosing one was never an option.

"You just couldn't wait, could you?" Renard glares down at Gabriel, their faces inches apart. His other hand holds something in the air. The tattered remains of my nightgown hang limply in his grasp. Renard's eyes blaze at me. "Very clever."

"I still beat you," Gabriel asserts, eliciting a snarl from Renard. I love watching their interactions. They fight tirelessly, compete endlessly to stake their claims, but at the end of the day I know they'll always be willing to share me. We have a unique love and one that I am endlessly grateful for.

"So you did…" Renard's gaze drops to Gabriel's cock, still shiny with my release. He drops the nightgown, lowering his hand to Gabriel's shaft. His long fingers wrap around his thick girth. Gabriel's head falls back as Renard pumps his length, using my slickness to slide effortlessly from base to tip, up and down, up and down. "She was soaked for you." Renard's tone is gravelly, dangerous, as he commands Gabriel's body with ease.

I bite my lip, getting off on watching the two of them

together. Gabriel never initiates anything physical between them, honestly I don't think Renard is his type. But Renard has been infatuated with Gabriel from the beginning and in moments like this, it seems Gabriel is unable to deny the chance to receive Renard's own unique brand of pleasure.

More hot arousal pools between my thighs. A moan slips from my lips as the unmet need deep within my core aches and throbs. Renard's eyes snap to mine. A wicked smile graces his sharp features as he ups his pace, eliciting a deep groan from Gabriel. "Do you want to play too?" The deep timbre sends goosebumps prickling along my skin.

"Yes, Master. Please..." I say breathlessly. Renard's eyes flare as they always do when I address him as Master. A title I only use when we're intimate.

"Then crawl to us."

I sink onto all fours, crawling eagerly. I stop before them, sinking back onto my feet. I stare up in hunger.

"Good girl," Renard praises. "I bet those pretty lips are good for more than just begging. Open up." He points Gabriel's cock toward my mouth and I obey, parting my lips and moaning as Renard feeds me Gabriel's length, relinquishing his grip as my mouth takes over where his fingers left off.

My jaw widens, drawing Gabriel in until he hits the back of my throat. His skin is salty and hot on my tongue. Gabriel wraps his fingers in my hair, urging me on. Renard moves behind me. He drops to his knees and presses his body against mine. His hand slides down my side, moving around front before descending to my throbbing clit. His fingers tease me and I moan around Gabriel's cock. Renard kisses my neck and shoulders, mumbling words of praise as I swallow Gabriel's length at a steady pace. When Renard's fingers dip inside me I let Gabriel slide from my mouth, drop my head back to Renard's shoulder, and sigh in relief.

"I think we've toyed with her enough," Gabriel breathes out. "Let's give her what she needs."

I squirm as Renard withdraws his hand. His fingertips trail through my wet center.

"What do you think, Fleur?" Renard's breath is hot on the shell of my ear. "Can you take us both?"

* * *

Renard

Fleur nods, depravity glistening in her pale-green eyes. We've got her so worked up I doubt she'll last more than a minute once we're both inside. I stand behind her, lifting Fleur to her feet along with me. "After you." I grin at Gabriel. Fleur's eyes go wide as she peers over her shoulder, noticing the elongated fangs that have dropped down between my lips.

"*Ma petite fleur*." Gabriel dips low, planting a deep kiss on Fleur's lips before hauling her up. She wraps her legs around his waist, gasping as he drives his cock deep inside her. He sheaths himself fully and then stills, waiting for me to join them. I drop to my knees, trailing my tongue across Fleur's lower back before dropping down to sink my teeth into the soft flesh of her ass. She cries out and I drink in the sounds as I lap up the small drops of blood that trickle forward. My tongue roves over the skin, soothing the wound before moving to dip between the cleft of her cheeks. She tenses, sucking in a breath as my tongue probes along the tight ring of flesh. I feast on her until she's squirming on Gabriel's cock and thoroughly dripping with my spit. "Renard," Gabriel forces the words from his clenched jaw. His body is already trembling. Between my hand and Fleur's mouth he's got to be close to bursting.

I rise to my feet, grateful that Gabriel and I are close enough in height—nowadays, anyhow—to make this erotic dance work. "Deep breath," I whisper in Fleur's ear, spreading her cheeks and pressing my tip inside her. She bites her lip as I work my way deeper, inch by inch. One of my hands moves beneath her thigh, supporting her weight. The other reaches across to grip Gabriel's shoulder, anchoring us together. I gaze into his blue eyes, watching them roll back as I begin to move. He matches my pace, slowly working in and out of her as we seesaw her body in deep, languid thrusts that have all three of us growling, groaning, and panting in pleasure.

Gabriel's cock glides along mine, his thick shaft pressing against me through the thin fleshy barrier that separates us. We work in tandem, somehow sensing the right time to move faster, deeper. Our movements build until we're tunneling into her with a savage desperation that has my balls tightening. Fleur's simpers rise in volume until she's screaming to the forest. Her muscles tighten, then clamp down around our cocks, making us both tense. We keep the pace steady, milking out every bit of pleasure from our Queen. My eyes lock with Gabriel's again and I see the same determination there.

"Another," I growl into Fleur's ear before sinking my fangs into her neck. Her back arches as her body jerks, spasms, and comes hard enough to make me wince. Every part of Fleur is fucking perfect. Gabriel's movements fall out of sync as his own release comes. I feel the steady pulsing of his orgasm as his seeds spills out into Fleur's sweet pussy. The sensation tips me over the edge and my orgasm roars out of me. Hot, sticky cum pumps into Fleur and she mewls as we fill her so fully. Blood thunders in and out of my pounding heart until it's all I can hear.

My head drops to Fleur's shoulder as I come down, the high of the climax still clouding my mind. I'm the first to pull out. Fleur whimpers as I slip free. Gabriel slides out next, setting Fleur on her feet. I catch her as she melts into a bone-less puddle of bliss. Her body is coated in a sheen of sweat as I pull her up into my arms. She's barely coherent, mumbling words of praise and thanks. We've fucked her into oblivion, again. I smirk at Gabriel who shakes his head, a wicked smile running away from his strong features.

"I think that's my favorite hunt yet." He brushes the hair from Fleur's face and bends down to kiss the scar that lines her fair cheek. That soft pink scar is a constant reminder of the past.

My gut tightens when I think of my days as the Beast.

Gabriel claps a hand on my shoulder, rousing me from my thoughts. "Let's get her home."

* * *

I wake early, unwrapping Fleur's arms from my waist and slipping from the bed. She rolls automatically, draping herself over Gabriel. The two remain peacefully asleep. They look perfectly placed in our large bed. There was a time when I thought I'd never be able to share a bed with a human again, let alone two. For so many years, I believed the witch's wrath, the curse of the Beast, was unbreakable. In those dark lonesome days I could not imagine a life filled with this much love.

I dress as quietly as I can. Catching my reflection in the mirror, I breathe deeply. Some days, I wake up in fear. Terrified that it was all a dream and I'm still trapped in a monster's form. The magic mirror is just a mirror now, but it reflects the truth of who I am. Seeing my human face reflected back at me, with Fleur and Gabriel fast asleep behind me, makes my heart swell with joy.

Somehow, we did it. My gaze falls on Fleur. If it wasn't for her, things would be so different.

Pale pink spills in through the window as the sun creates the morning sky. The boys will wake soon. They've always been early risers. Those two are a daily reminder of how beautiful life can be. Who knew life could change so much? One minute I was a monstrous Beast, now I'm a mortal man who two tiny humans call Papa. I grin, thinking of our two mischievous boys. They certainly keep me on my toes. If I want any time to myself, I'll have to take it now.

The castle is quiet as I wander its halls. The moment the witch's wrath vanished, the entire castle returned to its old self. Beautiful paintings and one-of-a-kind statues now line the halls. No more gargoyles and rows of thorny rose vines. Of course, that doesn't mean the roses have vanished completely.

I call for tea and head to the one garden on the castle grounds that the cursed roses still call home. It's a small space, surrounded by stone walls. The blood-red roses dominate every available space here, but have never ventured outside the walls or into another of the castle's gardens. Fear clutched my gut when I first discovered them, but as time passed, and I remained free of the witch's curse, I found myself venturing here more and more often. Several carved stones line the trunk of a pear tree. Each stone is dedicated to a loved one lost. There are markers for my family, for Gabriel's men, and several for Fleur's mama, papa, and brother. Even one for Aida, who lived out the last few years of her long life here in the castle.

"Special delivery." I turn to find Fleur pushing out a

trolley of tea and cakes. Her eyes are sleepy and her hair mussed. "I knew I'd find you out here."

"Is that so?" I sweep her into my arms, spinning her around. Her laughter fills the garden, satisfying some deep, contented part of my soul. "A Queen should not be serving tea." I cock an eyebrow.

"But I thought my master might be in need of company." She bites her lip and I give her mouth a playful nip. "Or would you rather reminisce about the darker days alone?" Now it is she who raises an eyebrow at me. "Surely you can't dwell on the past forever."

That's when I sweep her off her feet, carrying her to a stone bench, and we both sit. I trail my fingertips down the side of her face. "The past is where I found you."

"But the present is where you *have* me." Her green eyes sparkle. I draw her to me, and plant a soft kiss on her lips.

"And the future"—Gabriel's unexpected voice cuts into our tiny refuge—"is where we all live happily ever after or however those damned fairy tales go." He tilts a sleepy smile our way. Reaching her hand out to him, Fleur matches his grin. Gabriel joins us and the fullness of my heart grows.

Happily ever after.

Indeed, who could have predicted such an ending to a life filled with misery and suffering? The past is forever a haunting reminder of my unforgivable sins. But the present is more perfect than I ever dreamed. And the future? Well, if a woman as enchanting as Fleur could learn to love a beast, then I believe anything is possible.

A warm gust of wind blows through the garden, raining rose petals down around us. Fleur's smile grows as she plucks a single petal from my hair. Roses and the witch's wrath. How beautifully they've shaped our world. How lucky the cursed are, to know love after all.

THANK YOU FOR READING!!

Enjoy The Wrath of Roses? Please consider taking a second
to leave a review!

Keep going for a sneak peek of *Demons and Damiana*

The Dream Eater comes for the children, snatching them in
the night while they sleep. That is how it has always been.
Pru will do whatever it takes to keep the children in her care
safe from harm. But when tragedy strikes once again too
close to home, she's forced to make a life-altering decision.

She's going to kill the Dream Eater.

The spell has been cast, the summoning circle set, but
when the Dream Eater arrives, everything gets turned upside
down. In her haste to take the massive monster down, she
accidentally doses them both with a powerful aphrodisiac.
And now the two of them are trapped together, as the potion
sends them into a heat and need like they've never known.

All she has to do is make it until sunrise. But can she
avoid this undeniable pull to the Dream Eater? Can she still
kill him now that her feelings are hazy and fueled by lust?
Either way one thing is for sure. After tonight, nothing will
ever be the same.

SNEAK PEEK OF DEMONS AND DAMIANA

It's well into the night by the time I start my ritual. The cave I've chosen is deep in the woods and far enough off the beaten path that no one will mistakenly wander into the trap I've laid. The last thing I need is a human getting in my way when I have the Dream Eater in my grasp.

I paint my circle of sigils near the entrance, guaranteeing quick access to the outside world. I don't want to find myself trapped in the back of a cave if things go south. This way I can flee to the woods if the situation sours, which will at least give me a fighting chance. The full moon shines brightly down around me and I'm grateful for its offering of light. The darkness is suited for shadows and my eyes search the depths of the cave more than once. *I am guided, I am protected. I am guided, I am protected.* I repeat this mantra as I continue my work.

Each detailed sigil glows a deep crimson, their ancient power amplified by the addition of my blood to the mix. My nerves flutter through my stomach in an intense swarm as I prepare the final touches. I bite back a cry as I drag a purified obsidian blade across my palm, watching blood spring to the surface everywhere the black glass touches. I place the Dream Eater's claw against the broken skin, wincing as the sharp tip burrows into the wound. The broken talon sits heavy in my hand, its weight far more than what would process on the scales. My lips open to speak the incantation and I pause. There's a warning whirring through my mind, an inner voice begging me to turn back now. Fear clouds my determination, but one by one, the faces of my siblings appear to me, and I steel myself. I need to do this. For them.

"*Enorth me fa sahd, enorth me fah trud, syn yaht me col farth, syn yaht me col truth.* With Hecate guiding each word of my spell, and sending protection from creatures of hell. I call unto me now the Dream Eater's form. With my blood as the beacon, come crawling and warm. To atone for your sins, it is time to repay. For the Dream Eater's form, on this eve I shall slay."

The world around me sparkles to life as wind whips my hair across my eyes and the glowing sigils illuminate the cave. I brush my long, dark locks aside as my gaze remains fixed on the small summoning circle in front of me and I await the Dream Eater's arrival. My wrist shakes as I hold the obsidian blade high. *Strike quick, Pru. Don't hesitate.*

The winds die down and my pulse heats to a boil as I wait. Silence falls across the cave and the blood pounds in my ears so loudly I fear it may rattle the very stones loose from the ceiling, sending them crashing down around me. I suck in a breath, holding it tightly within as another sound reaches my ears. A low growling reverberates through the space and I whirl. There he is, no more than a foot behind me, in all his terrifying glory. The Dream Eater.

I stumble back, completely unprepared for the forced proximity that now greets me. The knife clatters to the stone floor as I throw up my hands, quickly working them in the familiar series of complex patterns, and sighing with relief as a small circle of wards forms a shimmering protective veil around me. The Dream Eater stands stunned, still recovering from the shock of the summoning. I use the brief moment of surprise to study him.

The Dream Eater stands at over seven feet, making him one of the largest creatures I have ever encountered. Everything about his form appears wrong. His body has been seemingly twisted inside out. A massive man's figure lingers beneath a mangled and mismatched skeleton that covers his outer body like armor. The bones are a horrific mashup of both human and animal parts. Upon closer inspection, I realize the bones are not just being worn on the outside, they are fused to his body. They sit grotesquely, half sunken into the skin and muscle of his pale gray flesh.

Massive black hooves stomp at the ground impatiently. They separate into clawed toes as he shifts his weight, then reform into their singular shape as he settles himself once more. His legs are wide trunks of heavy muscle, coated in rows of long, thin femurs. They lead up to his stomach, where his texture shifts, becoming a smooth layer of chiseled skin beneath an army of rib bones ranging from finger width to that of a great animal. More muscles than I've ever witnessed in a human flex along his abdomen with each breath he takes, bulging around the cage of ribs that protrude from his body. A wide torso gives way to a powerfully built chest where dozens of teeth, both small and large, all frighteningly sharp, line his collarbones and throat.

The most horrifying feature by far is the bony mask that covers his face. Or is it his actual face? Is there a man beneath? And what sort of animal is it exactly? A deer? A bear? The skull that sits melded into his skin shifts slightly, and I realize it's a new animal. Again it changes, morphing into an entirely different beast. The magic surrounding the ever-changing mask does not feel of this earthly realm.

Soft green moss grows over at least half of the exposed bone of his face, its color oddly vibrant in contrast to the mottled gray and white of the rest of him. The top of the skull is met with a pair of broad, slightly curved horns, at least two feet long and as thick as my wrist. The horns are as dark as his hooves, and lined with deep ridges. They remind me of an ibex, though I've never encountered one so large as to house these two weighty appendages. The vestigial features and pitch-black eyes are the only constant among the ever-changing skull. Even the moss seems to transform and grow. In fact, there are traces of greenery all throughout his body. Vines wind within the misshapen ribs. Weeds crawl up his thighs and weave between the clustered femurs. Small leaves and lichens dot the bones along his shoulders and arms.

A thicker tangling of vines ensnares his ankles and a light dusting of deep, dark dirt coats him from head to hoof. It's as if the earth is fighting a constant battle to reclaim his body. The plants struggling to subdue him are proof of the failed attempts to keep him buried in the ground, where he belongs.

The Dream Eater's body stills, and my eyes flick up and back to the wet, black pools of his gaze. He stares at me for only a moment before charging past my small, shimmering sanctum. He slams into the red outer sigil ring, sending sparks into the darkness and howling in rage as his path is thwarted. *What if he breaks through the circle?* I never anticipated it would go this far. He was supposed to appear in the small summoning ring, where I would stab him dead without a second's hesitation. Instead, he materialized right behind me and everything got turned upside down.

He rams forward with his horns again and again and I sense the magic beginning to wane. The steady stream of sparks he produces surrounds him in light, each small bit of fire glistening off his skeletal outer structure. It reminds me of the nights I lay beneath the sky, watching the burning stars fall to Earth. His intensity increases, and the red glow flickers. *I've got to do something.*

I drop to the ground, ripping open my satchel and digging through my apothecary bottles in a frenzy. I just need to stall him so I can make a plan. *Think, Pru, think.* A yellow bottle catches my eye. Chamomile? A sleeping draft! I set to work, my fingers flying as I mix one ingredient after another, preparing a powerful elixir. I curse as I realize I left my belladonna back home. Extra chamomile will have to do. I add enough of the pale yellow flower to affect six grown men. The delicate mixture dissolves down into one concentrated dose.

All he needs to do is inhale it, and it should knock him out cold. I take a deep breath, building my courage, then drop the wards around the small protective circle I've created. I move without hesitation, tossing the vial toward the Dream Eater, waiting for it to collide with his back. My heart leaps into my throat when he turns suddenly, his great hand whipping forward and smashing the glass potion while it's halfway between us. A cloud of vibrant yellow smoke envelops us both. I suck in a breath before I can stop myself and the airborne potion floods my lungs. *No.* I back away, quickly righting the walls of my personal wards. How could I let this happen? I just have to make sure he passes out before I do. It should only be a few moments more before…

I freeze as a sudden urge possesses my body.

Instead of drowsiness in my mind and limbs, a rush of warm blood surges between my thighs. That's…unexpected. The air surrounding me heats as a liquid buzzing itches beneath my skin. There is dampness on my dress, soaking through the fabric. This isn't right. I dig through my satchel once more, reassessing the ingredients I used. Panic seizes my overheated body as I reread the bottle of yellow flowers. *Damiana.* In my haste to create the draft, I mixed up chamomile with damiana. A sense of dread crashes over my charged skin. Damiana has one main purpose in potions and spells—it's a powerful aphrodisiac.

The world grows quiet around me and I pause. The Dream Eater has stopped trying to escape. My eyes snap up to find him very still, and staring straight at me in my tiny sanctuary. My gaze drops lower to where something very large, and very hard is now jutting upward from between his hips. That certainly wasn't there before.

Read this steamy dark romance monster short and the rest of the Darkly Depraved Monsters series on Amazon.

Chosen Shifter Mates Series

A Shifter Fated Mates Paranormal Romance

Frost and Fate

Alpha and Ivy

Lycan and Lark

Country and Clove

Darkly Depraved Monsters

A Collection of Steamy Monster Romance Shorts

Scream for the Scarecrow

Feast of the Vampire King

Frostbitten

Demons and Damiana

STAY IN TOUCH

Sign up for Violet's newsletter to keep up with the latest news about books, giveaways, and more!

Connect with Violet Taylor
Official Website - violettaylorauthor.com
Facebook - The Violet Pack
TikTok - @violettaylorauthor
Instagram - @violettaylorauthor

ACKNOWLEDGMENTS

A huge thank you to every reader who has taken the time to escape into this fairytale reimagining! You make every hour of writing, editing, formatting, marketing, and every other nuanced part of this job so worthwhile!

Thank you to my editor, Michelle, for always giving my words her utmost care and attention. You are such a valuable part of my team. I couldn't do it without you!

And of course, thank you to the love of my life, Travis. With you by my side, I get to live out my fairytale happily ever after now and forever! You're my prince, my beast, and so much more! Thank you for reading everything I write and for keeping me grounded every time I threaten to throw my current manuscript in the trash. I love you.

ABOUT VIOLET TAYLOR

Violet Taylor is a crystal and candle shop owner by day and a paranormal romance novelist by night. She spends her free time fantasizing about living in an isolated mountain cabin with her wonderful husband and herd of fur babies. She prefers her books with magic, mates, monsters, and plenty of muscles.

Shop candles and crystals inspired by Violet's books on violettaylorauthor.com

Printed in Great Britain
by Amazon

26839009R00162